"Do you have [barcode] [D0832082]

Dylan considered L... ...r. I'm usually
nearly naked body ...
a willing slave to women."

"And I'm an exception?" she prodded, forcing
herself to focus on the conversation instead of
the building ache between her legs. "Why?"

He slid his hands downward and recognized the
glint in her eyes. "I have no idea," he murmured into
her neck, "but when I find out, *you* can be in charge
for as long as you like." Dylan flipped her around
and bent her over the kitchen island, pressing
himself to her backside. "But not until I'm done.
And I plan to take my sweet time."

The shock of the cold countertop against her bare
nipples combined with the heat of his erection
pressed against the back of her thighs made Liza's
breath go rapid and shallow. She was *allowing*
him this little fantasy play, she thought as she fought
her desire. She was still in control. Wasn't she?

Then she heard the rasp of steel and chain. Her
breath stopped. Handcuffs. Never in all her wild
escapades had she ever been the one with the cuffs
on. So why let him do this?

Because I'm so damn hot I can hardly stand it, that's
why....

Dear Reader,

Okay, I admit it. I have control issues. I like to be in charge whenever possible. I can't help it. So I felt for Liza when she realized she had to make a change, and that change might have to start with herself. Giving up control (on occasion, let's not get radical here!) might sound easy, but when you do that, especially with a man in, say, an intimate situation…well, then elements like trust start to come into play and things can get pretty scary.

I knew I'd have to put Liza in good hands (among other interesting and capable body parts), so I put her directly in the path of Sheriff Dylan Jackson—he of the shiny handcuffs and imaginative ways of incorporating them into his personal life. Because sometimes the person learning to trust and give over control needs a little nudge. Or restraint, as the case may be. I hope you enjoy Liza and Dylan's adventure!

Happy reading,

Donna Kauffman

P.S. And don't forget to check out tryblaze.com!

Books by Donna Kauffman

HARLEQUIN BLAZE
18—HER SECRET THRILL

HARLEQUIN TEMPTATION
828—WALK ON THE WILD SIDE
846—HEAT OF THE NIGHT
874—CARRIED AWAY

HIS PRIVATE
PLEASURE

Donna Kauffman

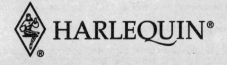

TORONTO • NEW YORK • LONDON
AMSTERDAM • PARIS • SYDNEY • HAMBURG
STOCKHOLM • ATHENS • TOKYO • MILAN • MADRID
PRAGUE • WARSAW • BUDAPEST • AUCKLAND

ISBN 0-373-79050-3

HIS PRIVATE PLEASURE

This edition published by arrangement with Harlequin Books S.A.

® and TM are trademarks of the publisher. Trademarks indicated with ® are registered in the United States Patent and Trademark Office, the Canadian Trade Marks Office and in other countries.

Visit us at www.eHarlequin.com

Printed in U.S.A.

1

THE MOMENT SHE SPIED that nicely formed male derriere sticking out of the tree, Liza Sanguinetti realized that giving up her career was going to be a whole lot easier than giving up men.

She slowed her shiny blue roadster convertible to a crawl. Which was only slightly slower than the speed limit posted next to the sign welcoming her to Canyon Springs, New Mexico. Population... "A hell of lot less than L.A.," she murmured. But definitely bigger than some of the one-horse towns she'd driven through. Canyon Springs looked like a festive place, with rows of quaint storefronts lining the main thoroughfare and banners streaming from the light poles, announcing some upcoming celebration.

The town was nestled in the foothills of the rugged Black Range Mountains, which, according to the brochure she'd picked up at breakfast in Santa Fe, were the source of the natural springs that fed down into the deep canyons and *rincóns*. Whatever the hell a *rincón* was.

All she knew was that she'd been drawn toward the dark shadowy mountains as if some guiding hand was pointing the way. The vistas here were downright awe-inspiring and pulled at something deep inside her. Which struck her as odd, considering she was a born and bred city girl. Her idea of a wild country weekend meant going horseback riding in a Palm Springs resort spa.

All she wanted at the moment was a bite to eat and the chance to wander around the antique stores she'd seen advertised on her meandering drive. Sounded like the perfect way to spend the afternoon. She was hoping the perfect housewarming present for Natalie and Jake would sit up and grab her attention. She smiled, picturing Natalie's face when she told her she'd been antiquing in the mountains of New Mexico. Not exactly on the list of Liza's normal haunts. But then, that was the point of this trip. Expanding personal horizons.

At the moment, however, the only thing grabbing her attention was the man perched in the towering corner oak.

"I could think of another way to spend a perfectly nice afternoon in Canyon Springs," she murmured appreciatively, staring openly at the fine masculine scenery as she tooled beneath the outstretched branches of the tree. An amazingly loud screech erupted a second later, causing her to swerve around the corner and pull to the side of the road. One hand clutching her racing heart, she climbed out of the low-slung car and shaded her eyes with her free hand. Just past the beautiful specimen of man was an even more exotic specimen of bird perched just out of his reach.

"Come on, Mango. Step up," the man beckoned, reaching his hand alarmingly close to that intimidating black beak.

The enormous bird was mostly white, with a vibrant orange plume that erupted all about its head as it spread its huge wings and shrieked once again. Liza covered her ears at the skull-splitting sound and wondered how the man managed to keep his perch a mere foot away without so much as flinching.

"Mango is a pretty bird," he cajoled, though now

Liza could see the muscles flexing along his jaw and neck. Perhaps the bird sensed the tension as well, since it lunged for the fingers being offered, as if they were a snack to be gobbled down rather than a lift to safety.

"Pretty, pretty Mango," he said, repeating the words over and over in a smooth, singsongy voice. A nice deep singsongy voice, Liza found herself thinking. What sort of things could that voice cajole her into?

"Come on, pretty boy, pretty bird."

Another piercing shriek split the air, making her jump.

"Pretty loud bird," Liza muttered, testing one ear, then the other. The bird flapped and ducked, bobbed and pranced in quite an ornate show of birdy fervor, but didn't move one speck closer to the outstretched hand of its brave savior.

"I don't think he's interested," Liza called up.

The man glanced down then, and Liza thought, *But I sure am!* Even frowning, he was quite gorgeous. Not Hollywood glamorous, but real world rugged. Mmm. Her afternoon was getting better by the second. *No, down girl, down.* It had been eight weeks since she'd gone cold turkey on men and she still got the shakes when confronted with a prime specimen. Surely that was natural. On the bright side, he'd be a real litmus test of her testosterone sobriety.

And test her he would. She couldn't make out the color of his eyes, but she could definitely make out just about everything else of importance. The close cropped blond hair, straight nose, sharp cheekbones and square jaw topped equally squared shoulders and a chest that did justice to the brown-and-tan uniform he wore. The shiny star on one pocket explained why he was up in the tree.

She'd never harbored uniform fantasies before, but

that fact was in rapid transition. Just because she couldn't play with him didn't mean she couldn't imagine what kind of playmate he'd have made. "Doesn't the fire department usually handle this sort of thing?" she offered oh-so-helpfully. Something about that scowl provoked her. She was an unconventional flirt, but this wasn't actually flirting. It couldn't be flirting as long as he kept scowling, right? "I passed a station on the way into town," she continued. She remembered because the guys had been out washing the trucks. Suds and muscular men with long hoses, always a good combination.

She sighed and wondered if there was a resort spa out here with a twelve-step plan to help her embrace celibacy. *Hi, I'm Liza Sanguinetti and I enjoy hot sex.* Probably the first step was truly grasping there was a problem with that. But she was working on it. At her own pace.

"If you'd like, I can drive over and ask them to send some help?" she offered. Who knew, maybe there were trucks still being washed. Another sobriety test in case she failed this one.

"I can handle things, ma'am," he said evenly, clearly not keen on his rescue mission drawing an audience. Even an audience of one.

Liza wasn't put off. She was still hung up on that "ma'am." All husky and direct, in that I-can-take-care-of-anything tone they must teach them at the law enforcement academy. She shivered, just a tiny bit. Apparently she'd repressed more uniform fantasies than she'd thought. "I can see that," she responded, smiling, not going anywhere. "Totally under control. I'm sure the citizens of Canyon Springs sleep better knowing that you're on the job. Protecting them from killer birds."

He merely stared at her. "Thanks for stopping. Please be careful when you pull back into traffic."

She glanced over her shoulder. He must be kidding. Traffic? Sure, the town had a steady little bustle of cars and trucks streaming up and down the main road, but traffic? Obviously he'd never seen Long Beach Freeway at five-thirty on a Friday.

"I think I can handle it, Officer," she said with great seriousness.

"I'm sure you can."

She smiled then. So, there was a real man lurking behind the badge. And that oh-so-official tone. She wondered what it would take to put a shudder in that "ma'am" of his. *No, bad Liza, bad.* No playing with small-town sheriffs.

But wasn't she on this personal odyssey for the express purpose of discovering new things, new ways of life? In addition to an appreciation for mountain scenery, she'd discovered she had appreciation for uniforms. That was totally new. Liza had spent the past eight of her twenty-nine years hopscotching around the globe, making sure her celebrity clients were all well pampered and cared for, and she'd never once lusted after a man in blue. Or brown and tan, as the case may be. So this could be seen as a positive step.

Maybe this was a test of another kind. "And maybe you're trying way too hard to rationalize an afternoon quickie," she murmured. But the longer she looked up in that tree, the harder it was remembering why celibacy had been an absolute rule on this journey of hers. Yes, she'd watched her oldest and dearest pal, Natalie, fall headlong into love earlier this year, and yes, her own heart had taken a tiny ding when she'd stupidly allowed one of her playmates to become more than a playmate. In her mind, anyway. And okay, so it had been more than a tiny ding.

More like a wake-up thwack in the head. And heart.
But those weren't the only reasons Liza had taken stock
and decided that success didn't always equal happiness.
She supposed she'd been heading toward that epiphany
for some time. Natalie's wedding and Conrad's infidelity
had simply been an impetus to examine why it was that
the more successful Liza got, the less fulfilled she felt.

Sure, she'd kicked ass as the hottest public relations
consultant on the West Coast, and just as certainly, she'd
enjoyed the wealth and the wide variety of perks it
brought her way. Hard work and hard play had made
Liza a very happy girl. For a time. But somewhere along
the way she realized that while she enjoyed the limelight
she garnered for her clients, at the end of the day, when
she went home to her glossy, Century City penthouse
condo, she went alone. She'd substituted clients for real
friends, and flings with the man of the moment for real
intimacy.

She could put together an A-list party at the drop of
a hat. But if she wanted someone to hang out with? Talk
to? Just kick back and be Liza with? Other than Natalie,
who lived three thousand miles away—or had before
meeting the man of her dreams—she had exactly no one.
In fact, outside of her work persona, she wasn't even
sure who the real Liza was. Hence her personal odyssey…and hence swearing off men until she figured out
how to have fun without one.

But…but if she knew it was just a fling, a teeny tiny
little detour, something to take the edge off—after all, it
had been two months, for God's sake, and a vibrator
could only do so much; she had needs, dammit—
wouldn't that be okay? Sort of a little reward for being
so good for so long?

That rationale took on more and more logic the longer

she stood there looking up at the sheriff's gorgeous chiseled face. Even his scowl turned her on. She had no idea why he was so irritated with her; she was only trying to help. Well, okay, maybe she wasn't helping, exactly. But she certainly wasn't keeping him from doing his job. And usually men were more than happy to let her help them. She'd built an entire career on that specific ability. Her clientele had been largely of the male persuasion simply because she understood their needs, their sense of pride and that little boy insecurity they never seemed to outgrow.

That was the part she missed most. Being needed, being the one they called to make it all better. She knew it was more of that faux intimacy thing, but without that, the gaping void in her life loomed even larger. Actually, it had sort of come as a surprise to her that she didn't miss much of anything else. Not the parties, the tours, the openings, the award ceremonies, the press conferences. The wild, uncontrolled sex with the Hollywood hottie of her choice. Okay, so maybe she missed that last part just a little bit. But she didn't miss the empty feeling that came afterward. The little pangs of neediness that postcoital snuggling no longer fulfilled.

Only, she wasn't quite sure how to transcend the arm-candy-at-the-latest-premiere followed by the fun-in-the-sack part. Probably she had to be friends with a guy first, find a man who satisfied her on levels other than sexual, a guy whose sole credentials weren't that he owned his own tux and looked damn fine in it. Then the rest would probably just happen. Wouldn't it? She thought of Natalie and had to grin. Her best friend had found her man in exactly the opposite way. An exclusive, purely sexual relationship that had led to real love.

So why couldn't it work that way for her?

Because it never has before, Liza, that's why. Nat had just gotten lucky.

Well, she'd like to get lucky, too, Liza thought with a wistful sigh as she watched Sheriff Sexy Ass lever that impressive torso of his up a bit higher, trying to reach his quarry. A quarry with an awfully big beak.

"Does he bite?" she asked.

Mango strutted some more and let out another one of his ozone-disintegrating screeches.

"Never mind," she called up. "Who needs the beak when you can defeat your predators by deafening them first?"

She thought she heard Sheriff Sexy Ass snort under his breath, but when he looked down at her again, his face was an impersonal mask. "Really, we'll be fine up here, ma'am. Thank you for stopping," he repeated. "Please be careful when you pull back into traffic."

Brown. She was pretty sure his eyes were brown.

"Do you always come to the rescue of your feathered citizens?"

"Do you always refuse to take a hint?"

She merely grinned.

He sighed. "I do when it's this one."

"She belongs to you, then?"

"God, no," he said, his tone one of horror. Mango strutted closer and he turned his attentions back to the bird. A minute or two passed, but he didn't look her way again.

She was being dismissed. Had been being dismissed for the past several minutes. Problem was, she wasn't ready to leave yet. An occasional drawback of hers, true, but more often a hallmark of her success. She never left something alone until she was done with it, no matter if it was done with her.

Staring at the flex of muscle in the good sheriff's thighs as he pushed himself up even higher, she freely admitted she wasn't done with him yet. In fact, right at that moment there was nowhere else she'd rather be than standing on a street corner in downtown Canyon Springs.

Suddenly Mango lunged, and Liza squealed and pointed. "Look out!"

He might not have flinched at Mango's scream, but he did at hers. Mango made a beak-dive for the nice, shiny star on his pocket just as he lost his balance.

Liza gasped. He slid from his branch and fell, butt first, into the V of branch and trunk just below. Mango flapped his wings and raced up and down the branch overhead, screeching the entire time as the sheriff cut loose with his own vocal tirade.

"I'm pretty sure they didn't teach you *that* in the academy."

"Nope, those I learned courtesy of Vegas street scum," he grumbled, trying to unwedge himself.

Las Vegas? Street scum? *Hmm,* Liza thought. She didn't think he was talking about Las Vegas, New Mexico. Which meant her sheriff had once run a much bigger town. A town filled with vice and sin. Fully intrigued now, she folded her arms and leaned against her car as she watched him try to extricate himself. He certainly appeared to have the upper body strength for it. A nice, thickly muscled chest, and incredible arms... Did they have a gym in Canyon Springs? she wondered. Somehow she didn't think her sheriff had paid a membership fee for those biceps.

"Are you sure you don't want me to run over to the fire department and get them to bring a ladder or something?"

"I'm sure," he growled, not bothering to look at her. His gaze was focused on Mango, who sat, quietly now, preening his magnificent tail feathers and looking as innocent as a little canary. "Escape artist," he muttered.

"So, he makes a habit of this, huh? Whose is he?"

"My mother's."

"Aww, that's so sweet of you, rescuing your mom's bird."

"There is nothing remotely sweet about this bird. Or my mother, most days, for that matter."

Liza thought of her own parents and nodded in understanding. She hadn't heard from her father since marriage number five, which, as several years had passed since then, was likely several "I do's" ago. Her mother only remembered to check in when she wanted something. Which was mercifully infrequent. "So, what kind of bird is Mango?" she asked. "I've never seen a white parrot before."

He gave her a long look, then sighed. "He's a cockatoo. Moluccan."

"He's really gorgeous."

"Yeah. Right. A real prince. Listen, maybe you can do me a favor."

Liza grinned. She knew she'd get to him eventually. "Sure."

"How good are you at climbing trees?"

Her grin disappeared. "You're not asking me to climb that tree."

He twisted a bit and looked down at her. He could smile, as it turned out, only there was nothing friendly about it. This was more like a take-no-prisoners kind of smile. Still, it managed to send those shivers through her again, anyway. She might like being taken prisoner by him for an afternoon...or three. But she drew the line at physical exertion of any other kind. That's what personal trainers were for—to sweat with her clients while she got her nails done and took another business lunch.

"I'm not what you'd call a climber," she said. "Social, maybe," she appended with a saucy grin. "Why don't you let me get you a nice strong fireman with a ladder?"

"Because Tucker Greywolf would love nothing more than to come pull me out of this tree."

"Ah." The pride thing. This she understood. "What exactly is it you think I can do for you if I were to climb this tree?" Not that she was going to, but she was nothing if not good at solving crisis situations. It was simply a matter of finding out who to call to fix it.

"My belt is stuck under a knob on this branch. I can't reach around for it without letting go. If you could climb up just a few feet and pop it off, I could maneuver myself out of here."

He was only about twelve to fifteen feet up. A person—meaning someone other than her—would only have to climb about three or four feet, reach the rest of the way, and presto. Shouldn't be too hard to wrangle someone walking down the street to do that. Only when she turned and looked around the corner, there seemed to be a sudden dearth of pedestrians. A few children down the block on their bikes and two elderly women crossing at the far corner—that was it. She sighed and looked up again.

He was staring down at her, waiting.

She glanced down at her perfectly gorgeous Jimmy Choo slings. They gave a two-inch advantage to her skimpy five-foot-four frame, but that wasn't going to be enough.

"I can't climb in heels," she said.

"Then kick them off."

"I really don't climb trees. I'm a city girl. L.A. by way of New York."

"This is a city."

She planted her hands on her hips. "A city with a perfectly good fire department two blocks down."

"Forget it." The sheriff redoubled his efforts, making the branch Mango was perched on sway wildly. The bird merely continued to preen, as if it were the wind blowing and not its rescuer flailing about. Then the sound of ripping fabric rent the air. "Well, shit."

"Shit! Shit!" Mango did a little hop from claw to claw, quite happy with his new vocabulary word. "Well, shit!"

Sheriff Sexy Exposed Ass let his chin drop. "Wonderful. This is all I need."

Liza was wide-eyed, staring both at the bird…and the patch of bright yellow smiley faces peeking out from those brown trousers. She focused on the former, though it cost her. "I didn't know Mango talked. What else does he say?"

"Only the things you never want him to. Listen, could we cut the chatter—" he glared at Mango "—from both parties, and get my belt unstuck, please?"

Liza shifted her attention from the prancing cockatoo to the smiley faces. After all, she *had* tried to focus on the bird first, hadn't she? "A briefs man, huh?"

"Wha—? Oh, that. Present from a friend. A joke, really. It's early when I get up and they were just what came out of the drawer next. Why am I explaining this to you?"

She shrugged. "That's what you get for dressing in the dark. Me, I prefer doing it with the lights on."

For a split second his gaze sharpened to such a fine

point she thought she felt it pierce her. Right where she wanted to be pierced, too. Then he sighed and let his head drop back, and it was like the moment never happened. Only it had. She knew it, and her libido definitely knew it. And wanted to be pierced again. And again. *Down, girl.*

"Please, I'm at your mercy here," he said. "Name your price."

Boy, talk about a test. The things she could come up with right now. But she met the challenge and said, "Do they serve lunch somewhere nearby?"

"Fine, lunch, great. Now could we— Oh, shit."

"Shit!" Mango mimicked happily. "Shit, oh, shit!"

Liza ignored the bird and turned in the direction the sheriff was looking. From his vantage point he could see past the corner. She took a step or two and craned her neck so she could see as well. A small, somewhat interesting contingent was heading their way. A strapping man in a form-fitting blue uniform, framed by two identical middle-aged women in identical business attire, fronted by a tall, rawboned woman wearing plaid Bermuda shorts, a pale green, long-sleeve pullover and a floppy straw hat. A long braid of shocking red hair lay over her shoulder. Her cane clacked against the cement sidewalk.

"Please God, just kill me now," she heard the sheriff say over her head.

"Greywolf and company, I take it?"

"I will pay any price if you could get me out of this tree before they get here."

Liza looked at the closing contingent, still a good block and a half away, then back up to the beseeching eyes of her sheriff. Definitely brown, she thought. And she *was* a sucker for brown eyes. Okay, so she was a sucker for green eyes. But that was only because she'd never seen eyes like his before.

"This is going to cost you big, you know," she said, still weighing her options. "Very, very big."

Then he grinned. A real grin. The Cheshire cat had nothing on this grin. "Oh, I'm sure it already has."

Liza sighed, then kicked off her shoes.

2

DYLAN HADN'T THOUGHT she'd really do it. But he was too damn grateful to tease her about it. He'd get his chance later. A vivacious brunette who liked the feel of a hot rod vibrating beneath her thighs was almost impossible not to have some fun with. And he might just be up for a little fun. As soon as he got out of this damn tree.

If he wasn't so annoyed at his mother's damn bird—and all too aware of the coming confrontation—he'd have enjoyed the hell out of watching Ms. Fancy Heels try to climb a tree. She wasn't kidding when she said she wasn't a climber.

"Dammit!"

She glared up at him as she lost the scant foot she'd gained and landed on the ground again. He had to admit he admired her spunk when, rather than quit, she squared her lovely, rounded shoulders and tried again. She wore a silky, aquamarine T-shirt that clung to her curves. A narrow band of smooth, honey-colored skin peeked from between the hem of the shirt and the low waistband of her white cotton pants. Pants that hugged her all the way down to just below her knee…and just above a very nice flare of calf muscle.

Must have gotten them from tottering around on those Popsicle stick heels, he thought, not uncharitably. Given her definite lack of athleticism, he figured she'd been born into those amazing curves of hers…and he was damn grateful for that, even if it didn't get him out of this tree.

He winced a little when her bracelets—she wore what looked like dozens of silver chains on her wrists—scraped along the gnarled trunk as her slender, ringed fingers scrabbled for purchase. He mentally added a manicure and possibly a trip to the jewelry store to the tab he was rapidly running up with her.

Another slide, another broken nail. She didn't even look at him this time. Instead she turned, shot a gauging glance around the corner, then shifted her gaze to her car.

Oh no. "*Now* you're taking off?" Not that he could blame her.

"Of course not. I always finish what I start," she retorted, then hopscotched barefoot on the hot pavement as she hurried to the driver's side of her car and jumped in. Literally. So maybe she was a bit more limber than he'd credited her with.

"What exactly are you—" He stopped as he realized her plan. She edged her car just beneath the tree, climbed back out, then scooted her fine little body onto the metal luggage rack bracketed to the miniscule trunk.

"Hold on," she called up to him.

"Oh, I'm not going anywhere." He couldn't believe she was actually going to all this trouble. But it was too damn entertaining to watch. Not to mention critical to saving his backside. Literally and figuratively.

He hadn't been surprised to hear she was from L.A. He could spot that movie-town gloss a mile away. Usually her type headed for Santa Fe and Taos, but occasionally they tooled down to Sierra County for the Balloon Regatta, or just to tell their friends they'd been to a town called Truth or Consequences.

None of which explained what a West Coast princess was doing crawling up on her car in downtown Canyon Springs. He watched her steady herself and carefully straighten, before looking up at him. Damn, but God had been having a really fine day when he put her together.

So, maybe Dylan would discover why she was here over lunch. And if he was lucky—and it had been so long since he'd even thought about getting lucky, he figured he was long overdue—breakfast as well.

Her short black curls whipped about in the breeze, dancing along a forehead presently furrowed as she reached once, then twice, for his backside.

Her nails were painted dragon-lady red. As was her mouth. And dear Lord, what a mouth. How had he missed that? Her eyes were a bright flashy blue that almost matched her shirt. But that bow-tie mouth… A man could waste large portions of the night fantasizing about a mouth shaped like that.

She reached up again. This time those nails scraped lightly along the swath of cotton the tear in his uniform had revealed. The way his body leaped to attention you'd have thought she'd stroked them down the length of his—

"Careful," he barked when she brushed him again. Jesus, it had been too long, if just the tips of her nails were arousing him so swiftly. It was bad enough his choice in underwear was being flashed to half the town. He really didn't need to reveal anything else, most especially not a raging hard-on.

"Get down before you fall," he ordered, when she made a little hop and swiped at his belt.

"I can get it, I just have to…" She crouched and

jumped a little higher and smacked the heel of her hand against the part of his belt that was stuck. "There!" she cried as it popped free, then shrieked when she lost her balance and did a slow tumble into the front seat of her car.

"Are you okay?" Dylan levered himself up onto the branch and looked down at the scene below.

She didn't answer. Not because she was hurt. Because she was laughing.

She was sprawled in the passenger seat, legs spread akimbo over the headrest and dashboard, arms flung wide as if waiting for him to hope down to join her.

"Don't give me any ideas," he murmured, then watched in amused fascination as she expertly untwined herself from the upholstery, levered herself upright, then pushed her wayward curls from her face, checked her lipstick in the visor mirror and settled in the front seat as casually as if she was merely waiting for her driver to show up. Yeah, definitely more limber than he'd given her credit for.

He'd never harbored hot-rod sex fantasies before, preferring the roominess of a bed—a big bed—thank you. But images of tangling himself up with her and all that soft leather were definitely appealing to him at the moment.

"Sure you're okay?" he asked, thinking he'd be a lot more okay after a cold shower. Or an afternoon drive into the countryside with her in that car.

"Oh, no problem, Officer," she said oh-so-innocently, then followed it up with a sly wink that was anything but. "But you might want to get down from there before..." She pointed behind him.

Oh yeah. "I have to get this damned bird down first." He'd forgotten all about Mango. His scowl returned as he looked up to where the cockatoo had been moments ago. There was a great flutter and flapping sound behind him. He swiveled just in time to see Mango stretch his huge wings—his huge clipped wings—and swoop ever so gracefully in an umbrella of white-and-salmon-colored feathers to land on—

"Look out," he shouted. "Incoming."

Ms. Bow-tie Lips turned just in time to see Mango land on the seat back behind her.

"Mango is a good boy!" the bird announced rather proudly, then attempted to prove his claim by prancing back and forth, bopping his head up and down, then extending one claw and, very sweetly, asking, "Step up?"

Dylan swore as he climbed to the lowest branch, then dropped to the ground. "Come here, you big pink chicken," he said as he approached the car.

But Mango was having nothing to do with him. He lunged and squawked, his crest fluffed out to its fullest extent.

"You know, I don't think he likes you," his rescuer murmured.

She really did have the sassiest mouth.

"He does prefer women. Go ahead, put your arm out for him. He's asking you to, so it'll be okay."

She laughed—a full-bodied sound that had those images flashing in his brain again. "Yeah, right. I've already lost three nails. I'd as soon keep the fingers they were attached to."

"He won't—"

"Why, there's my precious boy!"

Dylan broke off and looked up as Tucker and his mother rounded the corner. He had no idea where the Miller twins, Metsy and Betsy—one fraction of Tucker's personal fan club—had left off, but Dylan was glad for the reduced crowd. His mother rushed toward him. Rush being perhaps a bit too enthusiastic a term. Avis Jackson did everything at her own pace, even before she'd had to take to using a cane after a round of knee surgery.

"Come to Momma, my baby."

Dylan didn't turn or open his arms for her, knowing she wasn't referring to her only son.

Instead he casually leaned against the car and crossed his ankles, concealing the unfortunate state of his pants—both front and back. "Safe and sound," he said, trying not to grit his teeth as she cooed and fussed over her "sweet baby."

"Sweet my ass," he muttered.

"I happen to think it's pretty sweet."

He glanced down to find Liza sizing up the posterior he'd rested just beside her. But before he could respond to her whispered aside, his attention was pulled back to his mother and Mango.

"You really need to stay where I put you, baby," she was telling the bird.

"You really need to use that safe lock I got you after his last escape."

His mother merely clucked her tongue and scooped the giant bird up so she could cuddle him against her chest. "He doesn't like being all locked up. Do you, sweetie?" she crooned.

"Then you have to keep the windows—"

She turned on him, her frown emphasizing the deep grooves bracketing her mouth. "I'm not getting any younger, and I'll stifle if I have to sit all cooped up in some air-controlled trap. I like to feel the air move. Mango and the rest of the flock like the breeze, too."

She turned and her face became a wreath of smiles. "Don't you, sweet boy?"

Dylan had long ago stopped trying to figure out how a recalcitrant, oversize parrot could weasel its way into his mother's good graces when he'd spent the last thirty years trying to do the same thing, only to conclude no such path existed. For him, anyway.

"So, you new in town?"

Dylan shifted his attention back to the sports car. Tucker was leaning over the driver's side door, beaming that million watt smile he'd perfected back in his high school quarterback days.

She didn't answer directly. Instead she stuck her hand out and said, "And you would be?"

"Tucker Greywolf, town fire marshal."

"Pleasure to meet you."

Dylan scowled as he watched Liza give Tucker a thorough visual frisking. His frown deepened when Tucker returned the favor. And she didn't seem to mind.

Dylan cleared his throat. "We should get this car moved." He glanced at Tucker. "It's in a fire lane."

"So it is," Tucker said, still smiling. "Why don't you move it right around the corner to that lot there?" He pointed diagonally across the intersection. "Next to LuLu's. I'll spring for some lunch. It's nothing fancy, but—"

"I've already got a lunch date, Marshal, but thank you for—"

"Call me Tucker."

She merely smiled. "Thanks for the invitation, Tucker. Maybe some other time. I'm Liza."

Liza. Dylan groaned silently. No. This couldn't be happening. First the call from his old captain this morning. Then playing George of the Jungle. Now this. What were the odds her name would be Liza, of all things? And he'd thought his day couldn't get any worse.

Both Tucker and his mother had fallen silent and turned to look at him.

"Oh shit," Mango whispered.

His mother gasped and tucked Mango's head to her breast. "Dylan Benjamin Jackson," she hissed. "Tell me you did not use profanity in front of Mango."

For perhaps the first time ever, Dylan was almost grateful to the pink chicken for his timely interruption. "Mom, really, it's not like he—"

"You know how fond he is of reciting anything said with drama. If he so much as repeats that one time during bingo, I'll—"

"I'm sure he's heard far worse at the fire house. And really, it's not like the ladies have never—"

His mother cut him off with her trademark Glacial Glare of Doom, then flipped her attention back to Liza. Before Dylan could open his mouth to sidetrack her again, or better yet come up with a rapid explanation, she said, "So, you're the floozy keeping my son from getting married, hmm?"

Liza's blue eyes—which only a second earlier had been dancing in amusement at his maternal dressing-down—popped wide as she looked from Avis, to him, then back to Avis. "I beg your pardon?"

"Dylan's stripper. From Vegas." She turned to him and said, "I guess I should be happy you're getting it from somewhere. I'd almost begun to think maybe you were hiding something from me. Although you could have told me you were gay, you know. I'm hip. I'm…what do they call it? Down with that?"

Dylan's eyes bulged. "What? When did you come up with that idea?" And how many people had she shared her little theory with? He groaned, thinking back to the way the old-timers at Pete's Barber Shop had fallen silent the other day when he'd walked in. "And since when do you use phrases like 'down with that'?"

Avis had to raise her voice to be heard over Tucker's howls of laughter. "I have cable. I watch that cute Carson Daly on MTV. And what's a mother supposed to think when every young lady she introduces you to—"

"You mean shoves down my throat," he argued, forgetting Liza for the moment. "Like that poor woman who stopped by the VFW Hall last week during bingo to use the rest room?"

"Bingo!" Mango piped up. "B-12, N-35! We have a winner!"

Avis sniffed and stroked Mango's feathers. "Perhaps I've grown a bit desperate. It's hardly my fault. I want grandchildren to dandle on my lap while I can still sit upright."

As far as he knew, she'd never even dandled him on her lap. She'd been too busy feeding her flock. "And you think that accosting every—"

"Shush now," Avis commanded, then turned a forced smile toward Liza. "Introduce me to your stripper."

"I'm not a stripper," Liza interjected, looking amused once more.

"No," Tucker said, still chuckling. "She's a showgirl, Mrs. Jackson. Remember, Dylan told us all about how she could never find the time to visit due to the two-a-night shows she performs at the Tropicana."

Avis eyed Liza. "Doesn't look tall enough to be a showgirl. Aren't showgirls usually taller? She's got the boobs for stripping, though." She looked down at her own meager chest. "Saw a program on the Discovery channel about showgirls. Always thought it would be fun to wear those tassel things and…'' She looked at Liza, and in all seriousness, asked, ''Do you know how to make them swing in circles and—''

''Mother!'' Dylan felt his stomach burn, and automatically fished in his pockets for a roll of antacids. Only he didn't have any. That's why he was sheriff of Canyon Springs and not vice squad detective in Las Vegas anymore. So he didn't have to pop Tums like they were gumdrops. He gently tugged his mother away from the car. ''I'm sorry, Liza. This is all a huge misunderstanding.'' He turned to Avis. ''Mom, this isn't what you think. She's—''

''Really pleased to finally meet you, Mrs. Jackson,'' Liza interrupted, nudging her door open and climbing out. She bent down and scooped up her slings and slipped them on her feet, instantly adding a little showgirl length to those fabulous legs of hers.

Avis looked her up and down. ''Add one of those headdress thingies and I guess you could fill the bill.'' She transferred Mango to one sturdy forearm and stuck out a liver-spotted hand. ''Sorry if I offended. I just worry about my boy, is all. He's thirty-two, you understand. Pleasure to meet you.'' She shot a reproving look at Dylan. ''Finally.''

Liza grinned and winked at Dylan. ''Pleasure is all mine, trust me.''

What the hell did she think she was up to? As if this farce hadn't played out too long already.

Dylan squeezed between them, determined to straighten this out immediately. ''Mom, this isn't—''

''The place for formal introductions,'' Liza interrupted. ''Your son was just about to take me to lunch. We'd love to have you join us.''

Avis's face flushed with surprised pleasure. Dylan swore silently. He didn't know what Liza's game was, but he wasn't going to play along.

His mother patted her braid and adjusted her hat. "I'm not really dressed for lunch. I was out in the garden, weeding, when Mango pushed the screen out again and tried one of his little flying hops. He hates to be away from me. Don't you, boy," she said, snuggling Mango's salmon-colored head, which he'd tucked against her chest. "He's clipped, but the breeze lifted him, and next thing I knew, he was gone."

"Again," Dylan asserted, but no one was listening to him.

"You look fine," Liza assured Avis. She turned to Tucker and gave him her testosterone-booster smile. "I'm sure Marshal Greywolf wouldn't mind seeing to Mango, as he's been in the firehouse before, right?"

Tucker took one look at Dylan's obvious discomfort and stepped right in, all grins and helpful as hell. "Not a problem. Come on, Mango buddy. Let's take a walk."

He stuck out his arm and Mrs. Jackson gave the big bird one last cuddle, then said, "Step up, precious."

The bird dutifully did so, then looked at Dylan as if to say, "It's not women I prefer, just anyone but you."

Yeah, same to you pal, Dylan thought as he watched Tucker hold Mango close to his chest and saunter back down the block toward the station.

"Oh goodness, I almost forgot." Avis grabbed Dylan's wrist and turned it so she could read his watch. "I have a ladies auxiliary meeting. We're discussing the final plans for our Fiesta Day booth." She placed a hand on Liza's forearm. "You will be staying for the fiesta, won't you, dear? We're having our famous salsa-making contest. People come from all over. It's a real event.

Nothing fancy like they have in Vegas, I'm sure, but—''

Dylan stepped in, taking Liza's arm in his, mostly to get her out of his mother's clutches. ''I don't think Liza can—''

''Liza can speak for herself,'' Liza said, extricating her arm and smiling at Avis, who was looking well pleased at the way she was handling herself.

Great, he thought. Thirty-two years he hadn't been able to get on his mother's top perch and now it was suddenly two against one. How in the hell had this happened, anyway?

''I'm not sure of my plans at the moment, Mrs. Jackson,'' Liza was saying.

''And she has manners, too,'' Avis said to her son. ''I'm sorry I called you a floozy, dear.''

''I've been called worse,'' Liza assured her.

If Dylan's life hadn't been flashing before his very eyes, he might have smiled at the momentary blank look that crossed his mother's face.

''Yes, well, I suppose there are some with small minds who would make sweeping assumptions,'' she managed to murmur.

Never mind that she'd just done the same thing, Dylan thought. His mother definitely operated in her own universe, of which she was the undisputed center. He'd long ago learned it was best to stay in his own distant orbit.

Liza merely caught his eye and winked. ''Yes, sweeping assumptions can be a problem.''

Avis smiled. ''Come now, I'll walk you to LuLu's, it's on my way.'' She tucked her hand through Liza's arm and steered them back to the sidewalk. ''So, is being a showgirl so lucrative that you haven't found another line of work to bring you closer to my Dylan?''

"Mother, please." He thought about trying to explain the misunderstanding yet again, but one look at Liza's dancing eyes told him she'd only circumvent him. She obviously thought this was hysterically funny, and if he weren't so annoyed, he'd probably think so, too. He'd put an end to it as soon as he got Liza alone.

Which no longer entailed the pleasurable scenario he'd envisioned earlier. Now he was thinking that the sooner he got her out of town, the better.

"Actually, I've quit my job," Liza announced.

"Well, hallelujah," Avis crowed. "Does this mean you're coming to Canyon Springs permanently?" She reached over and rapped Dylan's ankle with her cane. "Why didn't you tell me? We would have thrown a party or something."

"I'm going to have you register that thing as a lethal weapon," he said, wincing as he flexed his leg. "And I didn't tell you, because I'm as surprised by this as you are." He sent Liza a pointed look.

She merely smiled brightly as they paused in front of the door to LuLu's. "Here we are."

Dylan stepped in, blocking the door and separating the two women at the same time. "Enjoy your meeting, Mom."

Avis frowned, clearly not liking being manipulated. *If she only knew.*

Liza opened her mouth—to say God knew what—but apparently thought better of whatever it was when she caught his eye. "It was a pleasure meeting you, Mrs. Jackson," she said instead.

"Why thank you, dear. And please, call me Avis. Where will you be staying?" She eyed the two of them.

Dylan placed a hand on Liza's shoulder and squeezed.

"We, uh, haven't worked that out yet," Liza said.

"I'll call you later, Mom, okay?"

Avis clearly wished she didn't have other obligations, but finally nodded. "See that you do. Have a nice lunch."

Dylan waved. Liza opened her mouth, but with a bit more applied pressure from him, simply nodded and waved.

Once Avis was around the corner, Liza turned, slid neatly from his grasp and reached for the door.

He shifted and blocked her entry with the toe of his boot. "Just what in the hell kind of game do you think you're playing at here?"

She looked up at him, her expression one of consideration, not guilt or apology. Why didn't that surprise him?

"Tell me one thing," she said. "Is there really a showgirl in Las Vegas pining after you?"

He opened his mouth, then closed it again.

She flashed those white teeth, aqua eyes dancing. "That's what I thought. Pretty clever. Coming up with an out-of-town flame to keep the matchmakers away."

"Not that it's any of your business."

"Not that it's working either, apparently. Did she really try to hook you up with a woman making a potty stop?"

"Just what is it you want from me?"

"Besides lunch, you mean?" She reached up and straightened his badge, which had become crooked during his descent from the tree. "Come on, you can always make up another imaginary girlfriend, right? I mean, no harm really done here." She sighed then. "Okay, I'm sorry, I got carried away. I just couldn't resist." Her lips curved again and she brushed a quick finger along the groove in his chin. "You have the sexiest scowl."

Dylan's gaze narrowed. "I don't have time for this." But he couldn't deny he'd like to make some. An hour or three, anyway. It had been a long time since he'd whiled away an afternoon with a willing woman. A woman who knew how the game was played, and what the rules of engagement were. Only, from what little he knew of Liza, he didn't think she was all that interested in playing by any rules.

She pursed those incredible lips of hers. "Come on, Sheriff Jackson. For a man who climbs trees, you don't seem to enjoy the concept of having fun."

"I had all the fun I could handle in Vegas. I didn't come here to have fun." That hadn't exactly come out how he'd meant it, but he didn't bother trying to explain himself further.

"A pity." Liza turned so that her body brushed briefly against his as she stepped behind him.

"What are you doing?" He almost leaped out of his skin when she snugged up behind him.

"I wasn't sure the citizens of Canyon Springs really wanted to know their sheriff favored smiley-face briefs."

Jesus. How had he forgotten about that? He knew exactly how he'd forgotten. One look at those party girl lips and far-too-knowing eyes and a guy could forget his own zip code. He scooted so his butt faced the wall, putting her a few merciful feet away from him at the same time. "I know I owe you a lunch, but—"

"Yes, you do. Wait right here."

"But, I can't go in there like—" It was too late. She'd disappeared inside.

She was out a moment later, dangling a navy-blue sweater from her fingers. "Here, tie this around your waist."

"Where did you get that?"

"From the coat rack. It was all the way in the back. Probably left here ages ago. Listen, I deal with these sorts of little crises all the time. You can always drop it back off later after you've changed clothes."

He fished his wallet out. "Fine. Great."

She frowned. "What do you think you're doing?" she asked as he peeled off a twenty dollar bill.

He took her hand and placed the bill in it. "For services rendered. Have a nice lunch on me. I have to get back to work and change. I don't have time for—"

"Oh. I see."

How she could put such a wealth of meaning into a couple of tiny words, he had no idea. And why he cared what the hell she thought of him, he also had no idea.

She folded the twenty very carefully and stuck it behind his badge, then patted his chest. "Thanks, anyway." She turned to walk away, then stopped and looked at him in that direct way she had. "Listen, I really am sorry if I caused you any problems. I don't know what got into me back there. I just—" She broke off, then shrugged and smiled at him. For the first time, that bright confident light didn't suffuse that ocean of blue in her eyes. "Have a nice life." She turned and walked away. On those impossibly sexy heels. She didn't look back.

Dylan swore under his breath. Just another eventful day in Canyon Springs, he told himself. Except there were no eventful days in Canyon Springs. He'd come here specifically to embrace the sameness of life that was Canyon Springs, New Mexico.

And then she'd strolled in and reminded him of just how invigorating change could be.

Before he could question his decision, or his sanity, he tied the sweater around his waist and said, "Wait."

3

JUST KEEP WALKING, Liza. She really had to work on her impulse control. Because God knew she'd totally failed in that department over the past half hour. And here was the perfect opportunity. She *really* wanted to stop, find out what sexy Sheriff Jackson had to say. She wanted to say outrageous things to him and watch that little divot in his chin appear, watch the light flash in those yummy caramel eyes. "But no," she said under her breath, "you've wreaked enough havoc for one small town in an afternoon. Time to move on."

Only she really didn't want to do that, either. In fact, this past hour was the most fun she'd had since leaving Natalie and Jake's ranch in Wyoming eight days ago. Hell, since leaving her condo in L.A. a month before that.

She had no idea what had gotten into her—okay, that was a lie. Sheriff Dylan Jackson had gotten into her. Her poor little libido had whimpered pitifully, and the next thing she knew she was letting his mother believe she was a Vegas showgirl. Although, and she doubted Dylan would be impressed with the significant difference, she hadn't actually told Avis anything that wasn't true. Liza had quit her job. And she didn't know where she was staying tonight.

But, dear Lord, she knew where she'd like to stay.

He was an ex-Vegas cop, her little libidinous voice

whispered. Not a small-town boy with those inconvenient, uptight small-town morals. Certainly not if he'd created a showgirl as his imaginary girlfriend. Liza smiled to herself. Maybe he enjoyed saying outrageous things, too.

All the more reason to keep on walking. She was supposed to be "finding" herself. Not finding a man to play with. But, dammit, one nice afternoon playing with Sheriff Dylan Jackson would sure as hell take the edge off.

She slowed, just fractionally, as her resolve wavered. Fortunately for her, it was just enough of a pause to allow Dylan to catch up to her. Her conscience clear—after all, she hadn't actually given in to her impulses, right?—she turned to face him. *Dear Lord,* she thought, feeling her skin heat up. Even with a silly blue sweater tied around his waist, he was every woman's pure, unadulterated authority-figure fantasy come to life. She'd never harbored any domination fantasies…but, hey, she was adaptable.

"If you'd like, I can go to the auxiliary meeting and explain everything to your mother," she offered.

She almost laughed at the look of horror that flashed across his rugged face. "That won't be necessary."

Liza folded her arms. It was that or reach out and trace those lips. They were so distinctly defined, almost hard looking. But she'd bet they were quite clever, that he knew just how to use them for maximum effect. *Like now,* she thought. The frown he was delivering was very effective. If she was the sort to be put off by that kind of thing. Which she wasn't.

When he didn't say anything else, she took a step back. "Well, then, I'll be on my way." It was a distinct invitation for him to stop her, to say whatever it was that had prompted him to follow her down the street. She could see the urge to do so warring with the resolve to simply nod, wave and wish her a safe trip. She knew all about that little internal tug-of-war. She lost those battles more often than she won them. She didn't use to mind. She wished she minded more now.

"Where are you headed?"

Good compromise, she thought with admiration. Not exactly a capitulation, but not a decisive victory, either. "Why?" she asked. "Did you want to escort me out of town before I get into any more trouble?"

His lips quirked, and for a moment she thought she'd be treated to another one of those I-dare-you-to-be-bad smiles. "I have a feeling that nothing stops you from getting into trouble if that's what you want to do."

"Why, Sheriff, I'm not sure you meant that as a compliment. But if you meant to say that I get whatever I set my mind to having...then you'd be right." *Stop flirting, get in your car and head out of town.* But this was fun. He wasn't like the flavor-of-the-month men she'd helped Hollywood churn out by the fistfuls.

The fact that she'd actually fallen for one of those prefab flavors still irked her. She'd never been susceptible to developing emotional attachments to the men she dated, and still had no idea why in the hell Conrad had been any different. Actually, he hadn't been any different. It was she who had been different. Needy. Emotional. Devastated when she'd found out he'd been sleeping with his own flavor-of-the-month. The fact that it had happened just as Natalie thought she was finding her real true love hadn't helped matters any.

"What makes you think Canyon Springs is a pit stop and not my destination?" she said.

"Call it intuition."

"The same kind of intuition that told me your Vegas dream girl was a figment of your imagination?"

He flashed her that smile, and her thighs actually went liquid for a moment. Damn, but he was potent. She could have done amazing things with that smile in her old line of work. The very idea of convincing Dylan Jackson to take a screen test had her suppressing a smile of her own.

"I have a fairly vivid imagination," he assured her, his smile shifting to a cocky grin. "But I didn't need to rely on that."

Oh yeah, he'd have tested off the scale.

"Have plenty of experience with Vegas showgirls, do you?"

"I've seen one or two."

"Personally…or professionally?"

He simply smiled.

Dear God. Liza pressed her thighs together. "So, is it the flashy car that pegged me as an outsider?"

"It's not the flash of the car, but of the occupant."

She laughed, not at all offended by his assessment. After all, he was right. He was also fun. And sharp. And eat-me-up sexy. Maybe she would hang around Canyon Springs. Just for a little while. And really, what harm could come of it? She was hardly going to break his heart. And her heart, despite recent bizarre activity, was certainly safe from a big-city-turned-small-town sheriff.

She may have decided that the superficiality of Hollywood had been slowly sucking her spirit dry, but wherever she landed, she was reasonably sure it would have more than two traffic lights. And at least one seriously upscale shopping mall.

"So, I'm flashy, am I?" She looked down at her capri pants and clingy silk T. "What's glitzy about me?" She was wearing only a few bracelets and one pair of earrings. No belly chain, no toe rings. Even her hair was relatively tame. Shoot, she was a total Plain Jane today. If you didn't count the shoes. But they were such sweet little heels, weren't they?

She glanced up just as Dylan stepped closer, and actually felt a slight tremble when he lifted his hand. Man, she hadn't reacted to a male this viscerally since…well, never. Probably it was the enforced celibacy magnifying her reaction.

But she doubted it.

He flicked a wayward curl from her cheek without actually touching her skin, then let his hand fall away before she could press her cheek into his palm. Not that she would have. Surely she would have resisted being that obvious. Surely.

"It's not the clothes," he said. "Some women just radiate flash."

She raised her eyebrows. "Oh, so now I'm 'some women?'"

"Ah. I suppose you're used to being singled out. Put on a pedestal. Worshipped. Is that it?"

She shrugged and tossed him her sauciest grin. "What can I say? Slavelike worship has always worked for me."

"Well, if it's any consolation, you're definitely not run-of-the-mill."

"Oh gee, my heart is all aflutter, Sheriff."

Now he grinned. "I do my best."

"So, if I'm nothing special, why are you standing on the street in downtown Canyon with a sweater hiding your smiley faces, stalling me from leaving?"

He took another small step forward. There was still plenty of space between them. To anyone passing by, it would look like a simple conversation between two adults. But she knew better. The air between them all but crackled. "Do you want me to keep you from leaving?"

"Maybe I just want you to admit that I'm special."

He smiled. "Surely you've heard that enough times, from enough men, to believe it by now. Why would hearing it from me make any difference?"

She'd just been playing with him, not serious at all, but his question made her pause. It shouldn't make any difference, anything he said to her. She didn't even know him. But she did know what he wasn't. He wasn't a player. He wasn't part of the machine, part of the hype, part of the world that never said anything, did anything, for anyone, without there being some angle, some hidden agenda. So, in that respect, it did make a difference hearing it from him.

A shame she'd just been teasing him. He didn't know her, couldn't possibly make an informed judgment on anything about her. "You're right," she said, feeling vaguely depressed by the admission, ridiculous as that was. "I guess it wouldn't."

He cocked his head. "Why are you in Canyon Springs, anyway?"

"I'm on my way home from a wedding."

"Albuquerque? Santa Fe?"

She shook her head. "Wyoming."

He laughed. "Sort of a circuitous route you're taking back to California, isn't it? Either that or you're really lost."

"You can't get lost when you don't have an itinerary."

"I guess that's one way of looking at it. But you do have a destination. Which is west of here, you know. West and a state or so away."

"I'm aware of that. I don't have to be back anytime soon."

"No new job waiting?"

She shook her head. "I'm on an extended... sabbatical."

"Must have been successful in your old job, to take an open-ended leave like that."

"Yeah, well, success isn't measured only in money," she said, then smiled. "But it does make sabbatical-taking a whole lot easier."

"Sort of like running away from home, but with an expense account, huh?"

"Is there any other way to run?" He really was an intriguing guy, she thought. Intuitive. Sexy as hell, good sense of humor, but with something a little dark and edgy on the fringes. Probably the part of Vegas he still carried inside him. A shiver of awareness raced over her skin as she wondered what he might have been like if she'd crossed paths with him when that darkness was still fresh. Visions of those authority-figure fantasies popped into her head again, complete with handcuffs, leather belts and—

And that was quite enough of *that*. She clasped her hands, surprised to find her palms a bit damp. "I guess I'll be on my way, then."

"I guess you will."

Neither of them moved.

"Head west, go past one state and hang a right, huh?" she said, after the silence stretched until her thighs got twitchy again.

"Or you could keep heading south. Since you're in no hurry."

"True. I'm not sure I'm done running away yet. I'm

sort of enjoying my little adventure." *Or I am now,* she thought.

His eyes suddenly narrowed and his entire body language shifted even though he didn't move a muscle. "You aren't running from something, are you? Someone?"

Liza felt the hairs all over her body lift at that sudden shift in intensity, all focused so deliciously on her. "Just the old me." She smiled when he only fractionally relaxed. "Although she does seem to be dogging my steps today."

"Meaning?"

"Old habits die hard."

He thought about that for a moment. "Rescuing men is a bad habit of yours?"

She laughed. "You could say that. Be thankful, though. My price used to be pretty steep."

"Hey, I tried to buy you lunch."

"No, you tried to buy your way out of lunch. There's a difference."

"You didn't honestly expect me to go in there dressed like this?"

"Half the town has probably driven past by now and seen you dressed like that. And, frankly, you don't strike me as the sort whose masculinity is threatened all that easily."

"I'll take that as a compliment. And typically, you'd be right. Anywhere except here. Hometowns have a way of making you feel you have to prove you're a grown-up."

"And not the roughneck rascal you used to be?"

He laughed. "How'd you guess?"

She could tell him her body knew a bad boy when it was around one, but he was so many things she'd never been around, it wouldn't have been entirely true. "So, why come back?"

"I was done being gone."

"Interesting answer. Surely there are other places besides Vegas and your hometown that needed a sheriff."

"I'm sure there are. I guess I needed to be someplace where I mattered on more than just a professional level. Good or bad, and there's some of both, Canyon Springs is that place for me."

Liza smiled. "So, is this a good day or a bad one?"

"Maybe a little of both."

"Ouch."

"Well, you did wreak a bit of havoc that I'm going to have to clean up."

"Guilty as charged." She stuck her arms out, wrists close together. "Take me in, Officer."

He surprised her by taking her wrists in one broad hand before she could drop them. His strength and speed shouldn't have surprised her…or soaked her panties like that.

"Maybe I'll do just that," he said.

She lifted her gaze from that big hand restraining her, circling hers so easily, so completely…. She hated not being in control. Really hated it. So why she opened her mouth and said, "Maybe I'll let you," she had no idea.

Those caramel eyes of his heated up. "Do I need to lock you up right now?" He stroked a finger across the pulse thrumming in her wrist…and his lips curved in a knowing smile. "Or can I leave you on your own recognizance until I'm off work?"

"Depends," she said, proud that she'd managed to get the word past her suddenly parched throat. "How long will I be left to my own devices?"

He grinned. "I'm thinking any amount of time is time enough for you to find trouble."

Liza merely smiled.

"Can I trust you to leave well enough alone with the showgirl story?"

"I don't know, that's asking an awful lot. I'm a people person. So I'm bound to meet up with some, and you know how it is, you get to talking and all." She tried hard to ignore the riot of sensations his gentle, but quite firm grip on her wrists was wreaking on her body. Christ, she'd have to be a saint to pull that off. And one thing she'd never be, no matter how long a sabbatical she took from the opposite sex, was a saint.

She shuddered just a tiny bit when he rubbed his thumb along the base of her palm. And she was pretty sure she was about to take a sabbatical from her sabbatical.

"To be—" She was forced to stop and clear her throat. She wondered if he had any idea how long it had been since a man confounded her like this. One look at the smile teasing that hard mouth of his and she figured he had plenty of ideas. Dear Lord have mercy. "To be on the safe side, why don't you fill me in on what you've told the general population here. So I can keep my story straight, of course."

"Of course." He relaxed his hold, but rather than sliding his hands up her arms and pulling her closer, which he had to know she was ready for, he surprised her once again by sliding his fingers down along her hands instead, all the way down her fingers to the very tips...before finally dropping his hands away.

Way more effective. Way.

"Tell you what," he said, his own voice just a fraction rougher. He fished in his pocket and came up with a set of keys. He slid one off and handed it to her.

Just full of surprises. She was off balance—badly enough that it rattled her a bit. This was so far outside the way these things typically worked for her that she reacted on instinct, meaning she used her mouth to put herself back on top. Figuratively speaking. "So, I've won the key to your heart already, have I?"

He didn't even blink. "Not a chance. This one unlocks something far less dangerous."

He was way too good at this. Almost as good as she was.

"It's the key to my place."

She laughed. "What kind of sheriff are you?"

"The kind that knows which is the safer bet. Trust me, there's not too much damage you can do at my place."

"Meaning you'd rather keep me tucked away, private, out of sight."

"Out of earshot is more like it."

She couldn't help but smile. "So, do you make a habit of giving strange women the key to your house?"

"You would be the first. And you're hardly strange."

She grinned. "Well, that's close enough to admitting I'm special to appease my inner princess." She eyed him consideringly. "Aren't you going to ask me if I'm in the habit of taking keys from strange men?"

He chuckled then. "Well, let's just say—and I know you'll take this the right way—I have a feeling you can handle yourself just fine with any man."

She could have told him he wasn't just any man, but she had little enough leverage as it was. "That may well be true. But I'd still be putting myself in a situation that would be hard to defend, if you chose to…overpower me." Dear Lord, where had that come from? So much for that pesky little domination fantasy she'd never had.

He pushed another curl from her cheek, this time just lightly brushing her skin. "I'm pretty sure the one overpowered here is me."

If he only knew, she thought, fighting the shudder of pleasure that threatened to ripple through her.

"But if you need further reassurance, I'd hardly do anything nefarious in my own hometown, where everyone's business is, well, everyone's business."

"You are the law, though. If you want something done, doesn't it get done?"

"You did stand under that tree an hour ago and watch me lose a battle with a bird, did you not?"

She laughed. "True. And your mother is a formidable woman."

"You don't know the half of it."

"You'd be surprised. Sometime we'll have to swap parent tales. I could raise your hair." *This is an afternoon fling, Liza, not* This Is Your Life.

"I could make the obvious observation here, but that would be too easy."

Easy. Sort of like some might think she was being at the moment. Only this didn't feel remotely easy. Still...

"When I said I rescued men, just exactly what did you think my former occupation was, anyway?"

Now he laughed. "Trust me, that was the last thing on my mind."

"So sure, are you?"

That dark edgy look was back in his eyes. "I worked vice in Vegas. I'm sure."

She relaxed. A little. "Okay. So I'm just supposed to head over to your place and sit and wait for you." She smiled. "I'm not sure whose fantasies we're fulfilling here."

"Is that what this is for you? A fantasy fulfillment of some kind?"

Oops. Oh well, in for a penny… "Didn't start out that way."

"But?"

"Well, at the risk of sounding horribly unimaginative, which, trust me, is so not like me—"

"That, I believe."

"Says the guy who created the floozy girlfriend."

"Showgirls work hard, they're not floozies."

"I won't ask how you know that."

He shrugged. "Your choice."

She grinned. "So maybe I will ask. Later."

"I suppose we both have some stories to tell. If that's how you want to spend the evening."

"Depends. What else did you have in mind?"

"Dinner. And—"

She raised a hand. "I might be willing to sit and wait, but I draw the line at cooking."

"Ever?"

"I don't recall us discussing more than this one dinner at the moment."

"At the moment, huh? I'll keep that in mind, too."

"Oh, I doubt you forget much of anything."

"You'd be right. You like grilled steak and a good red wine?"

"Add a tossed salad and we have a date."

"Deal."

"What else?"

"What else what? You want the dessert menu?"

She laughed. "I could make the obvious statement, but that would be way too easy. What I meant was, you

started to say something else earlier. Dinner and what?''
Something told her he hadn't been going to say ''hot
sweaty monkey sex.'' Although she might have been
perfectly fine with that.

''Dinner. And an evening spent talking on the front
porch, watching the sunset.''

''Sounds very nice. I guess we can discuss that dessert
thing during our porch talk, hmm?''

He grinned and dangled the key. ''I guess we can.''

She didn't take the key, not right away.

''I'm offering to be part of your adventure,'' he said,
looking at her in such a direct way she couldn't help but
stare back. ''Nothing more, nothing less.''

Liza was used to being the one in charge, the one
calling the shots, the one jacking up the atmosphere until
the man in her sights was reduced to a quivering mass
of need. Needs he believed—in that moment, anyway—
only she could fulfill. She was never the one trying to
sort out the dizzying swirl of emotions. Never the one
reduced to taking what was offered.

Of course, once she got him alone, there was nothing
to say she couldn't be the one in charge, the one driving
the course of the evening's activities. He'd told her he
was willing to be a participant in *her* adventures, hadn't
he?

So why, when he pressed the key into her palm, were
her fingers the only ones trembling?

4

HE'D TOTALLY LOST his mind. Dylan drove his Range Rover past the lightning tree and slowed as he approached the road leading to his house. What in the hell had possessed him to give her the key?

He thought about the way she'd looked at him, like she'd wanted to inhale him. The light in her eyes that told him she knew just how she'd lap him up. Slowly, and with great relish. He went hard just thinking about it.

And knew exactly why he'd given her his key.

"Dinner and some sunset conversation, my ass," he muttered. They both knew casual conversation was not her reason for taking that key. Which should have been an immediate turn-off to him. Of the fistful of reasons he'd come back to Canyon Springs, women figured prominently among them. Specifically, the type of woman he'd tended to run across in his previous line of work. Hard, cynical. Bored, lonely. He'd had too many of each, before realizing he saw himself in them.

But Liza wasn't like that. "That's just your hard-on talking," he told himself, shifting in his seat. Although that was partially true, so was his initial take on her. For someone taking a break from life, she didn't look used up or worn-out. Absolutely the opposite. *Alive, hungry, ready.* Those were words he'd use to describe her. He doubted she was casual about anything, even sunset conversation.

He wasn't that blinded by those aquamarine eyes and candy-apple lips. He knew a player was a player, no matter the league. Okay, maybe he was a little blinded. But they had one thing in common that intrigued him enough not to care. They were both escapees. And they wanted each other.

He smiled and pressed down on the gas. So maybe this wasn't the worst idea he'd ever had. At the very least it would be an enjoyable mistake.

His home, a soaring A-frame with more glass than any sane man with an aversion to cleaning would ever put in a house, appeared on the horizon. He smiled. So what? He'd spent long nights staked out in cramped cars dreaming of this exact house. And now it was a reality. And all his.

He topped the last hill and something in him settled, as it always did, every time he saw it. It was nestled perfectly among the tall pines and jagged rocks. He'd had to blast out some of it to make an area large enough to build on, but no one could say the foundation wasn't rock solid. The second-story deck afforded him a wide view of the *rincón*, or valley, below. A short walk to the other side of the mountain presented him with a spectacular view of the canyons where the springs originated.

He enjoyed sitting out on the deck with a cold beer, watching the sun go down as the few winking lights in downtown Canyon Springs flickered on, the endless sky full of stars overhead, the moonrise.

He kept thinking this feeling would wear off, that he'd get that same itch that had driven him from this town the day after he'd graduated from high school. But he'd been back a little over two years now. It had been eight months since he'd hammered the last nail on this place. And he still felt that sense of homecoming every time.

They said you can't go home again. But he was coming to believe that you couldn't really appreciate what home was until you'd left it for awhile. For all the annoyances that went with living in a place where everyone knew you, the sense of security, the steady pace of life, soothed the part of him left jagged and raw by his years in Vegas. That more than made up for the occasional bird rescue or irritating comments from the hometown hero–turned–fire marshal.

The sudden bleat of his cell phone jarred him from his thoughts. He thought about ignoring it, his body humming as he spied Liza's shiny little roadster parked in the drive. He reached over to punch the phone off, but stopped when he saw the number on the digital display. His gut tightened in that familiar way he'd hoped to never feel again. He pressed the Answer button. "How did you get this number?"

The deep voice on the other end chuckled. "Come on, D.J., I worked vice, same as you. If I want to find a number, it gets found."

"What part of 'I'm not interested' didn't Hannigan understand this morning?"

"You know the captain doesn't listen to what he doesn't want to hear."

Dylan let the truck drift to a stop, still a hundred or so yards away from the house. "And all you're going to hear is a bunch of silence when I hang up on you."

He felt the amusement leave his former squad member's voice even before he spoke. "You're the only one she trusted, D.J. She's ready to talk, but she'll only talk to you."

"I heard all this from Hannigan. She knows I'm not on the force anymore."

"That doesn't seem to matter. We've been trying to nail Dugan for—"

"I know exactly how long." The old bite was back in his voice. Dylan didn't appreciate being forced to use it. "It was my case, remember?" His stomach pitched and the acid burned his gut. One phone call and it was like he'd never left Vegas.

"Yeah, we all remember."

Dylan started to tell him where to get off, then bit back the words and sighed. "Quin, I'm out of that game. I'm not coming back."

"No one is asking you to come back. We just want you to conduct this one interview."

"To conduct an interview," he pointed out, "I'd have to come back."

There was a pause. "Not if we brought her to you."

Dylan went still, then his grip tightened on the phone. "Not a chance. I'm hanging up now."

"D.J., wait!" There was just enough desperation in Quin's voice for Dylan to keep his finger hovering over the End button without pushing it. Dylan could be gone for a hundred years and still never forget what it was like to be consumed by that sense of desperation, on the heels of which was always the realization that you'd devoted your whole life to bringing down scum like Armand Dugan. So if you failed…it meant your whole life was a failure.

"Dugan lost interest in you at exactly the same time you lost interest in him," Quin was saying. "He's been way too busy covering his tracks from the rest of us to worry about what your sorry ass has been up to. He also has no idea that we finally got Pearl to turn."

"How *did* you get her to turn?" Dylan swore under his breath when Quin said nothing. "It's a simple question. I worked on her for months. Never met a tougher broad than Dugan's ex-flame."

"Let's just say a woman scorned is a woman to watch the hell out for."

"He scorned her years ago and she accepted his sorry behavior as her due. So why turn on him now?"

"You asking because you're interested in helping out?"

"I'm asking because you're wasting my time with all this, so you might as well tell me the details."

There was another pause while Quin weighed what little leverage he thought he had. Dylan wished there were none at all, but he'd be lying if he said he wasn't at least interested in what had transpired on this particular case since he'd left Vegas. It wasn't the only one still open when he'd left, far from it, but it was one he'd poured a considerable amount of personal time and energy into. It was only human to be curious about how it was going, right?

He wasn't going back. But he might be able to help them out. "If I know why she turned, I might be able to tell you how to get a confession out of her without dragging me into this."

Quin sighed. "I'll take whatever help I can get."

"And owe me for it."

He laughed, but there wasn't as much humor in it. "Yeah, add it to my tab. Okay, here's the deal—"

"You sure you want to discuss this on the cell?"

"You aren't exactly giving me many other options here."

Dylan looked up at his house. His haven. A haven where a gorgeous and hopefully willing woman was waiting for him. He was not taking this into his house, for a lot of reasons. "If you think we're clear, go ahead."

"I'm as reasonably certain of it as I can be, or I wouldn't have said as much as I already have."

"Yeah, yeah, okay. Sorry. I have an appointment here, so give already."

"What, with the Rotary Club or something? What could possibly be going on in that one-horse town of yours at this hour?"

"We don't have horses. We actually drive cars now. And I didn't say it was a business meeting."

Quin hooted. "Some things never change, do they?"

"You'd be surprised," Dylan muttered. "So, why did Pearl decide to turn on her one and only true love?" Out of several Vegas casinos, Dugan ran an underground operation they'd been trying to break open and shut down for years. Despite his mob connections, Dugan played the role of family man. His extended family of aunts, uncles, brothers, sisters, nieces and nephews all benefited generously from not only his money—the part he kept clean—but also from his time and affection.

Five years earlier, word had leaked out that Dugan, who was forty-five at the time, had begun to despair of ever starting a family of his own. Family was sacrosanct to him, but he'd yet to meet the right woman who would help him continue his little dynasty. In the meantime, he'd run into Pearl Halliday, showgirl-turned-stripper. Definitely not the woman to bear his children, but Dugan hadn't minded getting her to bear his attentions for a while. What he hadn't counted on was falling in love with her.

Hopelessly in love. So much so that he'd tried to turn her into the proper woman his family would respect. He set her up with her own dance studio, as a proprietor and instructor. He lavished her with nice things, hired tutors to put some polish on her brass, basically did his best to turn his pearl into a diamond.

Only Pearl was simply Pearl. She wanted Dugan's love, not his things, not his Pygmalion-Svengali attempts to turn her into something she was not. She just wanted her Duggie, the man she'd made breathless with the sheer magnetic force of her attentions. So she made the fatal mistake of giving Armand Dugan an ultimatum: love me for me, or find someone else.

It had taken Dugan less than a week to find that someone else. A quiet young woman of good breeding—and obvious bad taste, if you asked Dylan, for falling for a slimeball like Dugan. It wasn't a love match, but Dugan had come to realize that passion distorted things, took away his ability to control. Elaine Bartoloni would be the perfect, malleable kind of wife he should have been looking for all along. He occasionally wished he could have had it all, but he wasn't stupid. So he took what was best. He graciously left Pearl the title to the dance school and the apartment that sat over it—what had once been their little love nest—and walked away.

Pearl should have hated him for that. Instead she was grateful for the chance to live quietly, out of the spotlight. She was pushing fifty now, but life had aged her beyond her years. Makeup, no matter how pricey, covered only so much. She was too old—in more than calendar years—to dance in the casino shows, and too aware of what real love felt like to take her clothes off again for leering, jeering drunks.

So she'd kept her school, made a life for herself and kept her mouth shut when it came to Armand Dugan. She wouldn't be used as the instrument for the downfall of the only man she'd ever loved. He wasn't to be blamed for the pressure his family had put on him. He was an important man. She was lucky to have had him for the time she did. She'd supposed she'd known all along she'd never be good enough for him. Giving him an ultimatum had just brought to an end what would have ended anyway.

"So why, after years of living quietly, has she finally decided to turn on him?" Dylan asked.

"That's just it, she won't say. She came to us three days ago, asking after you."

"You didn't tell her—"

"Please, no matter how much we hated you walking on us, we'd never do that to you."

"Don't expect an apology. There was never going to be a good time. So I did it on my timetable."

"Yeah, yeah, I hear you. Who knows, someday I might retire down there myself, if for no other reason than to drive you to an early retirement."

"I'm real amused here."

"Let us bring her down to you, you get the information we need to bring him in and get a conviction, then we'll disappear back into the night and leave you to your sweet little six-thirty appointments."

"Until the next time you need my help."

Quin laughed. "You weren't *that* hot a shot, D.J. Just this one favor, then we won't come knocking again."

The problem was, he had been that hot a shot. And they both knew it. They also both knew that one turn as a "consultant" would put him on their list. They'd come knocking whenever they needed to, with whatever excuse they saw fit to use to get what they wanted. "Liar."

Quin said nothing. "You going to help us or what?"

Dylan already knew it wasn't as simple as saying no.

If so, it would have worked when he'd done just that to Hannigan this morning. "I say no and you'll just show up in my office with Pearl in tow. So why didn't you just do that in the first place?"

"Professional courtesy?"

"That's an oxymoron if ever I heard one, especially out of our department."

Quin didn't rise to the bait. Probably because he knew it was true. Dylan was thankful enough that he had called first not to push it any further.

"Are you sure she knows anything? I mean, it's been years since she's been in the loop with Dugan. If she really knew anything important, he's had plenty of time now to cover it up. Otherwise he'd have never left her to her own devices in the first place."

"Maybe he knows she'll be loyal because she still loves him. Maybe he was stupid enough about her to trust her that way. You know we all think with our dicks half the time. Why not Dugan?"

"I don't know, Quin. It just doesn't sound all that solid to me. Did she give you any specifics of what she was going to spill?"

"No. But we have to pursue it, D.J. We don't have that many options with Dugan these days. So how does this Wednesday sound to you?"

That was only two days away. But it was probably best to get it over with. Dylan sighed and massaged his temple. Maybe he'd been wrong after all. You *could* go home again, but all the baggage you'd collected along the way came home with you.

"We'll come to your place. Keep this quiet and out of the local papers."

"No, not at the house." If he'd had the time, Dylan would have simply caved and gone to Vegas, done the interview and put it behind him. But with the festival coming up and all the attendant council meetings, there was no way he could be gone without making explanations he'd rather not make. He blew out a long breath and decided sleeping with Liza was moving way down on the list of possible worst mistakes.

"You pick the place, then."

Setting up secret meetings with ex-mob girlfriends wasn't exactly high priority these days, so he had to think about it for a moment. "Mims Motel. We keep this private." It was small, but nice enough, and more importantly, tucked away on the outskirts of town. "Reserve the room, an end unit, under the name Liza..." Damn, he didn't know her last name. "Smith." Lame, but he was thinking on the run here, and rusty at it.

"Hey, Boss, you trying to get the department to pay for your little shack-up?"

His jaw tensed. "You want my help?"

"Liza Smith it is," Quin said instantly, but not without a little amusement. "See you Wednesday, Boss."

"Yeah, great," Dylan muttered, but Quin had already hung up. Dylan tossed the phone on the passenger seat and scrubbed his hand over his face, then around the back of his neck. He wondered what his chances were of getting Liza to hang around Canyon Springs for another forty-eight hours.

He was certain his mother had mainlined the information about his supposed showgirl's arrival directly into the artery of the very active ladies auxiliary. The entire town was buzzing as he sat here. So, it would cause barely a ripple if he were to visit said girlfriend at a local motel. And there was the added bonus of gaining what little approval he could get from his mother over not allowing Liza to stay at his house. Why a thirty-two-year-old man gave a damn about that was simply too pathetic to contemplate.

Of course, Avis might be so thankful over his proved heterosexuality that she wouldn't care if he and Liza swung naked from the trees smack in the middle of town.

He shook his head at the image and climbed his truck the rest of the way up the steep drive.

She was waiting for him on the deck.

"I thought you were having second thoughts," she said, leaning over the railing. "And third and fourth ones."

He closed the truck door and climbed the spiral stairs to the second-story deck. "What do you mean?"

She turned to face him, but stayed by the railing. "Well, you sat down there at the bottom of the hill for so long, I began to wonder."

"Oh. Phone call. Sorry."

"Ah." She gestured behind her. "You have quite the view from up here."

"You improve it greatly."

She smiled at him. "Smooth, very smooth."

He shrugged and the whole problem with Quin and the upcoming interview slid to the background. Maybe he should arrange to come home to a beautiful woman more often.

"I try." Rather than move closer, which was what he wanted to do, and likely what she expected him to do, he leaned against the side door that led into the living area. The entire front wall of the house was sectioned glass. His bedroom was in the loft at the upper rear of the house and had a small balcony off the back. He wondered if she'd been up there yet and absently hoped he hadn't left too many stray socks lying around. "Can

I get you a beer or something? Or have you helped yourself?''

"Actually, I haven't been inside." She dangled the key. "I came up here and got cozy with the view instead."

"You could have at least gotten yourself something to drink." He'd assumed she'd make herself right at home. Maybe she enjoyed doing the unexpected, as well. Should make for an interesting evening.

She lifted a shoulder. "I didn't come directly up to the house." She grinned. "Now don't go frowning like that. I didn't talk to anyone. At least not anyone immediately related to you."

"In this town blood isn't necessarily thicker than water."

"Not to worry. It used to be my business to make sure only the right people heard the right things. I know my way around a grapevine."

"Well, Hollywood's got nothing on Canyon Springs when it comes to spreading the word. In fact, we could probably teach you all a thing or two. Who did you talk to?"

She merely laughed. "I think you're safe. For the moment, anyway." She walked over to one of the heavy Adirondack chairs and reached in a big, blue canvas bag with some gold designer logo attached to the front. "I did manage to pick up a nice bottle of wine." She pulled the bottle out of its paper bag. "My contribution to the meal."

He took the bottle and the house key she offered him. "Thanks. Looks good."

"It is." When he lifted a brow, she said, "Those who can't cook better know their wine. It's the only way we get invited back."

"Somehow I think you have a few other qualities that might recommend you as a repeat guest."

She smiled. "Somehow I'm not as flattered by that comment as I might be if someone else delivered it."

Now it was his turn to grin. "I guess I'd better get the grill fired up."

"It's your schedule. I'm just the guest."

He shook his head as he unlocked the door. Just the guest. He wondered what she'd say if he told her she was the first woman he'd had up here. Alone, anyway. He'd had the requisite housewarming, or should he say, his mother had. But other than that...well, he hadn't really pictured having a woman in his home, not quite yet, anyway. He figured he'd get around to developing a social life again at some point, but with his mother shoving anything in heels down his throat, he'd resisted a bit longer than he might have otherwise.

He glanced back at Liza, who was leaning against the railing, looking out at the view. He was enjoying the view as well. "Looks like the time for resistance is over," he murmured.

5

LIZA GLANCED BACK in time to watch Dylan disappear into his house. Her smile faded to a thoughtful look. She wondered just what kind of phone call he'd taken. Despite their banter, the dark edges were more prominent now. A slight tension to his jaw, a certain flatness to his eyes... And his voice was a bit more clipped, even though he'd been nothing but charming.

She laughed at herself. She'd known him, what? An hour or two? And already she was an authority on his moods? Maybe he was always like this at the end of a workday. On the other hand, she *had* built an exclusive clientele based on her aptitude for reading people, judging their needs, often before they even knew they needed something. She'd met Dylan under trying circumstances and seen him frustrated, irritated, annoyed. This... edginess she'd spied just now was totally at odds with the man she'd gotten out of that tree.

Danger, danger, Liza, her little voice intoned. This was just for fun. A nice dinner, mix in a little flirting, a little seduction, a few hours of intensely pleasurable sex...and she had no doubt he could deliver it. Some things a woman just knew. And some women knew better than others, she thought with a private smile. She'd be back to her journey of self-discovery by morning. Certainly a little discovery of Dylan Jackson first wouldn't do any harm.

Sure, he was enigmatic in a way she wouldn't have expected. Sure, she was intrigued by the big city–small town paradox he presented. But this was just an evening out. A little detour. He was offering to be part of her adventure. Nothing more, nothing less. She'd be a fool to pass up such a delightful and relatively safe proposition.

And Liza Sanguinetti was no fool. At least, most of the time.

Dylan reappeared on the deck with two glasses of wine and a bag of wood chips tucked under his arm. She took both glasses and set them on the small round table next to the railing. She wondered how many private little dinners had been set at this intimate table for two.

She sipped her wine, then motioned to him. "You changed," she said, faintly accusatory, although she admitted he looked damn fine in jeans and a soft ribbed Henley.

He looked down at himself. "Sorry, I forgot about the uniform fantasy."

"Somehow I doubt you forget much of anything."

He simply grinned. "Mesquite smoked steak okay with you?" he asked, his back to her as he set about opening the top to his grill.

"Sounds good." Nothing fancy there, she noted approvingly, just a regular, well-used grill. No tools and gadgets bought to impress, nothing that screamed bachelor-on-the-make. In fact, despite the stunning setting and interesting structure, the house looked to be more home than showcase. She hadn't gone inside, but she had looked through the windows. Heavy pine furniture stuffed with thick cushions in deep russets and golds were comfortably arranged on a rolled, handmade rug, fronting a cozy and also well-used wood burning stove.

No macho fireplace and fur rug type thing happening here. It actually looked like a place a man lived in, not a place designed for seduction.

What an interesting concept.

Liza sipped her wine and hid a private smile. God, she was so jaded. She took in a breath of the rapidly cooling evening air, so clean and crisp it almost crackled inside her lungs. So the jaded one was trying something new, she told herself. Maybe this *was* part of her journey, after all, and not a detour. As long as she didn't confuse this for something more than a pit stop, she'd be fine.

He came back out of the house with two steaks and a pair of foil wrapped potatoes.

"You were prepared, I see," she said, wondering if she'd read the setup wrong. After all, maybe men out here in the mountains didn't bother with all the seductive frills and finery meant to dazzle and impress. Meat and potatoes on the grill, meat and potatoes in bed.

It was effective, however, as she was developing a powerful hunger for meat and potatoes.

"Not really," he said. "I just happen to think nothing tastes better on a summer night than a grilled steak and a cold beer. So I always stock some of both. You got lucky with the potatoes, though."

"Ah, lucky me. But here I'm forcing wine on you. Feel free to pop a cold one if you'd prefer."

He'd turned back to the grill and didn't glance back at her as he spoke. "I'm a big boy. If I want beer, I'll have one, but thanks for the permission."

She grinned and sipped her wine. "It's been my experience that most men trying to get me into bed succeed more easily with flattery rather than censure."

"So now I'm 'most men,'" he said lightly. "I thought we'd covered that with you earlier."

"So we did." She noticed he didn't refute the "get me into bed" part. "And why I ever thought to compare you to most men is beyond me. You're one of a kind, Sheriff."

He shot her grin over his shoulder. "Why, thank you."

The punch of desire surprised her, the strength and potency of it. She'd certainly danced this dance before. And yet she didn't feel as surefooted as she usually did. She couldn't predict how he'd react to any given stimulus. Maybe that was the reason for her reaction to something as basic as a sexy grin. Uncertainty was a new emotion for her. She wasn't quite sure she liked it. But she didn't mind the way it heightened the tension between them.

Her gaze drifted to his denim clad backside as he turned back to the grill. She had the strongest urge to walk over and stand just behind him, feel the heat of him and the fire mingle together, seep into her. So wired into that scenario was she that when he pulled several citronella candles off the railing and struck a match to light them, she actually felt like he'd scraped against something inside her. Her thighs actually flinched.

She watched as he wiped his hands on his own thighs, and found herself running her tongue over her lips. Dear God. She jerked the chair out from the little table and made herself comfortable. Relatively speaking. She still felt a bit twitchy between the legs.

She really had gone solo for too long, she told herself, if she got this tightly wound over a mildly flirtatious bit of wordplay while watching a guy fire up a grill. He mercifully went back inside to get God knew what, allowing her to return her attention to the other view. She forced herself to keep it there when he returned.

"This is a spectacular site for a house," she said, needing to get herself back on the solid ground of innocuous first-date conversation. Sexual tension was one thing, but she really didn't like the way her body leaped about at the slightest look from him. She wanted this, wanted him, but on her terms. After all, that was one avenue of self-discovery she didn't need to traverse twice.

"Land belonged to my grandfather, but he never did anything with it," Dylan said. "I've always loved it up here and knew this was where I'd build when I came back. It took awhile and a bit of blasting, but I made it all fit."

And fit it did. Rustic wood jutting out of stone, with enough shiny glass to give it a veneer of polish. Just a little. Sort of like its owner. Why that was so damn sexy to her, a woman whose men usually matched her polish for polish, she had no idea. "Builder and sheriff, all in one package. Pretty handy guy."

He flipped the steaks and scooted the foil wrapped potatoes around on the grill. "I make do okay."

She just bet he did. She'd really never met anyone like him before. Secure, not working her for what else she might be able to do for him besides an evening or two of great sex. *Another good reason to leave the superficiality of Hollywood.* She supposed it was that very lack of calculation, the inherent honesty in everything he said, that undid her a little. He wasn't after anything beyond what she was after. And he didn't seem to care much if that worked out or not, either.

She wasn't sure how she felt about that. Relieved to know that dinner and conversation could be just that, no harm, no foul? Or a bit put out, wanting to push him into caring that they didn't let this opportunity pass them by?

Maybe a little of both, she decided, and took another sip as she contemplated just how to play this evening out.

He wanted her, and yet he wasn't knocking himself out to do anything to insure he got her, other than just being himself. An original concept where she was from.

She was still pretty damn sure she could get what she'd come here for. He wasn't the type to play coy, and he knew what was what. She wasn't going to have to be subtle. Except, in this case, she found herself wishing she didn't have to be the pursuer.

She paused midsip. Now where had that come from? She was *always* the pursuer. Even if the man was led to believe otherwise. Liza controlled what she got. That way she stayed safe and everyone had a good time. The one time she'd stupidly forgotten that rule, look where she'd landed. In the penthouse suite of the heartbreak hotel.

So, despite her mild flirtation with that domination scenario, letting Sheriff Dylan Jackson call the shots was definitely not an option here. Not that he was trying to, she thought, with the tiniest of pouts. He could be a bit more aggressive about things. That tingle of awareness raced through her again, along with a few stray images of just how she'd like him to be aggressive. Say, a pair of handcuffs. Maybe some persuasive…interrogation—

She hastily put her wineglass on the table. The alcohol, along with the crisp evening air, was obviously going to her head.

It was those damn dark edges that caught at her, she supposed. Dark edges she had no desire to smooth. In fact, she'd like to rub up against one or two of them, just for the thrill of discovering how they felt. "Danger, danger, Liza," she murmured, unable to stop picturing what it would be like between them.

"Medium rare okay with you?"

She blinked, startled from her hot little scenario by his voice. "I'm sorry, mind was wandering. What did you say?" Dammit, her voice was a bit hoarse. Maybe he'd attribute it to the wine. She knew he hadn't when he straightened and turned to face her, a long grill fork in one hand, a bemused look on his face.

There was the slightest twitch to his lips. "How do you like your meat?"

She laughed; she couldn't help it. "However you're having yours is fine."

His gaze remained on hers a moment longer. "It gets pretty cold up here when the sun goes down. You have a sweater or something?"

She could tell him her nipples were peaked for reasons that had nothing to do with temperature, but decided to forgo the direct approach for once. Besides which, she was pretty sure he understood her reaction was to him. A certain look in those melted-candy eyes of his told her that well enough. That he'd brought it to the attention of both of them only made her nipples pucker harder. "I've got something in the car," she said. "I guess I should go get it."

She wandered down to her car, privately smiling at the idea that for an evening that would likely end up with them both naked, it was oddly erotic to be covering herself up. "All the more for him to slide off of you later, Liza." She shivered and rubbed her arms in anticipation, all sorts of scenarios springing to feverish life inside her obviously sex-starved brain. Would he strip her? Or ask her to strip for him? Not that it would be the first time she'd done that for a man, but again, she was usually the one in control. In fact, handcuffs wouldn't be a new experience for her, either...unless they were put on her wrists.

"Okay, enough of this torture." She yanked open the tiny trunk and unzipped her leather duffel. She'd purposely taken her little sports car so she'd be forced to travel light, figuring that focusing on where she was going would be much easier if she wasn't lugging most of her past around with her.

Of course, that hadn't stopped her from buying and shipping home any little thing that caught her eye. She swallowed a wicked little snicker, wondering if she could mail Dylan Jackson home. He'd definitely caught her eye, all right, along with just about every other body part.

If only it were so easy.

By the time she got back to the deck, a thick white sweater buttoned at her throat keeping off most of the chill, he had plates and silverware set on place mats on the little table. Again, nothing fancy, but she was discovering the basic and simple held more appeal than she would have previously thought. "Can I help with something?"

"Just your appetite."

Oh, I definitely have that. "Famished." Noticing he was sipping his wine, she asked, "What do you think? Of the wine, I mean?"

"It's worthy of a repeat invitation."

She smiled. "For the wine, or for me?"

"I haven't made up my mind about you yet." He took another sip. "But the wine definitely passes."

"I'll take my brownie points and quit complaining then."

"Smart woman."

"So I've been told."

"I bet you have."

With both of them smiling, he turned back to the steak and she found her gaze drifting to the house. She wondered what his bedroom looked like. Basic, simple, down to earth, certainly. Big bed, small bed? Bathroom built for one...or two? "So you designed the house?"

"In my head, yes, but I paid a professional to put it on paper for me. I did a lot of the work myself, but hired out what I couldn't handle or didn't know how to do."

Practical. Secure. No need to brag, but there was quiet pride in his tone and, when he glanced at the house, in his expression.

"I can't imagine tackling something like this," she said truthfully. "I wouldn't even know where to start."

He laid his fork and tongs down and wandered over to the railing near where she sat. "What exactly was it you did in California?"

"Publicist. Celebrities mostly. I ran my own firm."

"Then I'd say you have some experience in tackling big projects. It's probably not much different. When you know what you want, I'm willing to bet you find a way to make it happen no matter how overwhelming the task might seem."

She stared at him, surprised by the insight. "I suppose you're right. The problem comes when you no longer know what you want, I guess. It's hard to make your dreams come true when you've achieved the only ones you ever had."

He crossed his legs at the ankle and took another sip

of wine. "Is that what you're doing? On this sabbatical of yours. Trying to find new dreams?"

"That's a good way of putting it."

"Some people just enjoy the dreams they've realized, consider themselves lucky for the opportunity. Why did you give up what you were doing?"

"Why did you give up being a vice cop?"

He didn't blink at the question, but handled it as directly as he handled her. She was really attracted to that quality in him.

"I had this idea that being a cop in a big city was more important than being a sheriff in a small one. I found out I was wrong. Crime is crime and no victim is more or less important than another. Keeping the peace anywhere, or trying to, is a rewarding experience."

"Some anywheres are more challenging than others, I would imagine. You strike me as someone who enjoys a challenge." She motioned to the house he'd blasted part of a mountain away to build.

"True, but one isn't less important than others. Las Vegas was definitely a challenge and I thought that was what I needed, would thrive on."

"How long did you work there?"

"Nine years. The last three in vice."

"That's a fair amount of time in a tough city."

"Felt like an eternity, if you want to know the truth. No matter what I did, how many people I busted, it seemed it never really made a dent." He took a sip of his wine, his gaze drifting to the winking lights of the town sprawled below them. "I realized I needed to make a dent. Challenge is one thing, but after a while I needed the satisfaction of knowing what I did mattered."

He said it matter-of-factly, but Liza had the feeling

the decision hadn't been so easily made. "You don't think what you did in Vegas mattered?"

"Maybe. I can't explain it. I suppose on some level, removing scum from the streets matters. But for every one I locked up, there was always another piece of slime ready and willing to slide in to take his or her place. In more cases than I can count, it was slime I'd already locked up before, out on the streets again. After a while, it starts to feel like you're shoveling sand against the tide. I guess I needed more tangible evidence that I was making a difference."

"So you came home again. And now you rescue cockatoos from trees." She didn't know why she poked at him, and she'd said it gently, with a smile, but she guessed she just enjoyed seeing him respond. It was never in a way she'd expect.

He smiled in return. "Yeah. But it's not always so exciting as all that. You just caught me in action."

She laughed. "So you're telling me it's all ho-hum and pushing paper? This is as rewarding as busting some drug lord or pimp?"

"You push paper no matter where you work. And no, I don't miss dealing with scum. I appreciate the sameness of life here, the fact that bodies don't end up in alleys and pushers don't deal crack on the playground. I actually enjoy dealing with the town council and the mayor on whether or not a new traffic light will slow down the occasional speeder, whether we need parking meters on the town square and what type of security measures we need to take to keep the kids safe at school. And just to make things exciting, I still get to throw the occasional drunk in jail and lock up the occasional crook. I also fingerprint kids at the school fairs and investigate who stole someone's bike from in front of the drugstore.''

"Do you think you'll ever get tired of that sameness?'' She realized she was asking as much for herself. She was looking for a new path in life and was interested to hear from someone who had done it and succeeded.

There was a brief flicker, as if she'd said something that reminded him of something he'd rather not recall. But then he looked at her and she was surprised by the avid and clear purpose in his eyes. "No. It's my town. My people. I'm responsible for them, and while it's occasionally frustrating, I like being the one who keeps their peace. Frankly, more than I ever believed I would.'' As if realizing an edge of fervor had crept into his tone, he banked it with a short laugh. "It's your typical town ruffian–turned–sheriff story.''

"That's right. The original Canyon Springs bad boy.'' She leaned forward. "So, tell the truth, were you really all that bad?''

"Let's just say when I left this place I had no intentions of ever coming back, and the town was probably hoping that wish remained fulfilled.''

"And yet they elected you sheriff. Go figure, huh?''

He grinned and she spied a little of that bad boy behind the man who now wore a badge. He shrugged. "Life hands you some unexpected lessons. It's all in what you do with what you learn, I guess. I consider myself lucky.''

"I imagine the town feels the same way,'' she said, and meant it, envying him his clear sense of purpose. She wondered if she'd ever feel that confidence in herself again.

He laughed. "Depends on who you ask, on what day.''

She smiled and nodded, but her attention continued to drift inward as she swirled the remains of her wine in the bottom of her glass.

"Life handed you some unexpected lessons, did it?"

He'd poked gently, too. She only wished she could answer as directly and honestly as he had. "A class load of them."

"Seems like you've done pretty well by them, from the looks of things."

"What makes you say that?"

"Well, I'm guessing you didn't walk away from your business because you had to, but because you wanted to. Or needed to. Two different things."

She tilted her head. "Since when did small-town sheriffs turn into psychologists?"

He didn't duck the question, but then he probably never ducked anything. "Actually, any Psych 101 abilities I have were learned pumping witnesses for information in Vegas. I discovered I got a lot more by paying attention to who I was asking, and acting accordingly, than by lumping them together into a faceless entity to bully information from."

She smiled a little. "I bet that comes in handy with the town council and the mayor."

"Don't forget the ladies auxiliary."

"No," she said in all seriousness, "I don't think we can ever forget them."

He grinned and downed the rest of his wine, but didn't leave the subject alone as she'd hoped. "The reason I assumed you'd chosen to leave was arrived at more simply." He gestured with his wineglass over the railing. "We've already deduced your ride didn't exactly roll off the used car lot. And I'm willing to bet those spikes on your feet didn't come from Payless."

"Ah, well, any good detective knows that things aren't always as they appear. Maybe I had family money. Maybe I just played at being a businesswoman."

"I don't think so." He grinned. "Instinct. When Psych 101 and deductive reasoning skills fail me, I rely on instinct." He set his glass down and folded his arms on the table. "So, am I right?"

"Let's just say I'm glad I'm not some perp you're trying to pump." He merely lifted an eyebrow and she couldn't help it, she began to laugh. "You're terrible."

He stood, and with an easy smile and complete humility, said, "No, I'm quite good, actually."

He walked over to retrieve their steaks and potatoes from the grill.

"That you are," she murmured, finishing off her own wine as she studied the continually confounding Sheriff Dylan. "Too damn good for me."

6

"THAT WAS REALLY FABULOUS," Liza said as she finished her last piece of steak.

Dylan nodded and wiped his mouth with his napkin. "Nothing tastes better."

He watched those eyes of hers twinkle. "Well, I could beg to differ, but as dinners go, you do have a point."

He'd forgotten how stimulating verbal foreplay could be with a woman who knew what real foreplay was all about. He swallowed a laugh at his own expense. Like he knew so much about women. But he did know that women in Canyon Springs didn't come with that kind of built-in savvy. And the women he'd met in Vegas had savvy of an entirely different sort, learned from a different set of circumstances.

This…this was refreshing. And damn if he wasn't ready to move past the verbal and on to the physical. He had a feeling Liza liked to move things along at her own pace and that most men didn't care as long as they had her undivided attention. Well, she already knew he wasn't "most men." Now she was about to learn that he had his own ideas about pace. Besides, it might be fun to see how she liked being pushed.

He stood and picked up their plates. "Why don't you bring the glasses inside? Grab the rest of the wine, too."

He saw her eyebrow flicker just the tiniest bit, but she merely nodded and scooped up their glasses and the bottle of wine. "I should tell you," she said as they entered his living room, "in addition to not being a chief cook, I'm also not much in the way of a bottle washer. But I load a mean dishwasher if you have one handy."

"Don't worry about it. Guests don't cook or clean."

"I like that rule."

She followed him as he wove through the living room into the kitchen and set the plates in the stainless steel sink.

"This is nice. Warm. Cozy."

"I put a lot of thought into this room." He imagined she'd seen places a lot snazzier than this, so he liked that she appreciated what he'd been going for in here. "I spent a great deal of time in our kitchen growing up. It was my favorite place. The one place the flock didn't intrude. Even my bedroom had brooders in it half the time."

"Brooders? Flock?"

"My mother's home is more aviary than house. Mango isn't her only baby. Avis Jackson is the original bird lady of Canyon Springs. We started with parakeets and finches when I was two. She was breeding them by the time I was five. I was seven when she took the neighbor's sun conure after the noise got to them."

"And Mango?"

"We ended up with him permanently when another neighbor developed an allergy to the cockatoo dust their feathers create. Then came Harris the blue-fronted Amazon, who was found in a gas station garage, all filthy and underweight, living in a rusted out cage. Pippin the African gray and Laslow the greenwing macaw were both found in a basement closet with a blanket thrown over them because the kids hated the noise they made. And well, before long she was the expert on bird rescue.

When the Internet came into play, she linked up with several people in the Southwest who also do rescues. Many of the birds get placed with other owners, some go to a sanctuary in Arizona. And some, like the gang I mentioned, she keeps.''

"Wow, sounds interesting."

"It's her passion. The birds are her whole life."

Liza cocked her head. "But not yours, I take it?"

He smiled dryly. "She does great work and it's sorely needed. But let's just say I was glad to stop being chief cage cleaner and vegetable washer when I graduated from high school and left town."

"What did your dad think of having his house taken over by exotic birds?"

"He was killed in Vietnam when I was a toddler. Actually, I think she got into it when he first went overseas. It gave her something to do, and I think she needed to feel needed. By more than me, anyway."

"I'm sorry. I'm the last one who should make assumptions about family units."

"That's okay." Dylan remembered Liza had said something to that affect earlier today. He didn't bother reminding himself that he wasn't trying to get to know her better, just to get her into bed. But damn if she didn't interest him. "I don't remember him at all," he added, "but Mom kept his letters and some of his things, so I got a sense of who he was. His folks were my only grandparents and we were close while I was growing up. I've got a couple of aunts and uncles and more cousins than I can name. It was one of my uncles who got me interested in being a cop. He's a retired captain out of Albuquerque."

Dylan grinned. "I think my mom put him up to that particular rescue mission. She was better with birds than people. Still is. But Uncle Pete knew from boys, having four of them himself. If it wasn't for him, God knows how I'd have turned out.''

Liza smiled, and there was something a bit wistful in it that made him wonder. "Big family. Sounds wonderful.''

He shrugged. "It gave me a place to go when I needed to escape the jungle, anyway.'' Again he wondered about her family. He wondered where they fit into her sabbatical.

He opened his mouth to ask, but she said, "Avis never remarried?''

"She gave her love to the flock. It makes her happy.''

Liza's gaze sort of penetrated him for a second, leaving him feel oddly vulnerable. "Sounds like you all found what you needed. That's good.'' Then she smiled and turned her attention back to the kitchen. "It's obvious you love this room,'' she said, clearly changing the subject. It was in the part of the house that snugged into the mountain, so he'd wanted to make sure it didn't look cavelike or dark. The walls were a rich yellow and the floor a warm, honey-gold tile. The cabinets were light pine with glass fronts and the center island, half stainless steel, half butcher block, had padded stools on one side and was ringed overhead with copper and stainless steel pots and pans.

"A lot of gear for a single guy,'' she observed. "You have a lot of parties up here?''

"I like to have the right tool on hand when I want it.''

She had a delightfully rich laugh. "I won't even touch that one.''

He closed the distance between them. "We'll see about that.'' She shifted ever so slightly and set the glasses down on the center island, but he took the bottle from her hand before she could pour, and set it down as well.

"I thought we might have another glass," she said, not moving away from him, but doing what he'd bet she typically did—steering the course of events back to her preplanned path. Or trying to.

"And I thought I'd see if your mouth tasted as sassy as it sounds."

"Oh."

He liked that little blink of surprise. It encouraged that bad boy part of him that had never completely gone away. So he tucked her small, tight body between him and the island and slowly pushed his fingers into her soft curls. "Oh," he echoed. "Yeah." Then he dipped his head to kiss her, only to stop just before making contact. "Do you always keep your eyes open during a kiss?"

"Depends on the kiss." She hadn't pulled away or stiffened when he'd moved against her. Nor had she opened up or invited him to go further. It was like she was hovering outside the intimate little circle he'd created, gauging, planning.

Well, he'd see about that.

"You'll have to let me know which kind this is, then." And he lowered his mouth the rest of the way. She tasted…warm. There was the spice of the wine and something else that was pure Liza. She tasted every bit as sassy as her personality, and it made him want to lap up each part of her. Something he might just be able to work out. He didn't push the kiss into anything heavy, nor did he try to seduce her into it. He merely took, tasted, tested…and enjoyed.

Not that she wasn't kissing him back, but there was a sense of gauging in her kiss, and he discovered he was a bit irritated by her somewhat removed, observatory attitude. At the same time, he was forced to admit he was anticipating what kind of counterassault she'd mount when it was her turn. And there was no doubt she saw this as a campaign of some kind, a strategic battle to be guided to a conclusion that would be most satisfactory for her. And perhaps him as well. He doubted she suffered many complaints.

But, just for the hell of it, he thought maybe it was time Generalissimo Liza discovered she couldn't command every soldier to follow her lead.

He explored her mouth slowly, enjoying the soft interior, the heat of her, the flavor. Then, just when he felt the slightest shift in her mouth, the tiniest tension in her tongue, a subtle move to turn control of the kiss her way, he moved from her mouth to the line of her jaw, robbing her of the opportunity.

He trailed the tip of his tongue along it, nipping gently at the point of her chin.

The slight stiffening he felt in her body, the quiet gasp he felt rather than heard, was immensely gratifying. He imagined most men were more than willing to let Liza do to them as she wanted. What man in his right mind would stop her?

Well, him, apparently. Not to annoy her, but more to provoke her into…well, he didn't know quite what. His instincts just told him it would be really gratifying to find out. And other than going another night without sex, what did he have to lose?

She moved her hands, which had been resting loosely on his arms, up along his shoulders, and slid her long fingers into his hair. He let the shudder of primal delight roll through him. He loved having someone's fingers on his scalp. And hers were particularly skillful. He felt her smile against his cheek as he pulled her earlobe into his mouth and bit gently, smiling himself when he felt her shudder in return.

She slid her hands down his back, then around his waist, and tugged lightly at the back of his shirt. He reached back and gripped her wrists to still her actions. "Not yet," he said against the skin of her neck, the skin he was busy kissing and nibbling.

She tipped her head and nuzzled his neck. "If you think my fingertips felt good stroking your head, I can guarantee you'll like what else I was planning to stroke."

He chuckled and pulled her hands to his chest, where he covered them with his own. "Of that I have zero doubt." The very part of him begging to be stroked twitched as he spoke, and he was pressed tightly enough against her for her to know it, too.

"Then what, exactly, are we waiting for?"

"I like to build the anticipation."

"Oh, excuse me," she said, untangling her fingers from his grasp so she could lightly scrape her fingernails over the soft cotton covering his nipples. "I thought we'd done that during dinner."

"You're doing a pretty damn good job of it now."

She merely smiled.

He pulled her hands from him altogether and pushed them back, pinning them on the counter behind her. "So, we'll just slow things down a bit."

Despite his grip on her, she leaned forward and pulled his bottom lip into her mouth, suckled on it for a moment, then let it go. "Will we?"

His body had hardened almost painfully at that unexpected little piece of action. Sliding both of her wrists neatly into a single-handed grip, he used his free hand to cup the back of her head, and angled his body against hers, giving her no choice but to look up at him. "Yeah," he said, his voice low and a bit rough. "We will." He ran his tongue along her lower lip, holding her head right where he wanted it when she tried to shift and come after him with her own pink-tipped weapon. "Uh-uh," he cautioned. "My turn."

"Says who?" she asked slyly, then ran that wicked pink tongue along her lips.

"Me." He swooped in and took her in a hard and fast kiss, snagging that tongue of hers and pulling it hotly into his mouth. He kept her head pressed to his as he worked her over…and over again. Not so much dueling as sampling at will, taking what he wanted. The instant she tried to turn the tables, he released her, sucking her bottom lip on his way out, then sliding his hand from her hair.

Surprised, she was left breathless, and swayed back before she could catch herself. So he followed her down, taking her mouth in another hard, drugging kiss. He kept moving her back until she was arching over the hands he still had in a grip behind her back. He moved his mouth down her chin, nipped her there, then kept on, running his tongue along her throat and the edge of her sweater, stopping at the glassy little button that held it together. That fell prey to his teeth, and the sweater fell open, leaving the deep V of her silky shirt bared to him…and his tongue.

She arched up and tried to lift her head. So he took that as a sign to pull one pouty, silk-covered nipple into his mouth. She rewarded him with a sharp gasp, followed by a long moan when he continued to work the wet silk and hard nub with his tongue.

She began pushing against his mouth, levering herself closer when he started to move away.

"Like that, do you?" he murmured.

"If you have to ask, you're not as smart as I thought," she said, a bit on the breathless side.

Chuckling, he let her hands go and supported her back as she straightened, then abruptly stepped back and reached for the wine.

"What are you doing?" She pushed her hair from her face, and he was pleased to see that her hand was a bit shaky. He wondered when someone had last gotten her off balance. And why he cared. He was enjoying the hell out of being the one doing it now, and that was all that mattered. Right? Eventually it would be her turn to make him pay. He could hardly wait.

But for now, he was liking his turn too much to relinquish it. "You said you wanted another glass of wine." He split what little remained of the bottle between the two glasses, then picked hers up and handed it to her.

She stared at him for a long moment, then reached for the glass.

"Uh-uh," he said, pulling it back. "I want to."

"You want to what?" Her tone was a tiny bit wary, but her pupils were still swallowing up all that aqua blue. He intended to keep them that way.

"Open your mouth." He grinned. "Without saying anything."

She smirked at him, then opened her mouth. But snapped it shut again just as he lifted the glass. "I'll have you know that wine doesn't come out of silk. Or white cotton for that matter."

"I imagine you packed other clothes, right?"

She actually spluttered. "You wouldn't."

He laughed and wrapped a hand around the side of her waist and tugged her close. "I'm not going to ruin those sexy, clingy clothes of yours. And if I do, I'll replace them. Problem solved. Now open up."

She glared at him and stuck her tongue out.

"Not exactly what I had in mind."

She merely left it stuck out there and shrugged, but her eyes were flashing, all but begging him.

"Fine then." He tipped the glass to his own mouth instead, took a small swig, then abruptly snugged her head to his and drew that pointed tongue of hers into his mouth...and let the wine trickle back into hers. He kept her tongue hostage until all the wine was gone, then ran his own over her lips, catching the tiny trickle that had escaped the corner of her mouth. "Mmm." He lifted his head, and offered her the glass. "You want to try some?"

"You'd trust me after pulling that little stunt?"

He smiled and dropped a quick kiss on her lips. "You want me to do it again, don't you?" He kissed her again, only held it longer this time. "Don't you?"

"I think you've done quite enough of the doing. It's my turn now."

"And here I thought you were the one with the uniform fantasy."

"You're not in uniform," she pointed out. "But even so, that was more curiosity than craving on my part. After all, I am supposed to be trying new things."

"Ah," he said, "so my instincts about you were right. You have a little problem with authority."

That wicked smile slashed across her gorgeous face. "Only when I'm not it."

"I'm gathering that."

She folded her arms, putting a bit more space between

them. "So this has been, what—a demonstration for my benefit, then? Showing Liza who the boss is going to be?"

"I'm pretty sure Liza was enjoying herself just fine. It merely seemed to me that you slide into that upper-hand position pretty naturally. And so, being the renegade type that I am..."

She snorted. "Says the town sheriff."

Now his grin was a bit wicked. "That badge might guide me...but it didn't tame me."

"I see."

And so did he. She'd crossed her arms again and it wasn't in annoyance. The wet spot he'd made on her shirt was a very revealing mood indicator.

"So women bring out the predator in you, is that it?" she queried. "You're used to women wanting that man-in-uniform fantasy? Maybe you do wear that badge in bed, symbolically speaking. You like being in charge on the streets...and between the sheets."

He laughed outright. "It's been so long I'd have to think about that. But off the cuff, no, you'd be wrong in that assumption."

"What do you mean 'it's been so long'? You haven't been out of town to see 'Liza' lately?"

"Just haven't gotten around to it, I guess." And realized the tactical error he'd just made as soon as the words left his mouth.

Her grin was wide and naughty. "Well, I'm surprised you're not on your knees begging for it then."

He laughed again, couldn't remember a time he'd enjoyed himself quite this much. And all he'd done was kiss her. So far. "As I said, I like to build anticipation."

"Hell, you've had months of it, years for all I know. Why waste more time?"

"You in a hurry?"

She sighed. "You're impossible."

"But worth the effort." He moved in again, framed her hips with his hands. "Like you, I imagine."

She let him playfully pull her close. "So what exactly is it that makes you want to push me around, tell me what to do? You have control issues?"

"Me? None. I'm usually a willing slave to women."

"And I'm an exception why?"

He lifted her chin and dipped his head, keeping his eyes on hers this time. "I have no idea. But I'm dying to figure it out." He dropped a quick kiss on her lips, then another, then another, before finally sinking into her for a long, wet mating of tongues that had them both breathless when he finally came up for air. "And just as soon as I do, you can be in charge. For as long as you like."

She grinned and he saw the gleam of intent in her eyes as his hands slid downward. So he flipped her around and bent her over the island, pressing himself snugly against that sweet, tight backside of hers. "But not until I'm done," he said against the side of her neck. He ran his tongue up to her earlobe, tugging it between his teeth for a quick nip. Her hips jerked in his hands and he felt her indrawn breath. "And I plan to take a long, long time."

7

SHE'D ALWAYS BEEN ABLE to handle anything. And
she'd handled a lot. Liza knew she could handle one
Dylan Jackson. Uniform or no uniform. She'd let him
get good and confident, thinking he had her at his
mercy…then find the right moment and have him however she wanted him. Until he begged for more. All she
had to do was wait for her opening.

However, the extremely nice pressure of that hard
bulge of his, pressing between the backs of her thighs,
was making it a bit hard to think clearly at the moment.
Her hips had a mind of their own and they wanted to
grind back against him, hard, push up a bit more so that
rigid length could press…just…right…. Dammit.

He'd pulled her upright when she'd been a twitch
away. Keeping her hands in his, in front of her waist,
he shifted just enough so that she could no longer feel
him pressed against her. She felt the pinch of his teeth
on the nape of her neck.

"You're pretty sneaky," he told her, amused.

"Your loss," she replied flippantly. But her breath
was rapid and shallow as she wondered what he had in
store for her next. She was only playing this little game
because it seemed to interest him, she told herself. It
was arousing her because it was arousing him. That was
all. She was still in control. In her mind, she was allowing him this little fantasy play.

Then she heard the rasp of steel and chain.

Her breath stopped. Her thighs clenched.

"What—what do you think you're doing?"

"Freeing up my hands."

She felt the cold metal brush her wrists as she looked down. And it wasn't her own bracelets. "Where did you get those?"

"Standard police issue."

"I mean right now."

"A good cop is always prepared." He slid one of the cuffs around her wrist.

"Dylan—"

"I like it when you say my name. Now hold still, this won't hurt a bit."

"Yeah, that's what they all say. Listen, I'm not sure this—"

"Tell me one thing," he interrupted. "Were you, just now, planning to take advantage of this situation at the earliest possible moment? Truth."

Why was it that his ability to climb inside her head was as arousing as it was threatening? Arousing enough for her to ignore the warning bells. "We're a lot alike," she said. "We both enjoy calling the shots."

"I'll take that as a yes."

He snapped one bracelet shut and she felt a spurt between her legs. Dear God, what was she getting into here? Out in the middle of nowhere, with a man she'd just met, letting him—

"I'm going to give you the key," he said, snapping the other bracelet on, then pushing them just tight enough so that they didn't slide off her wrists. He pressed a small key on a leather loop into her hands. "If you need help, you only have to ask me."

"Why not just tell me what to do and leave my hands free?"

He blew a soft breath along the back of her neck, stirring the hair there...and stirring her, as well. Not being able to see his face as he spoke, as he shackled her hands, was affecting her enormously. She was so ready for him she could barely stand upright. Never in all her wild escapades—and in her former line of work, she'd had more than a few—had she ever put herself in this sort of scenario. At least not with the cuffs on herself. So why let him do this?

Because I'm so damn hot I can hardly stand it.

That, and her curiosity was engaged. Both powerfully persuasive elements.

"Are you done figuring this out?" he whispered, nipping at her earlobe, then the side of her neck.

Dammit, she'd never been this obvious to anyone. "You know, if this is the only way you can get women to do what you want, it's no wonder you're so hard up for a date."

He pressed a soft kiss to the nape of her neck, then another along her collarbone. The tenderness of it, along with the bite of steel at her wrists, made her shudder. With pleasure. Dammit.

"Actually," he said, quietly amused as he continued dropping hot little kisses here and there, "I've had women beg me to lock them up. I have to say you're the first one who's ever actually compelled me to do it, though. Probably something to do with the fact that you'd be the last one on earth to ask in the first place."

Damn him, he made her laugh.

He slowly turned her around and looked her directly in the eyes. "Do you want me to take them off?"

She swallowed hard, the smile gone from her face

now. She could say yes, he'd take them off, and she was still pretty sure they could end the evening with some amazing sex. But there was something in those hot, candy eyes of his. Something pretty close to that wild, primal feeling he'd ripped to life inside her.

This was arousing him in a new way, too. And if she wasn't mistaken, despite his casually confident manner, he was just as surprised by it as she was. Which made her want to say no, and very possibly find herself somewhere she'd never been before.

After all, she was on a journey of self-discovery, was she not?

"It would have been easier if you hadn't asked," she said finally, unwilling to simply hand him the victory. "I have the key, you know."

"Yeah, I know."

She merely looked at him. She'd tacitly given her consent, and that was all he was going to get from her. After all, he didn't want this to be that easy. It wouldn't be fun for either of them then.

He stared into her eyes and she into his. *This is just about sex, Liza,* she reminded herself, fighting the sensation that she could easily wallow in all that warm, caramel brown.

His grip on her hips tightened for just a moment, then he slowly turned her toward the stainless steel end of the center island.

She resisted just enough to turn her head and look at him. "And I get my turn later."

He grinned then, only rather than relieve the tension now screaming between them, it only served to jack it up another level. "Oh, I'd be disappointed if you didn't."

She turned back to the table, grinning herself. He

wasn't so tough. Besides, how long could all this "anticipation building" last, anyway? Sooner or later he'd want inside her. Her smile turned wicked. And that would be a perfect time to start her turn, now wouldn't it?

She was merrily sliding down that quite satisfying little mental path when he abruptly raised her locked wrists and slid her shirt up over her head. Before she could pull her head free, he'd popped the front clasp of her bra.

She was still gasping at the sudden shift in action when, with her arms still held above her head, he slowly pressed her forward, his hips once again snugged up against her backside. The return of that rock-hard bulge to her now intensely sensitized inner thighs distracted her momentarily from her suddenly bared breasts.

Which made the shock of cold steel coming up against her engorged nipples a real surprise.

The rear juncture of her thighs all but burned with the heat of him pressed so intimately there, even as the cold island top sent numbing tingles all through her upper body. She was still sucking in air, unable to do more than simply feel the riot of opposite sensations he'd set off, when she felt a new one.

His tongue, his very warm tongue, sliding slowly down the ridge of her spine. He drew his big, warm hands slowly along her arms, brushing them down either side of her body, making her want badly to push up so he could cover her hard, cold nipples with those wide, warm palms of his. But he kept her pressed down...and kept his hands sliding down until he gripped her hips.

Just when it occurred to her to struggle, to try and pull her arms in so she could push up on her elbows and at least free her nipples from the shocking cold, he pulled her hips up, so that her toes just left the floor...and her slings dropped off her feet. She had to scrabble at the far edge of the table with her fingertips to keep from sliding forward.

She'd instinctively braced herself for the feel of him nestling between her legs, knowing, just knowing that that scant inch he'd lifted her would put that sweet hard-on of his right where she needed to feel it the most.

But instead of pulling her back up against him, he kept sliding her forward. And there was no sweet pressure. She whimpered before she could stop herself.

"You keep thinking I'm going to do what you expect me to do," he said quietly.

She said nothing, bit her lip to keep from cursing him, realizing it would just give him the satisfaction of knowing he was right. But whatever temper he might have roused fled an instant later when he slid his hands over her backside, holding her on the island, with the edge hitting her midthigh. She couldn't kick him, couldn't get any leverage, as her elbows were now hanging off the far side.

When he spoke, his lips were pressed against the small spot at the base of her spine. "Now, this I learned at the academy. However, I've never used restraint and control methods for quite this purpose."

He paused and she knew damn well he was waiting for her to say the magic word. Well, she wasn't going to give up so easily. But neither was she going to give in.

Which he probably also expected. Dammit. She hated being predictable. She was never that mundane. And yet her choices here were the proverbial rock...and the hard place.

She grinned, knowing he couldn't see it. It was precisely that hard place she was after. And damn if she wasn't going to get it. She kept silent.

But not for long. Just as he pressed his lips to that sensitive spot of skin, he slid his fingers from her backside to her inner thighs. One quick stroke of his finger along the center seam of her pants had her hips jerking…and her moaning.

"If you'd just stop plotting and planning long enough to relax and simply enjoy this…"

She had to bite her lip this time. Though she wasn't sure if it was to keep from swearing at him for tweaking her, or to stop herself from begging him to slide those fingers down there one more time. And slowly, please.

She would do neither.

She fought the shuddering response when he lightly drew a blunt fingertip along the back of one knee, then the other, before slowly following the inside seam of her pants. Pants she wished she could blink away. If he caught the scent of her, he wouldn't be taking so much goddamn time tormenting her.

The finger slid the opposite way and the heated epithet slipped out before she could catch it.

He chuckled softly. "You relax, you get what you want."

"I'm relaxed," she practically growled.

He simply sighed. "I'm thinking you don't know the meaning of the word." He started his finger's journey back up again, then stopped. "See, right there. You tense up the instant your brain kicks into gear. Do you ever let go? Completely, totally let go?"

"I'm not aware of my partners complaining at any lack of enthusiasm or focus on my part."

"Which is not at all what I asked."

She paused, smiling despite herself. "Which I'm fully aware of."

He laughed. "You take the term 'high maintenance' to a whole new level."

"Just give me what I want and you'll find I'm very easy to...maintain."

"Yeah, that's what they all say. Liza—" He broke off, then laughed again. "By the way, what is the last name of the woman currently sprawled half-naked on my kitchen counter, anyway?"

"Is it important?"

"You know mine."

"Sanguinetti."

"Ah."

She tried to pull her elbows underneath her to lever her torso up, but the shirt and bra straps twined around them hampered her movements. One slick slide of his finger between her thighs had her jerking flat again...and twitching with pleasure at the sudden shock of contact.

When she thought she could speak without begging him to finish her now—please God, now!—she said, "What, *ah*?"

"Italian women. Passionate, stubborn." He brushed his fingers along her inner leg, from knee to thigh. "Interesting combination."

"Glad you think so," she managed to say through clenched teeth. *Now* do *me for God's sake*. No man had ever played with her this way. This infuriatingly calm, controlled way.

Then she felt him tugging at the thin zipper that ran up the center of the back of her pants. *Finally*, she thought, and breathed a sigh of relief.

Slowly, torturously, he slid the tab down, and she

smiled against the cold tabletop, anticipating his reaction at what he would find.

"Well, that would explain the lack of panty lines in these fine white pants of yours," he said approvingly, but didn't touch the thin strip of white spandex that slid down between her cheeks.

"I find them functional," she said, ever so calmly. *And men find them erotic and hopelessly inviting,* she thought wickedly. Close, she was so close to having him where she wanted him.

He peeled her capri pants down and off, making her hiss as more of her came into contact with more of the island top. He moved between her legs, then nudged them just a bit wider.

She smiled and shivered in anticipation. It was wetly arousing, not being able to see him, to gauge his reaction to her as she revealed herself to him. But rather than pushing against that part of her that so badly required attention, he hitched his hips up on the table between her legs—facing away from her and all that she so gloriously had to offer him!—and lifted up, almost lazily, one of her feet.

"I—um," was as far as she got in her planned protest when his fingers started kneading the sole of her foot. In fact, she groaned and let her head drop back on her arm. "That feels amazingly good."

"Standing on those toothpicks like you do, I thought you might enjoy this."

She wanted to argue about what they *could* be enjoying right now. She wanted to pout and push her hips up at him, remind him of just how close she was and how easily he could take care of her real needs. But then he pressed his thumbs into her arch and the pleasure that radiated all the way up her calf was too damn distracting.

When he had that foot good and limp, he picked up the other. "This feels…almost better than sex," she said drowsily. "Almost."

It wasn't until he let her foot go and slid off the table that she realized just how relaxed she'd become. Boneless, that's how she felt. She hadn't thought of doing anything other than lying there and letting him work on her for a full ten minutes. Which, she also realized, was likely his plan.

"So who's sneaky now?" she murmured, not really able to work up a good mad. Who knew a decent foot massage could be so drugging? If managers of all the fancy spas she'd spent time in only knew about this, she thought, they could whittle their menu down to foot massages and make millions.

"Still plotting," he said idly, working those incredibly talented fingers into her calves.

"Not about you this time," she mumbled. "Spas should clone you. Make a fortune."

"Ah."

"Mmm. Ah." That last part ended up a long, satisfied groan as he deepened the massage on her legs. "On second thought, I want you all to myself." She smiled against her arm as he worked higher. "I'm greedy."

"Greedy can be good," he said, his voice a deep purr as his clever fingers continued kneading her flesh.

Drifting. For all that she was on a cold, hard slab, she could have been on a cloud. She'd had no idea how tense she'd been. Sabbaticals were a bitch, she thought, a smile curving her lips as her breathing deepened.

When she felt something warm and wet touch her between her thighs, she didn't even flinch. Tensing up was beyond her. The only thing she could plot or plan was feeling more of whatever he was doing now. It moved away and her hips lifted of their own accord, searching, wanting.

"Dylan—"

"Shh. Just lie there and feel. No thinking."

It sounded so easy, so wonderful. No thinking, no being in control, no worrying about her own agenda. Somewhere in the back of her mind, latent self-protective instincts tried to rear their drowsy heads, but then the warmth was back and this time it was sliding all the way between her legs. Closer to—sweet Jesus. She moaned and pushed, or tried to.

It disappeared again.

She frowned, but her body still felt so wonderfully pliable, it was too much work to make it move. The instant she released her breath, the warmth was back. Harder this time, pushing, probing.

She swiftly realized that as long as she didn't fight it, didn't try to force things, the sweet, tantalizing pressure would stay. And if it just stayed long enough—

"Ohhh, God!" She bucked hard off the table when his finger slipped beneath the thong strap and slid easily inside her. One slick slide and she went screaming right to the edge of a powerful climax, but hovered there when he did nothing more.

"Don't move," he commanded quietly.

She could only growl in response. But she held her hips completely still.

"You are so tight," he said, keeping his finger maddeningly still. "Hot and wet. But so damn tight."

"Mmm." It was all she dared say. Another syllable and she'd be begging him. She'd do what he said to get what she wanted, but she'd be damned if he'd make her beg for it.

"Slick heat," he added. "I wonder..." And he slid his finger back out.

"Ple—" She bit down hard on the rest of that word. Damn him.

Then she felt him again and her hips began to lift, doing some begging of their own. She couldn't help it.

He pressed her hips back down to the cold table, with just enough pressure for her to feel the steel press against her mound. But not enough to take care of her. Goddammit, when it was her turn, she was going to turn him inside out with wanting her.

Then she felt a new pressure between her thighs—still warm, still wet, but larger. Her hips twitched hard against the need to bear down as his fingertips—two this time—slipped beneath the thong strap.

"Take them off," she said. Commanding, not begging, she told herself.

"When I'm ready. I like the way they strap my fingers into you."

Whatever she might have said came out as a deep, gutteral groan of pleasure when he slid both fingers into her. With her hips still pressed flat as they were, she couldn't participate, couldn't move and push and, yes dammit, control the motion. By keeping her like this, he forced her to submit to his idea of how this should proceed.

He slid them back out, then pushed one back in, keeping the other one straight so he could press right where she—

"Thank you, God!" she grunted, then screamed as she came violently against his fingers. To his everlasting credit he kept them where they were until she stopped shuddering. She couldn't remember ever coming so hard with such little provocation. Although he'd primed her with a lot of provocation first. Still… She lay there and let the pleasure waves continue to ripple and twitch through her as he slid out of her.

Then she began devising her plan. Her turn now.

8

IT TOOK ALL of his willpower not to stroke himself through his jeans. He'd never felt such a desperate need to bury himself in a woman. But then, he'd never played kinky sex games on his kitchen counter before. Dylan wasted a moment trying to imagine any of the women he'd met in Canyon Springs sprawled, cuffed and naked, on his stainless steel island. Couldn't do it.

But Liza...she looked perfect. Too damn perfect.

She started to roll over and his hands shot out to hold her still. "Where do you think you're going?"

She started to lift her head, but apparently decided it was too much work. The muscles in her thighs were relaxed, pliable beneath his hands. For all he knew she relaxed this fully on a regular basis, but he didn't think so. She was on a vacation, of sorts anyway, and tied up like a knot.

"My turn," she murmured.

"Oh, not quite yet it's not."

Now she lifted her head, just enough to look over her shoulder. Sweet Mother of God, she was the most amazing thing he'd ever seen. And in his former line of work, he'd seen plenty. Her eyes alone were drenched blue sex.

"Oh?" she queried.

One arched brow and he twitched hard inside his jeans.

"Oh yeah." He slid his hands down over her thighs,

all the way to her calves. Slowly, until she sighed and laid her head back down.

"If you insist."

He grinned. Giving him permission, was she? What was it about her "woman on top" attitude that pushed his buttons? He hadn't been lying about letting previous partners have their way with him. He was more than happy to let the woman do all the work if she was so inclined. He was more than happy to do his share, too. Whatever Worked—that was his motto.

But this dominant streak she brought out in him—he couldn't think of any other term for it—was completely unlike him. In fact, given his line of work, he was generally very careful not to intimidate in intimate situations. Even when—especially when—his partner hinted she might like it. It simply wasn't his thing.

Well it sure is now, cowboy, his little voice taunted him. He had to agree. With her it was.

He slowly slid his hands up her legs again. Maybe, at some point during the night, he'd find out why. He stopped when his fingers were brushing the curve of her very fine backside. She twitched, just a little, but it was enough to elicit the same response in him.

The scent of her filled the room and made his mouth water. Maybe it was time to make that thong go away. He gripped her hips and rolled her onto her back. And his breath simply left him. Arms stretched over her head, dusky breasts bared to him and nothing but a scrap of white spandex covering the sweet spot below...she was every man's most carnal fantasy.

He didn't know where to begin.

"Stop drooling."

His gaze flicked up to her face. Her eyes were closed.

"Even if I promise to let you drool over me later?"

She lifted one slumberous eyelid. "Will I want to?"

He let the grin slide across his face. "Oh yeah."

"Cocky son of a bitch, aren't you?" Eyes closed, she let her head loll to one side. "The key word being *cocky*, I hope."

"Let's just say I don't get many complaints, either."

Now she smiled. Lazy and content, like a cat sprawled in a hot pool of sunlight. "Not what I asked."

"I know. You'll just have to trust me."

She laughed now, a deep rumbling purr that lifted the hairs on his entire body in the most pleasurable way. "Sheriff Jackson, you've gotten more trust out of me than anyone I've ever met."

"Good," he said, then gripped her thighs and slid her to him until her buttocks rested at the edge of the table. He slipped her ankles up to his shoulders.

The move surprised a squeal out of her. She lifted her head and started to pull her hands down in front of her.

"Uh-uh," he said. "Lie back down. I'm not done with you yet." He cupped her ankles and ran his palms down the front of her legs. She watched him, watched his hands. "Do it, Liza."

She lifted her gaze to his, and he knew she was dying to tell him where to get off. But then she wouldn't get off. Again. And she knew it.

She glanced back down to where his fingertips rested, curved around the inside of her upper thighs, then back up at him.

"Don't," he warned.

She merely widened her eyes in mock innocence.

"I don't want permission. I want your trust."

Whatever amusement there had been in her eyes fled. She held his gaze squarely and in such a way as to say, *Make me.*

"I'm going to touch you. However I want to. With whatever I want."

Her gaze remained on his, but her throat worked. And her nipples tightened, along with a fine tension that rippled beneath his fingertips.

"Lie back, Liza."

Holding his gaze almost defiantly, she did so. When he slid his fingers inward, to where he knew she wanted him to go, she gasped first, then sighed and let her eyelids drift shut.

"Oh no."

"Oh yes," she purred.

He smiled, beginning to realize why this was so enormously arousing to him. She was no pushover. But she was insatiably curious. He wondered if, put in the same position, he would acquiesce in the same way to her.

His smile spread to a grin. Probably.

"Open your eyes," he instructed. "Watching is half the fun."

"Oh, I don't know. I was having a great deal of fun a few minutes ago and my eyes were closed."

"And now you'll have even more." He slid his hands from her legs, then leaned in a little so he could brush the flat of his palms across the tips of her nipples.

She gasped and her eyes flew open. "Cheater."

"I never cheat. Going the long way around is too much fun." He brushed his palms over her nipples again, loving the way they pebbled harder. So hard they just begged him to roll them gently between his fingers.

Her heels dug into his shoulders and her hips lifted just a fraction off the table as she sucked in her breath…and closed her eyes. "Dylan—"

He lifted his hands. "Watch me, Liza."

She blinked them open. And he slowly leaned over,

testing her flexibility...and allowing her to anticipate the moment when his lips and tongue would replace his fingers.

She pumped her hips up and came close to brushing against the front of him as he lowered his head toward her breasts. He stilled. She swore. He smiled.

"Are your shoulders sore?" he asked, a millimeter away from touching her nipple with the tip of his tongue.

"I have shoulders?" she asked, a bit breathlessly.

Her arms still rested over her head, cuffed at the wrists, further bound by her shirt and bra.

"Stop procrastinating, dammit," she finally exclaimed.

"Bad move," he said, and started straightening.

"No! No, don't go. I'm—"

He stopped and grinned right in her face. "I'm what?"

She eyed him, pressing her lips together. "Not giving orders anymore," she said finally.

"Oh. And here I was pretty sure I was going to get the *S* word out of you. Silly me."

"You're getting a whole lot out of me. Don't push it."

"Oh, but I want to. You make me want to push at a whole lot of things." He leaned in and swiped the tip of his tongue over one nipple, then pulled the other into his mouth. She jerked, moaned and, he suspected, fought the urge to push her hips up. Hips that had to be seeking the same thing his were. He admired her control when she managed to keep them flat on the table as he continued to play with her incredibly responsive nipples. Because if she'd pumped up against him that time, when he had that velvety knob of flesh rolling against his tongue, he wasn't so sure he wouldn't have pumped back. Then ripped his pants off so he could pump some more.

He reached up and slid her legs from his shoulders, ignoring her whimper as he pushed her back just enough so that she could bend her knees and keep her heels on the table. He kept his hands around her ankles, and turned her whimpers into moans as he let his tongue trail from her breasts down along the center line of her stomach. When he got to the edge of white spandex, he took the elastic in his teeth and pulled. He glanced up and found her craning her neck to watch him. He grinned at her, knowing it likely looked feral with her panties in his teeth. But that's how he felt. Feral. Primal.

Her hips lifted. He let the elastic snap back into place.

"Hey!" she protested. "I was just helping."

"I don't need any help." He popped her heels off the table, grabbed her hips and pulled her up tight against him. He slid his hands up her torso and pulled her up to him, so that her handcuffed wrists came to rest behind his neck.

"I just need to give you something to do with that mouth of yours. Let's try this." He took her mouth, already opened in an O of surprise, and buried his tongue deep inside. She latched on to it, probably more as a protective instinct, but almost immediately took hold of it when he went to slide it back out.

So he continued the kiss, changing it whenever she thought to take control. Gentle when she wanted rough, hard and fast when she thought he wanted slow and sweet. Finally she sighed and let him have his way. He continued to kiss her until her arms tightened on his shoulders...and her legs came up to lock around his hips.

He unhooked her ankles and ducked out from beneath the circle of her shackled wrists. She started to say something, but at his warning look only pouted and stuck her tongue out at him instead.

"Watch where you wave that thing."

She merely flickered it at him, making him laugh even as she scowled.

"What, you aren't having any fun?"

She merely stared at him. But remained silent.

Then he spied that light in her eyes and caught her around the waist as she went to lie back again, her cuffed wrists resting at the apex of her thighs.

"Oh, no you don't. No putting on any shows."

She stuck that tongue out again.

"I warned you," he said quietly, then popped the button on his jeans and ripped the zipper down. The look on her face was so comically shocked, he had to laugh. "Hasn't anyone dared you like this before?"

She started to respond, then looked at him. "Permission to speak, master?" she said dryly.

"Permission granted," he said, as straightfaced as he was able.

She shot him a look, then said, "I've played in wilder little scenarios than this."

"Not what I asked." He held up his hand. "And I think I knew that about you right from the start."

"What is that supposed to mean?"

"You like to push things to the limit. And I would bet money that includes the sensual."

She snapped a nod of agreement.

He leaned in, gripped her wrists and pulled them to his open fly, pressed her flat palms against the rigid length of him. "But I'll bet everything else I own that at no time during those adventures was the guy calling the shots. If you've ever done anything like this before, I'm as certain as a man can be that you're the one stand-

ing, and they're the ones with their hands tied to the
bedposts." He curved his hands around hers, then peeled
her fingers away as she started to stroke him. "Tell me
I'm wrong, Liza."

She snatched her hands from his and let the key loop
slide off the thumb where she'd hooked it. She didn't
ask for help, but maneuvered the key all by herself, all
the while maintaining eye contact with him. The cuffs
fell to the tile floor with a clang.

She slid back on the table and hopped off the other
side, pulling her shirt the rest of the way off her arms
and untangling the bra from its folds.

"You didn't answer me. But then, I guess this is answer enough."

She spun on him, sparks shooting from her eyes, then
bit off whatever she'd been about to say and yanked on
her shirt, sans the bra, and began looking for her pants.

He scooped them up, then reached down for her shoes,
and snagged them with his free hand. He held them out
to her.

"Just like that," she finally spluttered. "It's your way
or nothing, is that it?"

"I don't believe I said anything like that."

She snatched her belongings from him. "You're on a
real power trip, you know? I'm not the one with control
issues here."

He took her elbow, turned her back around. "We can
go upstairs right now. Do whatever it is you want to do.
You can be in charge."

"You might think differently when you're the one in
handcuffs."

"Maybe. I've never had the pleasure. Might be the
best damn sex of my life. Given your presence, that's
highly likely."

Her mouth twitched despite her best efforts to keep the scowl on her face. "You can be that nonchalant about letting me shackle you to your own bed?"

"I doubt that anything that happens between the two of us will be classified as nonchalant."

"You'll let me do whatever I want?"

"Well, I'm not much for pain. I prefer pleasure. But then I think you know that about me by now."

He saw her throat work and felt his body leap in response.

She let her pants and heels drop to the floor and stepped closer to him. He took her arms and stopped her. "One thing."

"Ah. Here come the rules."

"No rules while you're in charge."

"So what is this one thing?"

"Once I let you have it your way, we come back down here and finish what we started."

A sly smile crossed her face, but not before he saw the flicker of not quite panic, but something close to it in her eyes. Frustration maybe. She covered it well. "You're thinking you'll still be able to do something else when I'm done with you?"

"I'm thinking it will be a demonstration of what I've been trying to get you to understand all along."

She tugged free of his grasp. "I don't need your lessons."

"Good, because I'm not in the habit of teaching. I had more an exploration in mind."

"What makes you think I want or need this little exploration of yours? You don't even know me."

"You're right. Sort of." He closed the distance and tugged her into his arms despite her initial resistance. "You said yourself you were here to find out something new about yourself. If we go upstairs, do things your way, it will be mind-blowing for sure, for both of us. I think we know that much. But will it be anything else for you? Anything new? Different?"

"I've never had you before. That will make it different."

The way she said it—"had you"—made him twitch. Made him wonder why in the hell he was pushing her in this direction, a direction that might leave him hard and alone, when he could have what they both wanted by saying the word and following her to his bed.

He still wasn't sure. Didn't know exactly what it was about her that provoked him to keep provoking her. Maybe it was instinct telling him there was something greater to be had here than the two of them just jumping in the sack together and going at each other like wild animals.

Which, when he thought about it like that, made him wonder if he was completely nuts.

"So, this is some kind of selfless lesson on your part. Teach poor Liza how to open herself up to the right man—you, of course—so she can get in touch with her inner submissive self."

"The only thing I asked you to submit was your resistance to letting someone else—me—be in charge." He reached out and traced a finger along her rigid jaw, then tucked his fingers into the curls behind her ears and tilted her resisting head back a bit. "Tell me this. Surely you've had men push their fingers into you, play with your nipples, suck on them, tease you." Her pupils widened instantly and he wanted to take her mouth and taste everything he saw there. He swallowed against the need. "But can you honestly tell me it excites you more when you demand your lover do those things to you, than

when I made you let me do them to you? When I took
away your ability to choose what happened and when?''

He felt her tremble, and damn if the power of it didn't
surge straight to his cock. ''What the hell is it you do
to me, Liza?'' he whispered roughly. ''You're strong.
Capable. Independent. All the things I prefer in a
woman.'' He pinned her to the table, pushed the ach-
ingly rigid length of him right between her thighs. ''So
why does making you tremble excite me like I've never
been excited before?''

He pushed both hands into her hair, gripped her head.
''Maybe I am the one with control issues, because I've
honestly never felt the need to be in control until you.
Maybe this isn't about just you, but both of us.'' He
lowered his mouth. ''So tell me, do you want to go upstairs and have it out and walk away with nothing new
to look back on?'' He brushed her lips with his and they
both shuddered. ''Or do you want to climb back up on
this table and let me finish this new adventure we both
started?''

9

DYLAN TOOK HER MOUTH with his, robbing her of the chance to answer. Thank God. Because she had no idea what to do with this man, this virtual stranger, who challenged her, intrigued her and damn well bewitched her.

One hell of a pit stop you decided to make, Liza, she thought as the rest of her was sucked back into the sensual vortex he'd created almost from the moment he'd looked down from that tree.

The shrill ring of the phone barely penetrated the thick fog of carnality she imagined almost visibly swirled around them. On the third ring she began to pull away, but Dylan gripped the back of her head, taking what he wanted, refusing—as usual—to let her call the shots. "Machine'll get it," he murmured against her lips, before slipping his tongue back between them.

But what Liza hadn't been able to do in person for the past couple of hours, Avis Jackson managed to do over an answering machine. And it only took one sentence.

"There's been a fire at the Mims Motel."

Dylan jerked his head up as if he'd been struck with burning cinders himself.

Avis continued, "Tucker says he has it under control, said not to bother you, but I knew you'd want to hear of it." There was a pause, then she added, "Hi, Liza. Sorry to intrude."

By the time the click of the phone snapped through the room, the fog had completely dissipated.

"Shit." Dylan settled her against the island counter, then hiked his jeans up and refastened them, his mind clearly no longer on seduction.

For her part, Liza merely folded her arms. "You don't trust your own fire marshal?"

"It's not that. Although Tucker knows protocol is to contact the sheriff anytime something like this happens."

"Which is how often in Canyon Springs?"

He tucked in his shirt. "Often enough. I know it looks like a small town, and compared to where you're from, it is. But it's bigger than it seems. The main part is in the valley, but there's a lot of sprawl—homes and places tucked all over the hills."

"Is this motel in a remote place?"

He shook his head. "Just on the outskirts of town."

"So, and I'm guessing here," she said dryly, as he finished tucking in his shirt. "You need to call it a night and head to the scene?"

He was tucking the handcuffs in the back of his waistband, but stopped and sighed. "I'm sorry." He tugged her wrists loose and pulled her close.

She resisted, but more out of form than because she really wanted to. "I'm not used to being so easily dismissed," she said, allowing him to weave her arms around his waist. That got a smile out of him, but she noted it didn't reach his eyes. "You take this small-town sheriffing thing really seriously." But then, she already knew that based on their dinner conversation earlier. She just hadn't wanted that reality to intrude on the nice fantasy scenario they were busily enacting in his mountain getaway.

So, a pit stop, after all, she thought, and sighed, feeling disappointed. More than she wanted to admit.

"This isn't just about a motel fire, Liza." He tipped her chin up, looked at her in that penetrating way he had. All the dark edges were prominent now, glowing from those vice-cop eyes of his.

Oddly enough, that made her wetter than anything that had happened between them so far. Which was really saying something. She wondered what it would have been like to bring the dark and edgy out in him this strongly when she was still handcuffed on the table. Her thighs clenched at the thought. Hard.

Dear Lord, she really was learning a few things about herself.

He was such an intriguing combination of things, so many layers. She'd love to peel some of them away and find out what was beneath. A shame it had to end now.

"I know this is asking a lot of you," he said, pulling her thoughts back to the here and now. "But I'd like it if you'd stay here."

Her eyes widened, more from surprise at the offer than any insult. "I've already waited for you once today."

His lips curved, but again the smile didn't penetrate those eyes. "And I believe that was working out nicely."

She smiled in return, though she was far more interested in what had brought that edge back than she was in any continued sexual banter. That realization shocked her so much she pulled away from him. She was only supposed to be interested in him for one thing. But she was finding that close to impossible the more time she spent with him.

She ran her hand through her hair and looked for her sweater. "Yes. Yes, I guess it was. But easy come, easy go, right?'' She shot him a look over her shoulder. ''Emphasis on the come part,'' she added, unable to pull off a sassy wink that would have sealed her casual, breezy exit. ''I'll just see myself out.''

He stopped her with a hand on her arm. His grip was like iron. Not painful, but completely unlike the firm, but gentle grip he'd had on her all night. She looked up at him, a silent question on her lifted brow.

''I'm not asking you to wait around for us to finish what we started, though I won't lie to you and say I don't want that. More than you can imagine. But this situation in town…there's more to it than you know. I need you to stay here until I check a few things out, make sure it's safe for you to go.''

''Safe? I thought you said the fire was on the other side of town?''

''It is.'' He ran a hand through his hair. ''We've talked about trust all night and I realize now how laughable that was since, despite where we were moments ago, we really don't know that much about one another.''

''I'd say we know a tad more than most new acquaintances.'' She'd meant it jokingly, but even as she said it, she saw that flicker of agreement in his eyes and knew they both understood it went deeper than sexual intimacy. Unexplainable really, considering, but true nonetheless. There was a connection here that defied conventional reason. If she were honest with herself, she'd admit she wanted to leave so she wouldn't have to face what came next. She could handle the sexual aspects of what they'd been about to do… Okay, so maybe even that was being pushed into a risky zone she'd never entered before.

She tugged her arm free and turned away from him,

suddenly far more confused than she'd realized. There were too many things roiling around in her brain, and she found it impossible to sort them all out and analyze with him standing there.

"Listen, you need to get to town," she said quickly. "It's really too late for me to be setting out on the road, anyway. Why don't I just go find a room for the night? If you want, we can meet for breakfast somewhere. Say whatever we need to say to one another, if you still feel the need, then I'll be moving on."

"Liza—"

"It's the best I can offer you. So unless you plan on handcuffing me to the table here until you get back, I'd suggest you recommend a hotel before I change my mind."

Mercifully, he didn't opt for the handcuffs, though she suspected he thought about it. So, as it happened, did she. Apparently he realized he'd pushed her as far as he was going to for one night. She was pretty sure she was happy about that. It was that sliver of indecisiveness that propelled her toward the door, before he came up with an alternate plan and she lost what little control she'd managed to snatch.

"Fine. You can follow me into town. There's a hotel near my offices. I'll get you checked in, then—"

"I can check myself in. Just point me in the right direction." She opened the door to the deck. "I'll meet you downstairs." She was gone, sliding the door shut behind her, before he could argue.

She paused on the deck, took a deep breath, tried to calm herself with a look out over the valley. Even in the dark, it was stunning. All the stars, the winking lights of the town. She could understand why he loved it out here, supposed it was a balm after a long day at work.

Maybe the balm was meant to soothe more than a day's work—rather, the years of work that had led him back to this place.

If any place could do all it, she thought, this one could. She'd always imagined she'd want her escape place to be on the shore, with the rhythmic sound of the waves, the salty tang in the air, the sound of wind chimes on the deck. She smiled as the chilly night breeze stirred her hair, and wondered what chimes would sound like up here in the mountains.

She shook her head and pulled her sweater on. Since when had she been so fanciful? She was the pragmatic one, not the romantic. Never the romantic. Her one and only trip down that lane had been an embarrassing disaster. Mostly because she'd been mortified at being played for a fool. She couldn't even fall in love right.

She imagined Dylan upstairs in his room, strapping on God only knew what kind of arsenal, probably standing by the bed she could have had him on at some point tonight.

Did she still want to get him there? Did she want to hang around in Canyon Springs until he had the time for her? Liza wasn't used to waiting around on men. But if she drove out of town tomorrow morning…would she always regret not finding out what could have been?

She snorted and headed down the spiral stairs. "Great sex with a guy who pushes buttons I didn't even know I had. What's to miss?" She could have great sex anytime. Okay, so maybe not whatever kind of sexual experience the two of them had been embarking on, but those were buttons perhaps better left unpushed, anyway. Besides, she really didn't need to get sidetracked here. One night was fun; two nights were almost like the beginning of something. Beyond that, things got…

complicated. She was trying to uncomplicate her life.

Dylan came down the steps behind her. "Listen, Liza, about tonight—"

She turned to him, pasted a smile on her face. "Dylan, it's okay. I'm a big girl. I realize you have a job to do and that's okay. I'll follow you to town." She opened her car door.

"You promised me breakfast."

"I'm not going to skip town before sunrise, if that's your worry," she said dryly. "I told you. I don't leave till I'm done with something."

He stepped closer, tugged her around and into his arms before she knew what was what. "That's just it. I want to know if you're done with me yet." His kiss took her right back to where they were before the phone call. Amazing, really. When he lifted his head, she tried to tell herself it was the thin mountain air that had her head spinning. But she knew differently.

"I'm...Dylan, I—" She should just thank him for an interesting evening and wish him a happy hometown life. Something Liza had never had and could never hope to find. Was a bit shocked to even think she might want to. "It's just that, maybe we—"

"Should have an early breakfast up here," he finished for her. "Alone. With no tongues wagging." He grinned. "Except ours, if we so decide."

She smiled, couldn't help it. "I'm beginning to see why witnesses never stood a chance with you."

His smile faded. "Do I? Stand a chance?"

She looked into those eyes and realized she'd never wanted so badly to say yes to anyone in her life. Save maybe her best friend, Natalie. That was terrifying enough right there, and reason enough to jump in her car and race away like a bat out of hell.

"How is it you have no problem giving me orders one minute, then look at me with huge, gorgeous puppy-dog eyes and ask me something like that?"

"Puppy-dog eyes?" He look honestly affronted, then surprised her with a fast, hard kiss. "Ordering you around is much easier when you're handcuffed and naked."

She was still trying to get her equilibrium back from that kiss. "You're getting entirely too good at that."

"Keeping you handcuffed and naked?"

"Sneaking kisses."

"Oh that." He grimed. "Yeah. I know." He sneaked another one, this time soft and sweet. It took her breath away.

"You confuse me," she said, not meaning to say it out loud. Or maybe she did. Just to see what he did with it.

"Then that makes us even."

She smiled. He brushed a fingertip over her lips.

"Okay," she said softly. "Breakfast. No promises. And no handcuffs."

He merely raised an eyebrow.

"Surely you can come up with some other way of controlling my wild and willful self."

The look he gave her then shot straight down her spine...and spread heat from there.

"I'm sure I can come up with something."

"We'll see about that." This time it was she who tucked in, stole a kiss. She'd meant to make his head spin a little, give herself some breathing space, a little control of the situation. But it had snapped back on her, leaving them both with the sensation of having been left dangling.

"How early is early?" she asked, hoping to mask the need and confusion in her voice.

He traced a finger over her lips, pushed the tip of his finger inside her mouth, then slipped it out again. "Sure you don't just want to stay here?"

She slid from his arms, far too close to saying yes. She might want him, might be confused by the needs he was stirring up inside her, but she'd never regain the perspective she sorely needed if she stayed here, in his lair, so to speak. And she definitely needed some distance. Because she'd heard the same need and confusion in his voice that he'd likely heard in hers. "You go tend to your fire. I'll be up here when I get up here."

He grinned. "I guess I had that coming to me."

She laughed, still feeling shivery with that delectable sexual tension that ebbed and flowed around them so effortlessly. "You haven't had anything coming to you. Yet. But we can discuss that over breakfast." She slid into her car before he could do or say something that would have her changing her mind. Or worse, tugging those cuffs from the waistband of his jeans and luring him back to his kitchen.

She gunned the engine and he leaned down, bracing his hands on her door. "Follow me," he told her. "And put the top up. It's too cold to have it down." He leaned the rest of the way in and snagged yet another swift, deep kiss from her, robbing her of the chance to tell him where he could stuff his orders.

She could only sit, dazed, and watch his very fine backside retreat around the back of her car and climb into his truck. "Big-time danger, danger," she whispered, rubbing her own lips as his engine roared to life.

She put the car into reverse and maneuvered around so she was facing downhill. She tucked her little car right in behind his big old police-issue truck. But, just to be perverse, she cranked on the heater and left the top down. Wiggling her fingers at him in a little wave, she laughed when he paused and looked pointedly out the driver window at her. Finally he shook his head, and she thought he might have been laughing as they headed down the mountain.

Halfway down, she put the top up, praying her fingers would thaw by morning. Making a point was only good when she didn't have to suffer personally to make it.

Besides, he'd gotten the message.

"Question is, Liza," she wondered aloud. "Have you?"

DYLAN PULLED OVER in front of the hotel, but Liza buzzed past him and swung into the small parking lot next door. She waved him on when he started to get out.

"Go play sheriff. I'll see you in the morning. Leave a message at the desk if something comes up."

He nodded. He didn't want to. He wanted to follow her inside, up to that room and into the bed. Forget all about his job. All about the meeting with Pearl. All about what was waiting to be dealt with minutes from now.

Because this was no simple motel fire. His instincts were already screaming and he knew he wasn't going to like what he found when he met up with Tucker at whatever was left of the Mims Motel. He closed the truck door, but waited until she was in the lobby before pulling away.

Normally his mind would focus fully on whatever task was at hand. But as he wound through the quiet night streets of Canyon Springs, his mind was more on what he'd just left behind than on what he was driving toward.

This entire evening felt surreal. And yet he had no doubts—just ask his body!—of what had taken place, or started to anyway, right there in his kitchen. God almighty, what the hell had he been doing up there with her?

Whatever the hell it was, he wanted to do it again. And go beyond. Liza Sanguinetti had cruised into his life mere hours ago, and she was already in his blood. He knew he was foolish to believe she'd really be there in the morning. She'd been as uncomfortable with what they were uncovering about each other as he had, maybe more so. Although if she knew the half of what he'd been feeling back there, she'd know she wasn't alone. Not by a long shot.

His lips twitched in a smile. Christ, she could tie him in knots with the arch of one perfectly plucked eyebrow.

He swung around the corner, the flash of multicolored lights over the trees ahead indicating he was almost there. Yet instead of contemplating how in the hell Dugan had found out about his little meeting with Pearl quickly enough to send him a warning, and what Dylan was going to do about it, he was thinking about swinging by Liza's hotel on the way back home. No matter the hour. She wouldn't expect that.

And, after all, doing the unexpected where Liza Sanguinetti was concerned had served him well up to this point.

He turned the last corner and slowed as he neared the scene. Two ladder trucks were still there, along with one emergency squad. He was heartened somewhat by the fact there weren't any others lined up. He hadn't heard any sirens heading out to the hospital on his way in, so hopefully that meant everyone had gotten out in time.

He hadn't radioed in that he was coming down. That, he admitted, was mostly payback for Tucker not following protocol. Dylan preferred his old friend not be prepared for their ensuing showdown.

"Dammit, Quin, who screwed up on this thing?" he muttered as he swung in behind Tucker's truck and shut the engine off. He should have made the reservation himself. But Quin had assured him no one knew about the meeting. Thinking how cavalierly he'd had Quin make the reservation in Liza's name, Dylan felt his stomach roll, just as it had when he'd heard his mother's message. He knew better than to involve civilians, even in name only. His lips twitched and he shook his head as he got out of his truck. He hadn't exactly used her real name, as he recalled. Because he hadn't known it at that point.

He paused and took in the scene, most of his brain already clicking into gear, processing information, noticing details, filing away questions with which to grill Quin. But as he strolled over to Tucker, a part of him couldn't help but wonder what the assembled group would think if they'd known what their sheriff had been up to before being called in.

10

LIZA FELL ACROSS the surprisingly soft hotel bed and simply lay there, trying to gather her thoughts. She rolled on her back and stared at the ceiling. That didn't help, either. Maybe a shower. A steamy cocoon, relaxing…

Images of her and Dylan, entwined in that steamy shower, assailed her. Images of them playing, toying, teasing… She sat up and grabbed the phone, and did what she always did when she couldn't stand to be alone with her own thoughts. She called Natalie.

She was planning her apology for calling so late when Nat's answering machine clicked on. "Great. Lovely." Liza clapped the phone back down on the base. "Desert a friend in need, why don't you." She rolled to her back again. "And do I ever have needs."

The sudden jangle of the phone made her jump. She snatched it up before the second ring. "Dylan?"

There was a pause, then a female laugh. "Nooo."

"Natalie! Oh, thank God. You saved me."

"Who's Dylan?"

"Wait a minute. How did you know where I was?"

"I was…occupied when the phone rang. But recognized that disgusted 'Great, lovely' and pressed star-sixty-nine to trace this number. What are you doing and where in the hell is the Canyon Springs Inn? Are you at a spa? You swore you weren't going to do anything normal. Normal for you, anyway. No hiding out, getting pampered while you ponder your destiny. And your destiny is not a masseur named Dylan, no matter how great his hands are.''

''He's not a masseur, he's a sheriff.''

There was a pause. ''A sheriff? Oh my God, Liza, what have you done now? Are you calling for bail money? Wait, you have plenty of money. Oh!'' Nat gasped, barely taking a breath. ''You need a lawyer. Okay, okay, well, I'm here now. Start from the beginning. Tell me everything. Wait. I need a pencil. And paper. And—''

''Natalie!'' But it was too late. And yet Liza was smiling, glad her friend had called back, even if she had interrupted her and Jake doing the wild—

''Okay, I'm back. Now, what did you do?''

Liza sighed, still smiling. ''First of all, I love you. And second, what happened to my oh-so-organized best friend? Since when don't you have a pad, pencil, mini-recorder, calendar and fax machine on your nightstand?''

''Since I left the fast track to become a small-town lawyer. But we're not talking about me. Wait a minute. Why are you calling the sheriff by his first name?'' There was a little huffed out breath, then she said, ''Liza…'' She'd dragged that last syllable into a warning note. ''Tell me you didn't break the no-sex-until-I-know-what-I-want-from-life rule. You only had one rule, for God's sake.''

For the first time in hours Liza felt like herself. No one did that better than the only person on the planet who understood her better than she did herself. ''Well…''

''Tell me you didn't call me in the middle of, well, the night, to crow about your latest sexual conquest, because you know I'm not going to congratulate you on—"

"There was no sexual conquest." At least not how Natalie meant it, Liza thought. Besides, if there'd been any conquest, it had been Dylan doing the conquering.

"No? So you didn't?"

"I can't tell if you're more shocked or relieved."

"So what happened? You had a sudden attack of guilt? No, that can't be it."

"Hey!" Liza retorted, but she was chuckling.

"No? So what, then—he was gay?"

"Well, his mother thought he might be."

There was another pause. "Okay, I was kidding. So you're going to have to start at the beginning at some point and explain that one to me. But assuming his mother is wrong—and how in the hell his mother got in the middle of this I am dying to hear—then I'm assuming some rule breaking of some sort was going on. Or will be going on."

"Well…"

"So I'm what? Your sex intervention squad? You want me to talk you out of doing it? Or, worse, you want me to tell you it's okay to do it? Where exactly are we on the sexual map here? I can't plan a strategy if I don't know where the battle lines are drawn."

"I'm still on the straight and narrow. Well, more narrow than straight, if you want to get technical. I just took, well, I prefer to think of it as a tiny detour. Finding my way around a sudden roadblock, if you will, on my journey to destiny." Liza pulled a pillow onto her lap and settled back against the headboard. "Which I still don't have a single clue about, by the way. And, for the record, technically speaking, I didn't break the no-sex rule."

"Yet. I heard the 'yet' plain and clear. And why, might I ask—technically speaking, of course—did things stop shy of a complete pit stop?"

"Fire."

Natalie burst out laughing. "Well, now that's a new one, even for you. What, did you get him so hot he forgot dinner was cooking? Or no, let me guess, you had him in the squad room and managed to catch the whole damn police department on fire."

"Hey, even I'm not that good. Or bad, depending on how you want to look at it."

"Don't sell yourself short."

"I'm going to take that as a compliment."

"You would."

"And you love me for it."

"Somebody has to. So, all joking aside, why *are* you calling me?"

For the first time in probably her whole life, Liza wasn't quite sure what to say.

"Wow. That bad, huh?"

"I'm not sure it's bad. Actually, it was damn good."

"You said you didn't—"

"I had an orgasm, okay? But that's not the same thing as sex."

"Depends on your definition, but okay, I'll grant you a stay on this one. Go ahead."

"It's just that— I knew I shouldn't have, but he's, well— And it was just going to be dinner, only we both knew— And he had handcuffs and I—"

"Please tell me you didn't leave him shackled up somewhere."

"The handcuffs weren't for him."

There was a moment of silence. "Oh."

Liza blew out a deep sigh, waves of remembered pleasure and confusion rolling through her at the same time. "Yeah. Big oh."

"But that's not like you."

"Tell me about it."

"So, tell me about him."

"I'm not sure how to describe him. He was a vice cop in Vegas, returned home to New Mexico to become a hometown sheriff when the big city slime started to eat down under his skin. His mom rescues big exotic birds and spends more time with them than him, but he seems to have come to terms with that. The town loves him and his high school rival is the town fire marshal. He's dedicated and straightforward, but he's got these dark edges to him. Probably all that time in Vegas. He's confident without being cocky. Assertive without being pushy. And sexy as all hell."

"Phew. You know, I think that's more than you generally know about a guy by the time you're already breaking up with him."

Liza shifted, suddenly uncomfortable. "Yeah, well, we talked over dinner. We said things."

"Does he know this much about you?"

"He knows some. We got, um, sidetracked."

"Orgasms can do that to a conversation."

Liza smiled, but it faded. "I don't know what to do here. He's...he's not like anyone I've ever met."

"Well, it's a little telling that you described the personality before the physical attributes. He sounds... promising."

Liza thought about that. "He also irritates me, frustrates me, pushes me."

"And it was the best orgasm you've ever had."

"What, you were watching?"

Natalie laughed softly, then said, "No, this just sounds kind of…familiar. That's all."

Liza ignored that for the moment. "Dazed and confused, that's the state he keeps me in. I think I have the upper hand one minute, and the next, pow. He's in control. I'm not used to this, Nat."

She was chuckling again. "No. No, I guess not."

"Yeah, easy for you to laugh. You weren't the one handcuffed half-naked on the man's kitchen counter."

"Kitchen counter? No, I'm not even going there. Question is, are you going back there?"

"That's just it, I don't know where this is going, or even if it should. Nothing like this was supposed to happen yet. It was just supposed to be a little detour, that's all."

"Uh-oh. We're not just talking about finding sexual nirvana among the kitchen utensils, are we?"

"It should be just about sex. We've both basically agreed it's supposed to be about sex."

"Only?"

"Only I don't know. And I don't think he does, either. He looks at me sometimes, Nat, and I…I feel things I don't completely understand."

"Whoa."

"Yeah. Big so-potentially-not-a-detour whoa." Liza sighed. "I think I understand now why it was so hard for you to tell me about Jake, in the beginning. It's so impossible to describe why it's different, but it is. Maybe it's the way he…pushes me."

"Pushes you how?"

"It's like he understands the way I operate. And he enjoys shifting me away from my comfort zone."

"Which is being in charge."

"Exactly."

"And you let him."

"Well, not necessarily *let*. He sort of, I don't know, made it worth my while that he be the one in charge. I could have stopped him."

"But you didn't."

She sighed. "No. And I think what was happening between us was as much a new path for him as it was for me. At least he said as much. I think I believe him." She laughed. "I'm not making any sense at all, am I."

"More than you think, sweetie," Nat said, all quiet and pondering again. "More than you think."

"What in the hell does that mean?"

"It means this sounds familiar. He's a rush, but confusing, scary because you want him really bad but you know it's probably really wrong to give in to it because it's supposed to just be about pleasure, and it is about that...but then he makes you look at yourself in a new way, and you know it could be about a whole lot more. Doubly scary given where you are in your life. Totally different from me, but yet a lot the same. Possible same outcome."

Now Liza laughed, but it wasn't the confident "yeah-right-sure" snort she'd intended. "Me? End up married to a small-town sheriff? I don't think so."

"Hey, watch it. You're talking to a small-town lawyer here."

"I know, I know." She gave a long sigh. "This isn't about falling in love, though. It's not like you and Jake, Nat. We're just...exploring. Things."

"Uh-huh. Sounds exactly like me and Jake, at least in that we swore that sex and pleasure was all it would ever be, could ever be. But that doesn't mean it can't be exactly what you both want. Whatever that might be." She blew out a breath and half laughed. "I can't believe

I'm telling you to go for this. Like you need to be encouraged to be incorrigible. But…well, I don't know, Liza. Something about the way you sound…it strikes a chord in me. The new married-and-in-love me, anyway. As long as you think you have a handle on things—''

Liza snorted. ''Haven't you heard a word I've said? Every time I think I have the upper hand, he flips things around until I don't know what end is up.''

''And?''

Liza didn't say anything for a long moment. ''And, maybe, I like it. Well, not like it,'' she added quickly, ''but I don't want to leave it yet, either. He wants to push me and I like to push back. We weren't done pushing at each other yet.''

''Because of the fire.''

''Yeah. He was called to the scene and, well, I checked into a hotel.''

''You must have some control if you're in a hotel and not waiting for him on his kitchen counter.''

''Ha ha. But that's just it. He pushes and retreats. It's a hell of combination. And he offered, but I said no.''

''But you're staying in town because of…?''

''Breakfast. And okay,'' she added impatiently when Natalie snorted. ''Because we're not done yet. I don't know what done is, but we're not there. Yet.'' There was silence on the other end, and it dragged on long enough that Liza finally said, ''Do you think I should just skip town and put this behind me?''

''What do you think?''

''I think I've been to enough therapists as a child to never answer a question with a question.'' They both laughed. ''I want to know what you think I should do.''

''Will you regret it if you leave now?''

''Yes. Maybe. I don't know.''

"I think you have your answer then. You didn't say 'maybe' first. Your instincts are usually dead on."

"Except where stupid-ass soap actors are involved."

"We both know that wasn't about Conrad. That was you figuring out that maybe you're hardwired more like the rest of us than you thought you were. He was just the man in your life when you came to that conclusion. Square peg, round hole. It was never the right fit and you know it."

"You're right. But it doesn't make this any less confusing. I've made so many changes recently. It's hard to sort out exactly what feels like the right thing to do."

"Well, I met Jake and then the changes came right in the middle, and we had to deal with that and sort them out. Maybe your changes had to come first and you met him right in the middle."

"You make this sound serious."

She heard the smile in Natalie's voice. "Honey, when you call me at this hour to talk about a man—a man you haven't slept with yet—it is serious." And while she let that little bomb of wisdom detonate and sink in, she added, "I love you. And I'll love you no matter what you do. Just make sure you stay safe."

"I've met the man's mother. No way is he going to do anything nefarious with me."

Nat laughed. "I still want to hear that story. And I wasn't talking about physical safety."

"Yeah," Liza said softly. "I know. Thanks, Nat. Sorry I interrupted, but not really. I'm glad you were there."

"Let me know how it goes, okay?"

"I will."

There was a muffled noise, then a giggle, then a man's voice on the line. "Nat has to go to bed now."

Liza smiled. "Hi, Jake. Bye, Jake."

"Good night, Liza." There was another muffled laugh, then a small shriek, then the line went dead.

Liza hung up and rolled to her back, still clutching the pillow. Nat was right. She *was* hardwired more normally than she'd thought. Because she wanted that. That easy intimacy, that easy banter.

That going to bed with the same man every night.

She'd known before leaving L.A. Had become more sure of it after spending several weeks with Nat and Jake in Wyoming. But she could never attach an image to the desire.

Well, she could now.

"One hell of a detour you picked for yourself, Liza."

11

"IT WASN'T AN ACCIDENT."

Dylan glanced at what had now been classified as crime scene pictures, then back up at Tucker. "I know."

Tucker hitched his hip onto Dylan's desk. "I know you know. I think you knew before you even got to the scene."

"A scene I only knew about because Avis called me," he reminded him pointedly, then waved his hand. He'd knocked heads with Tucker since their high school football days. Nothing much had changed since and he doubted it ever would.

Tucker, golden boy and gridiron hero, had stayed in Canyon Springs and become a real hero, charging into burning buildings, saving lives, shrugging it off with his million watt smile...but letting the ladies fawn over him nonetheless. He could have been the youngest fire chief Canyon Springs had ever had, but decided instead to turn toward the investigative part of things, and wound up fire marshal. Dylan, town renegade and gridiron bad boy, had left Canyon Springs and become an unknown hero, scraping slime off the streets of faraway Vegas. He could have been the youngest captain on the force, but no one would ever know that. Instead he'd come home and run for sheriff. He didn't court the spotlight and hated being fawned over by anyone.

Naturally, the town loved this dichotomy between its

two high-profile heroes. Tucker enjoyed the status, comfortable with his well-earned mantle. Dylan paid no attention to his, vaguely uncomfortable with labels. He just went about getting the job done. Their rivalry was more a town thing than a personal thing, except Tucker enjoyed tweaking him with it whenever possible. Dylan only sunk to his level when he couldn't help himself. Which was a bit more often than he'd like to think it was. He supposed the saying "boys will be boys" was coined for good reason.

"I had the scene under control," Tucker responded, as Dylan knew he would. "You'd have had my report on your desk first thing in the morning." He grinned and helped himself to Dylan's coffee. "Instead of hashing this out at 3:00 a.m. But hey, this is what we live for, right?"

"This is what *you* live for. I've had my share of this, remember? I'd be perfectly happy home in bed right now."

Tucker's eyes flashed. "Oh yeah, that's right." He pulled a face. "Poor Liza. Losing her man to the job, just when she'd finally gotten him where she wanted him."

If you only knew, Dylan thought. And he'd thought about it a lot. It didn't help that she was less than a block away, tucked in bed. All warm curves and contrary nature. He stifled a smile and pushed at the photos on his desk. "Any word back from the hospital yet? How's Payne?" The end three units of the strip motel were little more than a charred shell. The rest of the building had suffered both water and smoke damage. Luckily the few guests staying there had raced outside when the whole sprinkler system had been triggered by the one burning room.

Fred Payne, the night manager, had been taken away for smoke inhalation. He'd tried to fight the initial blaze with a fire extinguisher, then a hose, but it had quickly grown beyond his control and he'd retreated to wait for the fire department, which had shown up moments later.

"They're keeping him the rest of the night, but he'll be okay. I talked to his wife and she's staying with him."

Dylan had someone over there as well, with instructions to call him if Payne was discharged, and to report and detain any visitors other than family.

"We've put up the few guests in other hotels. The day manager is on call if we need her." Tucker started to pick up the motel booking log, but Dylan slapped his hand on it.

"That's evidence."

"Which, as marshal, I'm allowed to see."

"Only as it pertains to the fire. This goes to possible motive." And the longer he could keep it out of the local media that the room where the fire started had been reserved in the name of his supposed showgirl lover, the better. Dylan figured he had a few hours, tops, until Fred Payne got out of the emergency room. "You get the reports back on what accelerant was used?"

"Nothing sophisticated. It's what we thought. Gasoline on the carpet. Toss in a match and poof." Tucker glanced at him. "No one was trying to make it look like an accident." When Dylan didn't bite on that, Tucker picked up the photo showing the point of origin. "No one was checked into the room, though I got it from the day girl, Letta Sparks, that the room had been reserved earlier in the day. Specified an end unit. Interesting, isn't it?"

Tucker tossed the picture back on the desk and finished off the rest of Dylan's coffee in one swig. He pitched the cup in the trash across the room, even though there was one right next to him. "Nothing but can," he said as it sailed in dead center. Then, just as casually, he asked, "So, when are you going to tell me what's really going on here?"

"With Letta Sparks in your back pocket, or more likely, your front ones, what do you need me for?"

Tucker smiled, but didn't deny anything. "She said the caller was male, asked for a single room for a Liza Smith. We're having a real run on that name today, aren't we? Held the room with a credit card. You traced that yet?"

Dylan slid the pictures into a small manila envelope and tucked the flap in. He tossed them in the rapidly growing case file and flipped the folder shut. "Don't need to."

Tucker grinned. "Gee, now there's a surprise. Match the one in your pocket, does it?"

"No, as a matter of fact, it doesn't."

Tucker just shrugged. "So what happened? Your girl-friend come to town trailing trouble behind her?"

Liza didn't need to bring trouble with her, Dylan thought, biting back the urge to smile. She was trouble enough all by herself. He'd thought about just letting everyone continue to believe Liza was his imaginary showgirl, but now, with the fire and Dugan involved—and there was no doubt that he was—Dylan would have to explain. Which would also set tongues to wagging, but what the hell. It was the least of his worries at the moment. "She's not connected to this, Tucker."

"Then if it wasn't a jealous ex-boyfriend setting a jilted-lover fire, it was either a random act of violence—and we all know the chances of that are slim around here—or a warning. I keep asking myself, a warning for what? The room was in her name, yet you say she isn't involved in this. Then who is?''

''You know, you should have been the one to head to the big city,'' Dylan said. ''You'd have made detective young and been in your element. All those showgirls, high rollers, rich women. Think about it, Tucker.'' He grinned. ''Seriously, I mean.''

Tucker shot him a smile. ''I have. More than you might think.'' His smile remained, but his eyes blazed with the avid interest that underscored why his skills were wasted on a town the size of Canyon Springs. ''If trouble didn't trail her into town, then that means it's come to the only person she's connected to here. You.''

Dylan blew out a breath. Tucker might grate on his nerves from time to time, but he was a damn good investigator. ''It's something I was in before I left the Vegas PD. You heard of a guy named Armand Dugan?''

Tucker shook his head. ''No, what's he run? Girls, numbers, drugs?''

Dylan just nodded and Tucker whistled beneath his breath. ''What are you doing dragging that here? You're not sloppy.''

No, Dylan thought, *just horny.* His head had been in his pants when he'd been talking to Quin, otherwise he'd have listened to the tickle of neck hairs that had told him not to have that discussion on the cell phone. ''One of the guys on my squad called to set up a meeting. I covered it under Liza staying at Mims.''

''Good thing she wasn't.''

Tucker didn't need to remind him of that. Dylan was already worried that he should have sent her out of town the instant he heard about the fire. But Dugan wasn't targeting Liza, he was targeting Quin and Pearl. And, to a lesser extent, Dylan. It had been a warning to walk away from the meet. Dylan knew how Dugan operated. If he'd wanted Liza, or anyone else, hurt, he'd have made it happen. But that didn't mean he wouldn't up the stakes when Dylan didn't back off. And he didn't plan on backing off. It was personal now.

Dylan pushed that from his mind and stood up, rolling his shoulders and raking his hand through his hair. "I'm going to run by the hospital, check on Payne, then I'm calling it a night. I'll meet with you tomorrow afternoon, say two o'clock."

"You still going to set up the meet?"

Dylan wasn't ready to discuss that yet. "We'll talk tomorrow."

Tucker opened his mouth, then shut it again and nodded. "Fine." He stopped at the door, looked back. "Keep a close eye on her, Dylan. I know I don't have a scrap of your experience, but my gut tells me she could get pulled into this pretty easily."

Dylan could only nod. "Listen." He paused, sighed, and said, "You should know, she's not from Vegas, Tuck. The name was a coincidence. She has nothing to do with Dugan. With any of this."

Tucker just nodded, as if he'd known all along Liza wasn't what she purported to be. Whether or not he'd really suspected as much didn't reflect in his eyes. "Yeah, but Dugan finds out you've got a weak spot, he could have something to do with her."

"She won't be staying. Don't worry."

Tucker shook his head and laughed. "Yeah, you keep telling yourself that."

"I won't have to. She'll be gone tomorrow."

"I might not know about the kind of criminal element you used to keep company with in Vegas, but I do have you topped when it comes to keeping company with women.''

Dylan merely raised his eyebrows.

Tucker just grinned. ''Fine, fine. But she's not going anywhere anytime soon. Least not until you two burn each other out of your systems. With the way you've had one eye on that phone and the other on your watch half the night, I'm betting that hasn't happened yet.''

''You have no idea what you're talking about,'' Dylan retorted, but he was talking to the back of his office door. ''Pain in the ass is what he is,'' he grumbled, then grabbed the folder and his gun and headed out in turn.

After his trip to the ER, it would be close to five by the time he got home. Unless he went back to the hotel instead. Tucker's warnings echoed in his mind, but Liza wasn't a target now, and she wasn't going to become one later. Dylan had spoken with the night manager at her hotel anyway, just as a precaution. She'd made one call to a Wyoming number, taken one call. No visitors, no room service.

He climbed in his truck and tossed the file on the passenger seat. He needed to have a talk with Quin, but had been unable to do so with everything else going on. So his plan was to hit the ER, find a place to make contact with his old squad mate, then be back at the hotel by seven to wait for Liza. He'd already written off their breakfast—and anything else that might have come after. As tired as he was, he smiled, hearing her response to that in his head. *Come being the key word, Sheriff.* He wished.

But it was best to get her on her way and out of the line of fire. He put the truck into gear and tore out of the lot with a bit more rubber than necessary.

TWO HOURS LATER he was one county over and on the phone of the local law. ''Come on, Quin, answer the page,'' he muttered beneath his breath. He'd put the word out early for the surrounding counties to be on the lookout for the man Dylan was all but certain had set the fire: Tunny Stubbs. Dugan was nothing if not consistent with his personnel. They'd never been able to nail the little bastard and use him against Dugan, and it was likely they wouldn't have more than circumstantial on him now. But Dylan could slow him down a bit, and it was worth a few more sleepless hours to put what screws he could to Dugan.

He'd gotten a radio call at the hospital that Stubbs had been picked up, so he'd headed south to see to it personally. He knew the police captain here from a class they'd taken on new strategies for busting racketeering networks several years earlier, when they'd both worked for bigger departments. Captain Henry had retired to Las Cruces, then ended up running a department in the county.

Dylan had finished with Stubbs for the time being and was using Henry's office to place a page to Quin. Now all he had to do was hope Quin was wearing his pager. The phone rang a moment later. ''What the hell happened?'' Dylan snapped as soon as he heard his voice.

''I don't know, man. I'm tracking it. I thought we were in the clear.''

''Obviously not. Everything okay?'' Quin would know he meant Pearl.

''Yeah, I'm taking care of things.'' Meaning he had Pearl with him.

''You got help?''

''Yeah. We'd planned for that. We just had to put it into motion a bit sooner than scheduled.'' They'd have known she would need a safe place to stay until trial, once Dugan was finally arrested.

"Will it fly now that the cat's out of the bag?"

"It has to—she's all we have. Listen, we need to do this thing ASAP. I can't make a move until I have the information."

Dylan paused, sighed. It was too late to wish he'd never met Pearl Halliday, but it didn't mean the sentiment wasn't there. Meeting in Canyon Springs was out. But now with the fire, the town would be in a tizzy, plus the fiesta was coming up. "I'll come, but it's going to be an in-and-out." Meaning he'd fly in on a private charter, do the interview and fly out. "Your boys will be picking up the tab."

"Not a problem. Page me the info. I'll see you there."

"I'll have it set up shortly."

"Great. And…thanks. I wouldn't have contacted you like that if I'd known—"

"I know, I know. Just make sure you have things closed down tight."

"We do. Did you find our favorite little firebug?"

"Yeah, I'm down in Dona Ana County now working out getting him sent back up to Canyon Springs."

"Have anything that will stick?"

"No, but I can jam him up for a while before he'll get cut loose. Listen, any federal interest in this yet? Anyone who can put some pressure on Stubbs for me?"

"Dugan's still ours and I plan to keep him that way."

Dylan knew what he meant. It had happened enough times on other cases. They'd bust their asses to put the whole thing together, then the feds would waltz in and take over in the eleventh hour. Dylan wasn't worried about garnering glory, but it rankled not to be the one to finish what he'd started. His thoughts switched to

Liza. As they had far too often this night. Another thing he'd started that he wouldn't be able to finish. As it was, he'd have to hurry to take care of her and set up the flights in and out of Vegas.

"Yeah, well, we'll put a nice fat bow on it tomorrow. Just keep it out of my town from here on in." He ended the call with Quin, thanked the captain for his assistance, finalized the details on transporting Stubbs the next day, and got back on the road. A quick look at the dash clock told him he'd be at the hotel by eight. He only hoped Liza wasn't an early riser. He wanted to catch her before she headed back to his house.

No point going there now.

He worked hard to focus on the glorious sunrise...and not what could have been taking place in his bed this morning. As stunning as the morning colors of the sky were, it ran a poor second to images of Liza tangled up in his sheets. Blue eyes, tawny skin, a tangle of dark hair.

Maybe, he thought, when this was all over, he'd work it out to contact her, see her again. His laugh was harsh and hoarse from his going a night without sleep. "You were a side trip, Jackson." Once Liza Sanguinetti tooled out of town in that hot rod of hers, she wouldn't be passing his way again.

12

LIZA WAS STEPPING OUT of the shower when someone knocked on her door. "No housekeeping needed," she called out. "Thanks."

The knock came again, more insistent. She wrapped herself in a towel and dripped out to the door. "No house—"

"It's me, Liza."

She froze. Dylan. "I thought we agreed I'd come up to your place. I know I was running a bit late, but…" She peeked out of the peephole, then yanked the door open a second later and pulled him inside. "You look terrible."

He smiled, though it wasn't the full voltage grin she'd gotten the night before. "Thanks. I try."

"You haven't gotten any sleep at all, have you?" She guided him into the room and pushed him down on the edge of her bed. "Don't worry," she teased, trying to conceal her concern. "I don't plan to take advantage of an unarmed man."

His smile did flicker to a grin. "I am armed."

"Oh. Well." What was it about this whole cop-with-cuffs thing that turned her insides into libidinous jelly, anyway? She tried not to be obvious with the little shiver of pleasure that intruded, along with images of what they'd been doing with those cuffs the night before. Gauging from the flare of interest in his oh-so-tired eyes, she failed. "I'll be right back. Make yourself comfortable."

"Okay." He snagged her wrist and dragged her into his lap. His mouth found hers a second later and she forgot to be mad about his heavy-handed, take-what-he-wants-when-he-wants-it attitude and— Oh dear God, but he tasted good in the morning.

"You taste like sugared coffee," she murmured, when he trailed his lips down to her chin, nipping it as he had the night before. She really liked that, she decided, that little chin nip.

"Elixir of life," he said, his voice all hoarse and raspy. A shame it was from fatigue and not passion, although he was doing a pretty decent job of getting her worked up. "Of course, this isn't a bad second," he mumbled, then pulled her mouth to his again.

She thought about kissing him back, turning it up a notch, taking over…but his lips were soft, not hard and demanding like last night. And his arms seemed to cling to her, rather than lock her into place. It made her want to…well, take care of him.

This was a role she was used to, albeit usually professionally rather than personally. But being caretaker also afforded its own balance of power, and she thought it might be a good idea, strategically speaking, considering how weak-kneed one kiss had already left her, to gain any leverage she could early on. Shore it up for later, when she might need it. He slid his tongue past her lips, pulled her more deeply into his need for her…and she forgot all about strategic campaigns and simply relaxed in his arms and let him kiss her. She'd worry about control issues later. This was…nice. And a little scary, if she let herself think about why it was so nice. So she didn't.

But just as she was sinking under, he was surfacing. "I'd better stop here or we'll be crawling under the sheets."

"And?" she said, shifting just a bit in his lap. Yep, he might be tired, but he was ready.

"And I'd embarrass myself by tucking you against me and falling dead asleep on you. Not the morning either of us had in mind, I'm sure."

She was shaking her head, but mostly because she was trying to deny just how incredibly appealing that suggestion had sounded to her. And she was the one with a good night's sleep under her belt.

Liza was typically not a snuggler. She was an action girl, then she liked unencumbered space to sleep. Bless the soul who had created the king-size bed. Because a well-rested Liza was a happy Liza in the morning, when adventure and acrobatics could continue. Her partners tended to appreciate her all-fun, no-work attitude. No awkward physical entanglements that led to messy emotional entanglements.

Not that she was emotionally entangled here. *Yet,* her little voice whispered. She hadn't even had sex with him. Which, of course, when she thought about it, made her sudden yearning for snuggling even odder. Since when was sex not the priority?

"I shouldn't have started this," he said apologetically, but made no move to get her off his lap. "I hadn't planned to."

See? Messy entanglements already. She should have just shoved him back on the bed and taken away whatever little willpower he might have had left in him. Not much, judging by the ragged look of him. He clearly hadn't shaved and was still wearing the same henley and jeans he'd left in last night. Why he looked so endearingly sexy, all rumpled and tired, she had no clue. She liked her men sharp, well dressed and most definitely alert.

And look where that got you, her little voice piped. Enough, already. It was too early and he had her too confused to deal with this…this libido bait-and-switch. What should have been about mind-blowing sex was suddenly seeming like it was about something else entirely. He'd just said he hadn't meant to start something. Well, she could help him out with that, too.

She pulled away and stood, clutching her towel to keep it on. "So I take it that was a goodbye kiss?" Fine, she was cool with that. Only instead of shrugging it off and waving him out the door, she heard herself ask, "What changed your mind since last night?"

Ack! She didn't want the answer to that question. No woman did. Which was why she never asked. Actually, she never had to, being the one who usually ended things first. Maybe she'd been prodded to say it because, while his mind might have been changed, his body was clearly still on the same page as hers. And, dammit, she hadn't finished with him yet. She hated not finishing what she started.

And he'd definitely started her the night before.

Recoup and recover, she told herself calmly, praying he'd assume the question was rhetorical. She strolled to the corner, where she'd laid out the few clothes she'd brought inside with her last night. If she thought she could have pulled it off, she would have casually dropped her towel and dressed, showing him just how unaffected she was by his little announcement.

Only she wasn't unaffected. She wasn't angry at his rejection. Her ego wasn't fragile. But she was… disappointed. Yes, disappointed. Surely that was the real emotion behind what had actually felt a whole lot more like hurt. Liza never got hurt. Conrad notwithstanding. And as Natalie had already pointed out, her little…whatever, with Conrad had really just been a case of happily-ever-after envy.

This…well, this wasn't anything. A private little pleasure detour was all this had been. So what if it had ended more abruptly than she'd have liked? She was already over it.

And yet she still took her clothes to the bathroom to change. No point in advertising what he wasn't willing to work for, she told herself.

"You look beat," she called out, leaving the door open just to prove how little he was affecting her. "If you want, you can just catch a little sleep here. Checkout isn't till eleven. I'm taking care of the bill on my way out, so just close the door when you leave." Perfect. Breezy, casual, *so* not affected.

Then he appeared in the doorway, just as she was pulling her flower-print cotton sundress down over her hips. No knock, no clearing of throat, just there he was. And there was absolutely nothing casual, breezy or unaffected about the way he looked at her.

"I'm sorry about breakfast. About…this."

She found a smile somewhere, though her lips trembled a bit. Dammit. "I understand," she lied. Well, she did, really. He was tired, he was busy, he didn't have time for dallying with her. She just didn't want to understand it. She collected her toothbrush and makeup bag and turned sideways to slip by him. Only he turned that big body of his so that he blocked the door.

She didn't move back, though it took serious willpower. No doubt her reaction to being so close to him was quite obvious through the thin cotton of her dress.

So what? Let him deal with it, she thought, studying the tiny row of buttons marching down his chest.

"Look at me."

She glanced up through her lashes. "You don't stay to play, you don't get to order me around anymore."

His lips quirked, but the humor didn't reach his eyes. He looked so weary, as if the dark edginess had invaded and sapped the warmth, the life out of them.

"And don't go pulling handcuffs out of…wherever it is you stash them." She wagged a finger, falling back on the moxie she used to keep men off balance, a little unsure of themselves in the face of her oh-so-sassy confidence.

It took serious effort this morning, and she doubted Dylan was falling for it, anyway. Even when he was dead tired, those eyes of his…saw things. Things most men didn't notice. But what the hell did she have left to throw his way? Except herself.

Don't even think it, Liza.

He lifted a hand, as if to brush away a stray curl on her cheek, only her hair clung to her head in wet ringlets, not brush-awayable, and he let his hand drop without touching her at all. She had to work to stifle the yearny little sigh of disappointment.

"You're not an easy woman to walk away from."

"Yes, I know." She beamed a phony smile as her heart clutched. Her heart was supposed to be unclutchable. "It's one of my finer points. Now if you'll excuse me…" *Please let me get out of here while I still can.*

"I want to. In fact, if I'd been smart, I'd have just called you this morning instead of showing up."

She fluttered her lashes and tried like mad to unclutch her damn heart. "Honey, you know it's always better to do it in person whenever you can." He didn't laugh, didn't smile. He just looked at her, in that way of his that went past her phony repartee, straight into her eyes and right down into her soul.

Now she pushed past him, not caring about the contact and the shivery way it made her feel to brush up against that hard, muscled body. She forced a light, sexy grin and looked back at him, telling herself she didn't care if he saw through her. Phony repartee served a purpose in times like this. It allowed both parties to retreat with pride intact, so that both could nurse their wounds in private. Always preferable over some messy public implosion.

"I do appreciate that you made the effort to stop by. And it's just as well we don't take this further, you know?" She tossed her makeup bag and toothbrush into her leather overnight clutch. "I'm not really that into bondage, and despite what you think, you'd have probably gotten weird when it was my turn at the controls." She scooped up her pants and shirt from the day before and her sleep T and panties, not bothering to fold and pack them carefully. She was a decent actress in moments like these, but this performance was straining even her talents. She grabbed her purse and her bag. "This way we can each fill in the details of what might have happened according to our own personal fantasy."

"That's just it," he said, crossing the room, "you are my own personal fantasy."

She laughed even as he closed the distance between them. "Oh, I don't think so. You like your women willing and pliable. I'm flexible, but only in the way that leads to incredible orgasms."

"Not a bad place to start."

She crossed her arms, sending her mind and her heart

back to their separate corners. "You need to make up your mind here."

Now he laughed. "I know." He rubbed his hand over his face, then through his short but already rumpled hair. "I have a serious case on my hands that's top priority."

"The fire?"

"That's part of it. I have an out-of-state meeting in a couple hours and will very likely be tied up for the next couple of days. I don't have time for—"

"Me."

"For anyone." He laughed again, but there was no humor in it. "The irony of which overwhelms me at the moment. For years in Vegas I tried to force relationships into the cracks between my job, but my job didn't leave too many cracks. So I came home, made a grab for a life that actually leaves time for one. And when I finally get around to wanting the relationship...my old job comes back to bite me on the ass."

Her eyes had widened at the *R* word. "We don't have a relationship."

"Exactly."

She shook her head. "I'm missing something here."

He stepped closer and gently unfolded her arms. "Exactly." He pulled the bag from her shoulder and tossed it on the bed. "Letting you walk away from me now, before I even get to figure out why it is you make me crazy and hot all at the same time, is missing something."

"See, if you'd let me be in charge last night, we'd have ended up in bed and be out of each other's system by now," she said with a laugh she didn't feel. Wishing she didn't understand exactly how he felt.

"You think so?" He tugged her closer. "I'm not so sure."

"Dylan—"

"See? Just my name on your lips—" he pulled her up tight against him, wrapping a thick arm around her waist to hold her there "—does that to me."

"You have meetings," she said, a bit breathlessly. Which made no sense. She had made men hard for her before. *But not just by saying their name. Not in the way it is for him.* Nonsense. They were all the same.

Except they weren't. Because Dylan wasn't like any man she'd encountered before.

"An important case," she added, scrambling to find her footing physically, emotionally.

"I know."

"So you shouldn't do this. You should go."

"Absolutely."

They stared at each other for one long, screamingly tense moment. *Pull away, Liza. This has advanced beyond the safety zone. Abort, abort. Detour over.*

She drew in a shaky breath. "So either throw me on the bed and take me right now, fast, hard, until we both can't remember our names. Or let me walk out the door."

Okay, so that wasn't exactly the firm dismissal she should have delivered.

Her heart thundered in her ears and she honestly didn't know which choice she wanted him to make. Another lie, but no less scary, and hard as hell to admit.

"I should let you go," he murmured, then slid the spaghetti-thin straps off her shoulders. "Because I have this feeling," he continued, as she tried to suck in enough air to form some kind of response, but instead just stood there, riveted by the look in his eyes as his fingers brushed down her arms. "That once I get inside you—" he leaned down and nipped her shoulder, a light pinch that made her gasp "—they'll need to send Tucker's entire department over here with fire hoses to blast us apart."

"Dear God," she finally said, exhaling shakily and knowing she'd truly lost the battle. She reached for the hem of his shirt, but he gently pushed her hands back to her sides.

"Just let me have you the way I want, the way I need to have you."

Oh boy. The ache between her thighs had already reached viselike clutching proportions. She could only nod. Something about the fatigue and the need in those caramel-candy eyes of his prevented her from trying to turn this around. But it wasn't like last night, either, where he was pushing her, prodding her. This was a request, by him…made for his own needs.

So she kept her hands by her sides, and felt the shudder of anticipation climb higher as he skimmed her dress over her hips and left her standing before him wearing only a thin scrap of panty lace.

His hands dropped away and she saw his fingers close into fists, then open again. His body was rigidly fixed to the spot, tension emanating from him in waves. Then his shoulders shifted, just a fraction, as if he was willing himself to relax, to slow down, to appease his needs at a pace that lent itself to true enjoyment of what was going to happen between them.

His gaze never left her, and there was a strength there, almost tensile, that held them both in place. He finally reached out and traced one blunt fingertip along her collarbone, then down the center of her chest. She shuddered hard and her breathing came in hitches and puffs. But she stood still, squeezing her thighs together and wondering how in the hell the brush of one finger could make her burn like this. Need like this. Want like this.

He drew it beneath the swell of one breast and she held her breath, willing him to cup the full weight in his palm, give her some relief for the sudden need in her nipples. But he merely traced his finger over to the other one.

"Beauty," he whispered. "Pure beauty."

She might have swayed, just a little, at the reverence in his tone. She felt unworthy. And at the same time wanted to plead with him to touch her, hold her, taste her, do something—dear God, anything!—to her.

"Please." The hoarse whisper was hers. And she was past caring that he'd made her beg. She'd do that and more right at the moment, if it meant...

Her breath came out in a long sigh of unadulterated pleasure when he cupped the weight of both breasts in his palms. Then she sucked the air right back in when he flicked his thumbs, oh so lightly, over her now painfully puffy nipples.

"Yes," she gasped.

"Open your eyes."

She hadn't even been aware they'd drifted shut, and opened them without questioning herself over the wisdom of following his every order so obediently. She was doing this as much for her own pleasure as his, and besides which— Oh God, she thought, losing track of all thought when he rubbed his thumbs more slowly over and around her nipples.

She pressed her thighs together, moaned softly.

"Exquisite," he whispered, as if in awe himself of what he wreaked from her.

She couldn't help it; she arched, slightly, toward him, a silent plea for more attention. His gaze lasered into hers as he rolled her nipples, making her gasp, making her shudder. Then slowly, exquisitely slowly, he lowered his head. It took every ounce of control she had and some she wasn't even aware she possessed not to grip his head and hurry him closer, to do what she so badly wanted him to do.

She curled her fingers against damp palms and felt the rush of anticipation build so high it made her dizzy. The first flick of his warm tongue actually made her knees dip, the spear of pleasure was so true and deep. He grasped her hips with his wide, strong hands, steadying her. Then he was at her again with that warm, wet tongue. Rolling, circling, suckling, flicking, until her head thrashed and her nails dug into her palms and moans were ripped from somewhere deep inside her.

And just when she thought she'd simply collapse to the floor, he traced his tongue downward and slid his hands down her thighs as he shifted to kneel in front of her.

Dear God, if she'd all but climaxed with his tongue on her breasts, the idea of… She clenched and almost came just in anticipation. "Lay me down," she managed to gasp, knowing she'd never withstand such an incredible assault and be responsible for remaining upright. "Must."

"Shhh," he replied, then nudged her back a few steps until her spine met the wall. And there, wedged between the dresser and the desk, he drove his tongue inside her and made her come so hard she saw stars.

She sought purchase by slapping her palms flat on the wall, as he ruthlessly drove her up again. Her hands were so damp they slid, as she wanted to. But he wouldn't let her. Again he teased her quivering nerve endings right to the limit of endurance, then shocked a scream of plea-

sure out of her when he slipped a finger inside her just
as he flicked at her with his tongue, jerking her over the
edge.

She trembled, her body shuddering as the aftershocks
continued to sizzle inside her, and he pushed his finger
deeper, not allowing her to withdraw and recoup. Her
body tightened down hard on him and she was moving,
sliding, trying to stay upright and at the same time get
him deeper and deeper without sinking to the floor in a
tumble of quivering need.

"Again," he said.

She shook her head. She couldn't. She was almost
limp and there was nothing left. He'd wrung her dry.
She felt an almost hysterical bubble of laughter surge up
her throat. Hardly dry! Still, there was no way—

And then she was over his shoulder, sputtering in surprise at the sudden shift in her pleasure-clouded universe. "What the—!"

And then softness met her back as he tumbled her
from his shoulder to the bed. Before she could think to
react, to even move, he was pulling off his shirt, shuck-
ing his jeans, and she had no words of censure as long
as he planned to climb on top of her in the immediate
future. She was vaguely aware of heavy things thumping
to the floor along with his boots and clothes—likely his
cuffs and his gun and God knew what— She stopped
thinking altogether just then because he was pulling her
ankles, sliding her to the edge of the bed and—

She tried to prop herself up on her elbows, thinking
she might sob in frustration if he didn't just— "Please,
Dylan, I—"

"I know." He pushed her back on the bed, then rolled
her over. She heard a short tearing sound and his breath
hitch as he slid on a condom. She clenched hard at

that, and the distraction cost her, because he gripped her hips, pulling her up and back, then was kneeling between her thighs before she knew what was what.

She pouted, not minding the position except she wanted to feel the weight of him on top of her, to look in his eyes when he was inside her and— She shut down that track, then every other one when he slipped a hand around her thigh and probed with his finger as he slid slowly, and oh so tightly, inside her.

Her long groan of satisfaction was matched by his own. Once he was all the way, deep inside her, he ran his hands up her torso, lifting her off the bed so her back was to his chest. He lifted her arms over her head and draped them back around his neck.

He throbbed inside her, but didn't move. She'd never felt so full, so…taut.

"Keep…your hands…there," he ordered.

She was panting, the feel of the hard length of his body behind her, the hard length of him inside, robbing her of speech. Not to mention the vulnerability of having her whole front exposed to his hands.

He tilted her head back against his, traced his tongue down the side of her neck, bit her earlobe at the exact same moment he tweaked her nipples with his fingertips. She gasped, moaned, clenched.

He groaned and moved within her, several strokes, until he got himself under control.

"Jesus," he breathed.

"Mmm." All she could manage was a murmur.

Then his hands were toying with her, sliding down her stomach, pressing her back into him as his fingertips crept through the curls, found her, teased her.

"I can't—" she gasped, right before he proved her wrong. Just as she snapped over the edge—again—he plunged deeper, his fingers on her, holding her against the thick slide of him inside her.

He growled against the damp skin of her neck, pummeling her both with another orgasm and with the incredible feel of him filling her right up.

It was amazing, intense, like nothing she'd ever felt. And yet it wasn't enough. She wanted the weight of his body on hers…and the weight of his gaze—the latter far more powerful than the former. She refused to let herself think why, just knew she had to have it.

"Dylan," she gasped. "I want— Let me just— I need you to—"

But it was too late. His body jerked forward, sending her to her hands and knees. He wrapped an arm around her waist and held her tight to him as he thrust again and again. The growl of his release shuddered through every cell of her body.

Liza felt the dampness on her cheeks, knew they were tears, ignored them. Never, not once in her whole life, had anyone taken such masterful control of her body, given her what she hadn't even known she could have. The downside of always being in control. You can't test your own limits when you don't know where the boundaries are.

Dylan had known. Or suspected. Either way, he'd proved his point gloriously. She should be grinning deliriously over such an intense hour of pleasure.

"Mind-numbing," she murmured as he shifted and slid out of her. "I knew it would be."

He didn't say anything, but pressed a kiss in the center of her back before moving off the bed. A moment later she heard the water running in the bathroom. She didn't move, didn't even raise her head. *Truly remarkable,* she thought, and forced subsequent thoughts down the same path. There was absolutely no earthly reason to feel anything less than one hundred percent satisfied. So she concentrated on the bliss…and carefully avoided the niggle of disappointment creeping just below the surface.

So he hadn't stayed to cuddle. So she hadn't looked into his eyes when he was inside her. When had this ever been an issue? And in the face of the pleasure he'd wrung out of her, it seemed awfully greedy to want more.

She rolled over to her back and looked unwillingly toward the open bathroom door.

Dammit. How had that happened?

And more importantly, what was she going to do about it?

13

DYLAN CLEANED UP, then braced his hands on the sink and stared at his reflection. *Now what are you going to do, hotshot?*

He knew what he wanted to do. Pull the drapes tight, crawl back into bed with Liza and sink into sleep with her all soft and warm, curled around him. And a few hours from now, wake up and sink himself back into all that soft warmth. Only this time he'd control himself, let her take them where she wanted them to go.

What it was about her that got his primal instincts all riled up, he had no idea. He'd taken her like a damn caveman or something. His lips quirked. Okay, so maybe he'd taken a bit more care with her, but still, that's the way she made him feel. Me man, you woman. You all mine.

Jesus.

But it didn't matter what he wanted to do. He had to go. He had to be at the airport an hour from now. He should hop in the shower here and save the time, drop by the office and change into the spare set of clothes he should have changed into at some point the endless night before. And just the idea of taking a hot steamy shower in Liza's hotel room brought all sorts of images to mind, none of them having to do with efficiency.

"She's in your blood," he told his reflection, then reached to turn on the shower, only to find an erotically rumpled Liza standing in the doorway. Something about the tangle of linens she'd pulled around her was far sexier than if she'd simply appeared in the flesh. Flesh he found he was dying to taste again.

He wondered if she'd heard him, what she'd think of that little revelation, but all she said was, "Shower for one?"

There were a hundred things he wanted to say to her, not the least of which was how he'd love to spend the day making love to her, in the shower, on the floor of the bathroom, on the desk in the other room…. But what he said was what he had to say. "I have to be somewhere in an hour."

She simply nodded. He should appreciate that. He'd known going in that she understood what was happening between them was an interlude at best. Instead it irked. Not that he wanted whining or temper or, God forbid, begging. Mostly because he was close to doing all three himself. But a little pout wouldn't have hurt any.

"You keep going on no sleep like this and you're not doing anyone any favors," she said. "Surely the meeting can be rescheduled. If you're that irreplaceable, they'll wait."

He smiled. "I bet you were really good at what you did."

"I was," she said matter-of-factly. "Do you want me to make a call, work this problem out for you?"

His lips quirked. He had no doubt she could do just that. "Unfortunately, it's not that easy. If you're so good at your job, why did you leave?"

The sudden shift in conversation made her pause, and he realized she didn't really talk a lot about herself. Most women of his acquaintance loved to feel important, and that often manifested itself in long monologues of how they spent every minute of their days. Maybe it was because she'd spent so many years deflecting the spotlight to her clients that she simply didn't realize she'd closed herself off in that way. Or maybe she was just a really private person.

No, that wasn't it. *Shy* and *retiring* were two words that would never be used in conjunction with Liza Sanguinetti. Which was also why she'd probably been good at her job.

The odd thing was, he wanted to hear about every second of her day, about what she'd done as a public relations person, where her family was, were they proud of her, what her dreams were and… *Jesus, Jackson, one little roll in the hay and you've gone right over the edge.*

"All work and no play left Liza without a real life," she answered bluntly. "Actually, my work *was* playing a great deal of the time, which was the real problem. I needed to get off the party-go-round and grow up, I suppose." Short, succinct, nary an extraneous detail.

He smiled, and continued pushing despite her obvious desire to leave the subject alone. Maybe because of it. "And what do you want to be when you grow up?"

"Still working on that." Before he could ask her anything else, she said, "So, where is the meeting?"

He thought about ignoring the question to prod her some more, but he was standing naked in her bathroom and he did have a meeting to attend. "Vegas. I have to be at the airstrip in an hour."

Her eyes widened a bit. "Vegas? Oh, right, you said your old job had come back to rear its ugly head. Then the fire at the motel is related to something you were involved with in your former line of work? Is that why you thought I might be in danger? Because I was with you and you were the target? But why the motel? I don't see how that could be connected to… What? What's so funny?"

He swore he could almost see the gears in her mind spin, and damn if that didn't turn him on, too. He tugged at the linen sheet and she shuffled closer. He couldn't help it. It didn't matter that he had to walk away at some point and that she was going to drive away even if he didn't. He wasn't walking yet and she was standing right there. And he had to touch her. "I just enjoy watching you be you, that's all. You fascinate me."

She grinned, but there was something almost a bit…nervous dancing in her eyes. He liked it that he could make her nervous. He suspected not many men had. God, here he went with the caveman thing again.

Then she pressed a red fingernail in the dent in his chin and he found he didn't care what game they were playing, as long as it meant she was right here in his arms.

"Glad I can amuse you, Sheriff." She trailed the finger down to his chest, and damn if she didn't have him stirring again. Whatever nerves he might have seen were gone now, replaced by a mischievous light that he knew boded trouble. Problem was, he wasn't all that put off by a little trouble just now.

"Just how long a drive is it to the airstrip?"

"Twenty minutes, give or take. But I have to stop by the station and—"

Her hand trailed lower as the steam from the running shower began to billow around them. "That gives us, what, at least a good ten, twelve minutes to work up a decent lather." She let the sheet drop. "What do you say?"

His pulse kicked up, along with other parts of him. "I soap you first?"

She stretched up and kissed him, then stepped behind the shower curtain. A long, very appreciative groan followed.

Dylan didn't even bother berating himself for letting her get to him. Again. After all, he was only human. And she was…she was like a fever on perpetual spike.

He followed her into the shower and a moment later was groaning as well, but not just because the hot water felt so good.

She'd sabotaged him with body soap. Followed quickly with clever little hands that lathered him in all the right places.

"Liza—"

"Turn around and hold on to the towel rack," she instructed. "Eight minutes left and I plan to use them wisely."

Soap-foamed fingers and her slippery body sliding past him encouraged him not to argue.

She started at his ankles and worked her way up. His knees threatened to give way when she cupped him from behind. His groan of appreciation was met with a slide of slick skin up and over his buttocks. Breasts, nipples, belly and… "Don't stop," he demanded hoarsely.

"You wish."

He did wish. In fact, he could make a number of wishes right at that moment.

"Turn around."

He did, gladly. Because she continued her ministrations, tipping her head back so the water rinsed the soap bubbles from his skin…and cascaded down over her kneeling form. He knew it shouldn't affect him so, seeing her kneeling before him, knowing she was the one that held all the power—literally—in her own small hands. But it did, viscerally. Which became immediately obvious to her as well.

She grinned up at him, mouthed ''my turn'' and slipped him fully into her mouth.

He could have come right then. And if he hadn't just climaxed less than a half hour earlier, probably would have. But that didn't mean he couldn't enjoy the ride.

Far too soon she was letting him go, turning off the water and reaching out for towels.

He might have whined. In fact, he was pretty sure that whimper of disappointment had come from him.

''Sorry, Sheriff, time's up.'' She wrapped a towel around her body and tossed him one. ''I'd help, but you have a meeting to make.'' And then she was gone, leaving him standing in a dwindling cloud of steam.

''You should have let me have my turn earlier,'' she called out, as if she'd read his thoughts. And he wasn't entirely sure she couldn't.

He stepped out of the bathroom, towel around his hips, to find her back in her sundress, combing out her hair in front of the dresser mirror. When she said nothing, he reached for his clothes, glancing at the bed, then at her, and wondering how goodbye had come rushing up at him like this. Only it hadn't really rushed. In fact, he'd postponed it longer than he should have.

She scooped up her purse and bag as he slipped on his boots and tucked in his shirt.

''So, that's where you hide them,'' she said, fingering the cuffs he'd stuffed in the back of his waistband. Right next to his gun.

She led the way to the door, then turned when he didn't move from the foot of the bed. She arched a questioning brow. ''Lose something?''

''My sanity?''

"What, you mean you don't often spend the morning performing lewd and lascivious acts with strange women not a block away from your office?"

"Shh," he said, nodding toward the open door at her back. She merely smiled back at him. "There was nothing lewd about it," he said, crossing the room. "And you're no stranger to me." He pushed the door shut and pulled her into his arms. "Not anymore." His kiss caught her off guard and he willingly silenced her gasp with his lips and tongue. He pulled her under with him until his own head spun. When he finally straightened, she was struggling for equilibrium, judging from the dazed look on her face. He took advantage of that, too. "Lascivious, now that I might cop to," he said with a grin. "Don't check out."

She'd started to shoot back a retort—never one to be thrown for a loop for long, not Liza—then stopped herself. "What? What did you just say?"

It had been hard enough the first time. But he made himself say it again. "Don't leave. Not yet." He pressed his finger across her lips, buying time to explain. He only hoped he explained it to himself at the same time. "I know I asked you to wait for me once before. I'm asking again. I'll be back late tonight. Be here." He slid his finger from her mouth. "Please."

Her lips curved slightly, but her eyes bored into his, and those nerves fluttered within them once again. "Why?"

"You said you didn't leave something until it felt finished. This doesn't feel finished to me. Does it to you?" He pushed his fingers into her damp curls and tilted her head. "Does it, Liza?" he queried softly.

She stared into his eyes for what felt like eternity, then

slowly shook her head. He let out a breath he hadn't even been aware of holding.

"So? Does that mean you'll stay?"

Slowly, so slowly, her bow-tie lips curved into a smile that was definitely both lewd and lascivious. His heart picked up speed. He knew enough now to understand the promise behind that smile. And if physical bliss was all he could count on with her, then, for the time being, anyway, he was happy to take what he could get.

He could push and nudge and prod for more later.

"Twenty minutes to the airport?" she asked.

Confused, he nodded.

She reached around his waist and pulled the door open, even as she leaned in and kissed him. This time he was pretty sure he was the one with the dazed expression on his face. "Then that gives you twenty minutes to convince me, Sheriff." She nudged him into the hall and pulled her keys from her purse. "You want to drive, or shall I?"

DYLAN HAD TO ADMIT her little car was fun. He'd always gone for trucks, as tucking his long frame into a small death trap had never appealed to him. He supposed it was that remnant of renegade that got a hot thrill from the high speed and the tight way it hugged the mountain curves.

He glanced at Liza, at her curls dancing wildly around her head in the wind. "I can see why you love this little demon," he admitted. "Suits you perfectly." All tight curves and high speed, indeed.

She laughed. "Yeah, and you're just hating it. You've got more demon in you than you think."

He shot her a grin. "Something about you just brings that out in me, I guess."

She buffed and examined her nails. "I try."

You succeed, he thought, turning his attention back to the road. *Boy, do you ever.* His focus should be on the meeting ahead. He hoped it went down smoothly and they got what they needed from Pearl without too much hassle. He needed to get back to town for the meeting with Tucker, then there was the council meeting the following day he had to prepare some notes for. And at some point, he needed some sleep. But all he could think about was when he'd get Liza alone again. Surprisingly, it wasn't even about the sex, though he wasn't going to lie to himself and say he wasn't looking forward to the possibility of more of that, either.

But just having her next to him on the drive to the airstrip, all sexy smiles and bouncy curls, made him feel good…and spiked his curiosity. It was as if there was some dormant part inside him that had dried out, like a sponge laid out in the hot sun for too long. And now he wanted nothing more than to fully saturate that long-ignored facet by absorbing every last bit of her. Being around her was like irrigating his soul.

Jesus, Jackson, you have been out in the hot sun for too long. Irrigating your soul? He sounded like one of those *Chicken Soup* books.

But when he glanced back at her again, took in her profile as she took in the stark scenery around them, with that oddly compelling mixture of clear-eyed wonder and sharply focused attention, it somehow didn't feel as ridiculous as it sounded.

"So, what got you into public relations in the first place?"

There was a pause and he glanced over to find her looking at him somewhat warily.

He smiled. "What? Is that such a strange question?"

She shrugged and turned her attention back to the scenery. "No, I suppose not. Why do you ask?"

She might as well have said, "What does it matter to you? Aren't we just having sex?"

"Do you always separate yourself like that?"

Now she looked honestly surprised. "Like what?"

"Well, I think I can safely say you are a woman who is pretty direct about things. Pretty honest about what she wants and not at all shy at going after it."

She didn't smile, but simply nodded. "You'd be right."

"Which is all fine as long as you're doing the directing."

She sighed. "Are we back to my supposed control issues again?"

"Maybe. But I'm not talking about sex. You don't seem to have any problems communicating with your body."

She didn't take any offense at his statement, merely nodded in agreement. "I've never had anyone misread my signals, if that's what you mean."

"See?" he said. "That's one of the things that attracts me to you. You don't play coy. You take a direct statement as it's intended. No reading between the lines, assuming some other meaning lurks behind the words."

"Well, I do assume that by saying I can communicate with my body, you inferred that I don't do all that well verbally."

"Oh, I don't think you have any problem verbally when *you* want something."

"Clear and direct articulation of one's needs is important in my former career. I happened to be quite good at it."

"Exactly."

"Meaning?"

"As long as you're in charge and directing the conversation toward your interests, you handle yourself with absolute aplomb." He slowed and looked directly at her. "But let someone else try and direct the conversation, probe to the woman behind the words...and suddenly this wall comes down. Wham! That's what I meant about separating yourself."

"Just because I don't want to spill my guts to strangers doesn't mean I can't 'let my hair down.' Which is what I think you mean."

He swerved to the side of the road, making her grasp the door for balance. The dust from the gravel shoulder swirled around them as he swiveled his body as far as the tight compartment would allow. "Strangers? You honestly think of me as a stranger?" He lifted his hand. "And don't tell me that sex isn't the same thing as intimacy. I know that. And a lot of what we've done together has been about feeling good, not about forming some sort of intimate bond."

"You're yelling," she said calmly. But her blue eyes were wide and not so clear.

"I know." He took a moment, and a slow, deep breath. He looked out the windshield and tried to compose what he wanted to say, but the words came out in a tumble, anyway. She did that to him, too—jumbled him up. "The sex was great. Mind-blowing. Out of this world." Then he looked at her. "But any two people who put their minds to it can probably achieve that." He waited a beat, some part of him wanting her to refute that, tell him it had been different with him. Because, though he believed what he said, believed that a great part of what they'd had together was purely physical, it didn't negate the feeling, the deep-in-the-pit-of-his-gut feeling, that beneath the tingling nerve endings and brain-numbing climaxes, there was another connection being made. One that had nothing to do with bodies talking to each other, and a lot to do with souls reaching for one another.

But he couldn't say that without sounding as ridiculous as he knew it had to be. *Had* to be. But somehow wasn't.

"You don't mind me getting to know you in every carnal sense of the word," he said quietly. "But the moment I try to get to know the intimate you, the stuff that makes up the best parts of what you are, or seem to me to be, you shut yourself off. Why is that? How is it that a person can be so good at facilitating the lives of others, at meeting the needs of others, and so fully close off her own needs?"

She sat there for what felt like an eternity. Saying nothing. Dylan thought about just pulling back on the road, heading to the airport and wishing her a good life. He could get a deputy to come pick him up when he got back. It would certainly be the smart thing to do. He already had one major complication to deal with, get rid of, so he could go back to his new, quiet, life. Why in God's name ask for another? Hell, he was practically begging for it.

"You think you're pretty damn clever, don't you?" she said at last. Almost too quietly.

He looked to her, but her profile was averted, so he couldn't see her eyes, or what was in them.

"For someone who just met me, you seem pretty damn sure you have me all pegged." She turned to him, and what he found was not what he expected. He'd expected irritation, maybe even anger. But not hurt. Never hurt. He didn't know her well enough to hurt her, didn't mean enough to her to hurt her, wouldn't have if he did. Realizing that he did—and had—stunned him into silence.

"I guess all those years grilling perps and witnesses makes you a pretty good judge of character. Because you're right. Most people see the confidence, the directness, the control, and think I have my act together. Well, I do. Precisely because I know how to close myself off. I've been taking pretty damn good care of myself for a very, very long time. And I'm very good at it. Mostly because I learned early on that sharing pieces of yourself didn't guarantee that others shared back. And pieces given away don't always regenerate themselves. It seemed smarter to me, still does, to take special care with those pieces. Protect them, and therefore myself, from harm." She turned away, looked straight ahead. "It's worked out pretty well so far."

He stared at her proud profile and didn't know if he wanted to yell at her, break through that wall with the sheer force of his will, or pull her into his arms and hold her, then demand to know who had so stupidly squandered those precious pieces.

"So you took care of other people's precious pieces," he said, almost to himself. "Protected them, coddled them, made sure no one abused them."

She said nothing, but her shoulders rounded slightly. The rigid line of her neck softened a bit.

"So, maybe the question shouldn't have been why you got into your former line of work...but why you left it?"

There was a long pause, then a sigh, then she said, "Why bother to explain further? I'm sure you'll be telling me, anyway." She looked at him, and some of the hurt was gone. But what replaced it was far worse. What replaced it was…absolutely nothing. It was like staring into a mask. "I know why I left Hollywood. Any shrink with a framed piece of paper on the wall could tell me without even seeing me why I left my former life. It was ultimately unfulfilling because in putting those pieces in protective custody, I'd effectively put myself away. My whole life was my job and I enjoyed it, I was good at it. But it wasn't enough. I watched my best friend fall in love, talked myself into believing I was, too. I wasn't. But what I learned was that I needed more than job satisfaction. Somewhere along the way, I'd lost myself. So I walked. Toward what, I have no earthly idea. I haven't a clue what I want to do with myself now. I'm still figuring out who that self is and what will make her feel whole. But until I do, those pieces are going to stay under lock and key."

Now he did reach out. Even if she pulled away, he had to make the gesture. Because he simply couldn't not make it. She stiffened, but didn't recoil when he stroked his fingertips down her cheek, along her jaw. Very softly, he said, "Did you ever think that maybe you're going to have to bust that lock if you ever want to find out who you are? That maybe it's the risk of exposing those parts to the light of day that allows them to reflect back on you?"

"I—I never thought of it that way," she said with abject honesty, shifting slightly away from his touch. "But…" She held herself very still, then sighed. It was a deep, shuddering sigh that seemed to deflate her usually abundant innate strength. When she lifted her gaze to his, those oceans of blue were clouded with tears. "Maybe it's been so long, I've forgotten how."

Her voice caught and Dylan could see that she was struggling very hard to hold it together. "Come here."

She shook her head, sniffed once and went to move away. "Just get back on the road. You're going to be late."

"I don't really give a flat damn at the moment."

His quiet vehemence startled a glance from her.

"Right now my only concern is you."

She tried a cocky smile, and managed a shaky one. "I don't need your concern."

"You need a whole lot of things."

"And I suppose you think you're the man to give them to me, right? Well, I don't need—"

He tugged her against him, held her there. "Yes, you do need. Maybe that's a good place for you to start. Admitting you need. That you're not a completely self-sufficient unit. That it just might feel good when you share a part of your real self with someone who cares about you, who you care about. I know I do, Liza." He bent his head to hers. "I think you know it, too." He took her mouth, but rather than demand she respond, he gentled the kiss, coaxed her to respond, to give back to him. To give something of herself, even if it was just a kiss. A kiss not designed to seduce, but to comfort, to soothe. He realized he hadn't had too many of those in his life. Maybe none. And he'd be willing to bet she hadn't, either.

"Maybe we both need to find a way to expose those little pieces," he murmured against her lips. "I want to try. With you. And I want you to try. With me." He kissed her again, and reveled in the joy of feeling her gradually respond, if not in words, at least in action.

When he finally lifted his head, his own eyes were a bit cloudy. He didn't try to analyze the emotions, the illogical reality of them, considering the short time frame of their acquaintance. At the moment, he only knew he'd found the most significant piece of himself. He was holding it in his arms. And he was damned if he was going to simply let it walk away.

"Stay," he said. "With me. Explore this, yourself, us, whatever. With me." He brushed his hand over her hair. "Please."

She was quiet, tucked against his chest. He could feel her heart pounding, but her breathing had steadied. Just when he thought she wouldn't answer him, she said, "I'll stay." His heart was already leaping, his pulse kicking, when she added in a soft whisper, "For now."

14

STAY. Liza tried to keep her focus on the scenery as they turned onto the narrow road leading them to the airstrip. But it was Dylan's request that echoed in her ear, and his hand covering hers—as it had for the remainder of the trip—that cornered her attention.

She'd been teasing him earlier, when she'd hoped he'd convince her to stay. She'd wanted more playtime with him, sure, but that had changed the moment he'd started his little analysis. She should have known he wouldn't play by the rules, that he'd keep probing at the parts of her she'd just as soon remain untouched. And she'd be a whole lot more pissy about it…if he hadn't been so damn right.

But that didn't mean she wasn't irritated. Or, dammit, intrigued. No one bothered to look behind her in-your-face attitude and see that she was more than the sum of her smart mouth and savvy brains. And now that someone had, she wasn't quite sure what she was going to do about it. Or worse, what he was going to find now that he'd looked.

This was one exploration she wasn't sure she wanted to make. And yet in the weeks she'd been on the road to personal enlightenment, this was the first time she honestly felt like she was getting anywhere.

Stay.

"Dammit!" Dylan smacked the wheel and stomped on the brakes.

Liza was jerked from her thoughts in time to grab the dashboard…and to see a small plane take off from behind the hangar-shaped white building and control tower they'd just pulled up to. "Would they take off without you?" she asked, confused. But there were no other planes on the ground. "I thought it was a private charter?"

Dylan merely grunted and swung around the building, then slowed to a stop as they both spied a dark blue sedan pulling away from the tarmac. When it turned and started toward them, Dylan surprised her by placing his palm flat on her head and pushing her down. "Keep low."

"Wha—?" Whatever else she might have said was swallowed hard when he spun the little sports car around and headed back toward the main road.

"Damn, damn, damn. I should have never—"

Then there was honking coming from behind them.

Another string of expletives floated through the air above her head, but the car slowed, and Dylan finally let up on her. "I'm going to kill that son of a bitch."

"Which son of a bitch would that be?" Liza asked calmly, as if she hadn't just been crammed down into her tiny seat. She smoothed her dress, fluffed her hair.

"Stay here," Dylan barked, slamming the car into Park, then leaving it right in the middle of the road as he got out and shut the door with a resounding thump.

"Sure, no problem, master sir," Liza murmured wryly, then swiveled in her seat and watched him stride back toward the sedan. The window was down and an attractive Hispanic man was leaning out the window. His bright smile remained intact, despite Dylan's immediate and lengthy harangue. She couldn't make out exactly what he was saying, but with the arm gestures and rigid body language, Liza could only assume it wasn't a friendly hello.

He spun on his heel, leaving the man in midsentence, and stalked back toward her car. If Liza had thought she'd seen the dark, edgy side of Dylan Jackson, she now realized she hadn't come close. And why in hell seeing him like this made her nipples hard, she had no idea.

Then a woman leaped from the sedan and began running after him. Liza's eyes widened in surprise, but she was smiling by the time Dylan slowed, then stopped, hung his head and took a deep breath before turning to face the woman. Not that Liza enjoyed seeing him in the midst of what was apparently a situation gone badly out of control, but he was just sexy as hell when he displayed this cop-with-a-heart side of him. She couldn't help it.

Of course, the appearance of the woman also made the situation hard to take too seriously. She looked like something out of a bad B movie. She was tall, or maybe she just seemed that way. Her bright red hair—no way a natural tone—had been teased to the limits of endurance. Just as the clothing she was wearing had been stretched to theirs. Her tight, black leather skirt ended high on tanned, surprisingly toned legs. Legs made even longer with the spiky, black plastic heels she wore. But it was the furry lime green tank top, encasing amazingly proportioned breasts that seemed to defy gravity, that really made the ensemble...special. It was a hell of a combo on a woman who looked to be pushing fifty.

"Now *that's* a Vegas showgirl," Liza muttered, as

Dylan braced himself and the woman launched herself into his arms.

"Detective!" she squealed, quickly smoothing her hair and tugging her skirt down as Dylan disengaged himself from her clutches. "Don't go off mad," she said with a pout. "I made him bring me here. I was afraid. I'm sure Duggie knows I'm ratting on him and I don't trust anyone but you to keep me safe."

"Pearl, Dugan knows we were set to meet here," Dylan said, jaw clenched. He swiveled his attention to the Hispanic man, who was now out of the car and approaching with his hands up, palms out, as if beseeching Dylan to calm down. "What in the hell were you thinking, Quin?"

"We need her testimony, D.J. If I didn't get her out of town, she was going to leave on her own."

"I thought you had her under lock and key?"

"Yeah, well, she managed to talk Moriarty into getting her some nail polish and—"

"Nail polish?"

Liza thought Dylan's eyes were going to pop right out of his head.

"Honey, I wasn't staying in that place a moment longer," Pearl stated flatly. She folded her arms, plumping her already bulbous breasts until they came dangerously close to spilling out of the low-cut tank top altogether. Judging from Quin's anticipatory expression, it was a calculated move on her part.

Liza smiled. This was someone who knew how to turn a situation around to her advantage, and who was unafraid to use whatever tools she had available. Liza admired that.

"I already suffered a great deal from letting a man pretend to take care of and protect me," she said huffily.

"Right on, sister," Liza said. Apparently louder than she intended, as the woman turned toward her.

"Who's this?" she demanded, eyes narrowing. "Another cop?"

"No," Dylan said flatly, then turned to Quin, not bothering to explain further. "Why didn't you take her to a third location, alert me, and I'd have filed a new flight plan? I told you I didn't want this here."

The redhead's unnaturally full lips quavered. "You didn't want me, either?"

"Pearl—" Dylan began.

"Don't start!" she screamed, waving him away. "Take me back," she informed Quin as she stalked past him, strutting amazingly well on four-inch heels. Liza's respect continued to climb.

"I might as well let Duggie kill me for all the good living does me," she said, then stopped suddenly and dabbed at her eyes with the side of her thumb.

Liza looked at both men, neither of whom seemed to know what to say, then sighed and got out of the car.

"Liza, don't—" Dylan began, but she ignored him and walked straight over to Pearl.

"Men can be morons," she said bluntly.

Pearl sniffled, then slowly turned to look at her. "Damn straight. I don't know why I agreed to this in the first place." She glared at Dylan. "I thought there was at least one decent man left, but I guess I was wrong."

Liza forced her lips to remain flat, no matter how badly they wanted to twitch when Dylan scowled. She waved him back when he stepped forward, and was surprised when he stopped, albeit reluctantly.

"Who are you?" Pearl asked.

"A woman who's been burned by a man," Liza said. "Came home and found him in bed with another chick."

Pearl sniffed and patted her on the arm. "That's awful, honey. Me, I'd have pumped one or two in his humpin' ass."

"If I'd had a gun, I might have," Liza admitted. "But I'm glad I didn't." She grinned at Pearl. "Waste of lead. He was a jerk and didn't deserve me, anyway."

Pearl's lips twitched slightly, then quivered again. "Yeah, at least my Duggie had the decency to break things off with me before he found Elaine."

Liza reached out and fluffed the fur on Pearl's shoulder. "Nice. Where did you find it?"

Pearl smiled now and dabbed at her mascara again. "Half-price sale at Thompson's, just off the strip. I call it my purr fur."

I bet you do, Liza thought. "I'm too short to pull off something like that. You're lucky."

Pearl snorted. "Yeah, that's me all right." Her lip quavered again. "Protected his ass for all these years. All these years I knew I was his special one. Sure, he married Elaine. I knew from the beginning I wasn't going to be the missus, you know? His family demanded he marry better." She shrugged, but Liza could see the hurt in her eyes. "So it wasn't no real surprise when he ended it. He didn't love her, you know, but he had balls enough to not screw around with me on the side once he got hitched. I admired that in him." She picked at the fur between her breasts. "I knew I was still his special lady. In his heart." She sucked in a short breath, then another, then the tears started to spill down her cheeks. "At least I thought I was. Until…until that bastard—" It was all she could manage between sobs.

Liza took her hands and pulled her into an awkward

hug. She sent a sharp glance toward Dylan and Quin and a brief shake of her head when they went to step forward. She patted Pearl's back. "It's okay, sweetie, let it all out."

And she did. Boy, did she ever.

"You're wrong, you know," Liza said quietly as Pearl cried. Noisily.

Alternately gulping and sniffling, Pearl lifted her head. Mascara had tracked heavily down her wet cheeks. "About what?"

"About being good enough for him. A man who truly loves a woman doesn't care what anyone thinks. She's worth his respect no matter what."

"You saying he didn't truly love me?"

Liza shook her head. "I'm saying he didn't love you enough. Enough to respect you. You thought he respected you enough to walk away, but he should have respected you enough to tell his family to take a flying leap."

Pearl nodded miserably, but said, "I don't know. His family ain't like a regular family, if you get my drift. But Duggie, he did love me." She gulped down another sob. "What you said, though, about that respect thing..." She swallowed hard and had to try several times to continue on.

"It's okay, nothing you say will surprise me. I used to work in Hollywood. There's nothing I haven't seen," Liza said with a wave of a hand.

Pearl perked up immediately. "Hollywood? Really?" She hiccuped, then wiped at her nose with the back of her hand.

"The guy I was telling you about? You ever watch the soap opera *Steam?*" Liza knew she shouldn't be saying this; she hadn't told anyone but Natalie what had happened. But there was some perverse pleasure in sharing it with Pearl. "Conrad Jones? He plays—"

Her eyes widened. "Straker. Wow. And I thought he was a hottie. Scum, huh?" She sighed, then hiccuped again. "Figures." She smiled wistfully. "I always had this dream about going to Hollywood. Pretty silly when you think about it. A girl like me?" She shook her head and dabbed at her mascara again.

"What? 'A girl like me,' my ass," Liza stated. That seemed to startle Pearl. "Just because some jerk-off doesn't appreciate you is no reason to think he knows his butt from a hole in the ground. What did this bastard Duggie say to you to make you think you weren't good enough?"

Pearl surprised her with a laugh. "Oh honey, he was just one in a long line of people who have made that pretty damn clear. Club owners, boyfriends, girl-friends…my own ma, for Christ's sake." She shrugged. "I got worth, don't get me wrong. This ain't no pity party. But I know my limits, too. I wasn't from the right stock for Duggie. I knew that. I didn't have no silver spoon in my mouth, more like picnic plasticware. It didn't mean he couldn't love me anyway, just that we weren't meant for each other in the long term. And he set me up nice when he left." She tugged at her shirt, stood a little taller. "I run a school, you know. Dancing."

"See? That's great. A businesswoman. Successful, too, I bet. So what happened? You protected him all these years, he took care of you. Why give him over now?" Liza could almost hear Dylan gnashing his teeth behind her, but she ignored him. She had put two and two together pretty easily and knew why Pearl was here, and under police protection. She also had a pretty good idea of who had set that fire…and why they'd chosen that motel.

"I protected him is right," Pearl said, almost fiercely. "Kept his ass out of prison. Then, after all the years of trying, Elaine finally went and got knocked up." Pearl looked up. Her dark brown eyes were blazing, then just as suddenly filled with tears. "She said no fun time in the sack no more until after Duggie Junior arrived. So he…he—" She choked back the sob. "He thought I'd be willing to resume our relationship while his wife was…was with child. Like I was some kind of…some kind of—" She huffed and sucked in a breath as she scrubbed the tears from her face. "Well, I'm a lot of things, but I ain't no whore. What is your name, anyway?"

"Liza," she supplied.

"Like the singer!"

Liza just nodded, feeling an affection for the woman despite, or maybe because of, her wacky, up-and-down nature. She was this endearing combination of weary street smarts and naive, wide-eyed wonder.

"Well, Liza, I know a lot of people might think less of me because I took my clothes off for money. But, like I said, I ain't no whore. Never have been." She laughed, her voice hoarse with tears. "Maybe I should have. Probably coulda retired in Florida, be feeding the birds by now."

"I think you should talk to Dylan," Liza said abruptly, gripping Pearl's wrist when she would have pulled away. "Men can be assholes, but the only reason Dylan wanted you away from here is because Dugan set a fire to your first meeting place. He was worried about you."

"He's worried about the information I have, you mean."

Liza nodded. "Sure, he *is* a cop. You knew that coming in. But there are a lot of other cops in Vegas. You chose to talk to this one. Surely there was a reason you trusted him and not the others."

"He was…nice to me. Back a long time ago, when they first tried to take Duggie down. The others, they didn't, you know, show any respect." She shrugged, then looked at Liza consideringly. "You trust him?"

She smiled now, and it was the sort of look that only another woman would understand. "Honey," she said, leaning in, "he's hard not to."

Pearl smiled back, and pushed at her hair, straightened her shirt. "You two…you're, you know, together?"

Liza shrugged and nodded. "For now, anyway."

Pearl sighed and dabbed at her lipstick, then adjusted her bra. "Yeah, well, if I was you, I'd do whatever I could to keep my hooks in that one." She sighed. "He's a bit young for me, anyway." She leaned down and shot Liza a wink. "You didn't hear that from me. Most men don't guess I'm as old as I am." She moved away, mercifully keeping Liza from having to answer that one, and crossed the road. "Okay, Detective, I'm ready to talk. Is there somewhere around here a girl can fix her makeup and get a soda and some fries? I do better when my digestive system is evened out."

Dylan smiled. "Sure. No problem." He corraled her toward Quin's car, sending Liza a look she couldn't interpret, but figured she'd hear all about momentarily. "You two follow us," he told Quin. "I know just the place."

As soon as she and Dylan were back in her car, Liza

turned to him, all set to tell him to back off, that she'd done him a favor, only he beat her to the punch.

"Thank you."

Her mouth dropped open, then snapped shut again. "You're welcome," she said, nonplussed.

He smiled as they headed away from the airstrip, and continued on in the opposite direction from town. "What, you think I'm going to beg to be the one who has to handle the angry, hysterical woman?"

Liza smiled, but answered him seriously. "She wasn't hysterical. She was humiliated. She thought this Dugan character held her in some kind of esteem because he'd taken care of her financially and had the decency to end their sexual relationship before finding himself a more suitable bride."

"You're angry. Is this personal?"

Liza shrugged. "Maybe."

"Someone pass you over for that reason? I have a real hard time believing that one."

She shot him a smile. "Brownie point earned. And no, not me. But my parents could both write books on the subject. Thankfully, neither has an interest in literature."

Dylan chuckled, then apologized. "I'm sorry, I'm not laughing at their misfortune."

"Don't worry. I learned a long time ago they brought their misfortunes on themselves."

"I take it you're not close, then?"

She hadn't meant to talk about them, didn't really want to now, but she supposed this was a step toward revealing a couple of those little pieces. It wasn't as hard as she thought it would be. "They were always pretty self-involved, even when they were together. It's easier and certainly healthier to leave them to their own destructive devices.''

''I'm sorry.''

She shrugged. ''Don't be. I'm not. It just is what it is.'' She glanced at him. ''I always wondered what it would be like to have a big family. I think I would have enjoyed having an escape hatch like you did. I can't imagine a houseful of people, all related to me.'' She laughed. ''The very thought used to make me shudder.''

''Used to?''

Her smile wavered, then steadied as she held his gaze. She nodded. ''Till recently. Very recently.''

He smiled, looked back to the road. ''Thank you,'' he said at length.

''For?''

''The little piece.''

She glanced over at him, but he kept his eyes ahead. *What do you know,* she thought, shifting her own gaze forward, her lips curved in a slight smile. It didn't hurt to share a little. In fact, it felt kind of good.

He was silent for a long while. Normally Liza didn't mind the silences, but she discovered she was curious about this one. Curious about what he was thinking, curious about a lot of things regarding Dylan Jackson. Everything, really. ''Pretty quiet over there,'' she said casually. ''You thinking about Pearl, the case?''

''Honestly?'' He darted a quick look at her. ''I was thinking that I enjoy the way you put things into words.''

''What? Where did that come from?''

''I was thinking how much I enjoy just having you with me. I enjoy talking to you, listening to you. You're interesting and entertaining.''

She didn't know what to say. She'd honestly expected

some cop shoptalk, even an "I can't discuss a case" response.

"You're witty, with a sense of humor that is dry and clever without sounding flippant or petty," he continued. "You've got this ability to put everything in perspective with a quick, common sense approach. And you read people very well." He shifted a little and glanced briefly at her. "You handled Pearl really well."

Liza shrugged, caught totally off guard. "It's a gift, what can I say?"

Dylan laughed. "Now you're being flippant. What, you can't take a compliment?"

"I can take a compliment. It's the observations that are harder to swallow."

"Was I off the mark?"

She glanced at him now, and smiled. "I'll just say thank-you and shut up." When he merely stared at her, she reached over and nudged his face to the front again. "Keep your eyes on the road, Sheriff."

"Chicken."

She smiled, then laughed. "Okay. Let's just say you read people well, too. Maybe too well."

Dylan grinned. "Then we have something in common."

"Learned in completely different worlds, but maybe you have a point."

"Just about that?"

She smiled but didn't look at him. She could feel his glance. "Maybe. Maybe more." Liza rubbed at her arms despite the hot, dry air that teased her curls as they drove on. But it only enhanced the tingling sensation she was feeling. Perhaps the same thing he was feeling. A connection that belied the short time frame of their acquaintance. Natalie had worried about the very same thing when she'd met Jake. And Liza had told her then that maybe sometimes a heart simply knew. She stole a glance over at Dylan's hands, hands that had pushed her, prodded her, brought her indescribable pleasure.

Much like the man himself.

She shivered again, both in anticipation of where this thing between them was headed…and where it could end.

"You joked about your parents writing a book," Dylan said into the quiet rush of air. "Maybe *you* should think about writing a book. I bet you could tell some tales. About the insights you gleaned from your former business," he added quickly. "Not about your parents."

She smiled, honestly surprised by the suggestion. "When I first decided to leave my business, I thought about writing a screenplay, figuring maybe I could do for myself what I had done for others. Bask in my own spotlight." She gave a dry laugh. "I discovered I didn't have the main ingredient."

"A good imagination? I find that hard to—"

"No, talent."

"Oh. Well."

"Yeah, that's what I said. And I also realized that basking in the spotlight wasn't what I needed, anyway."

Dylan grinned. "Still, book writing is different."

"If it's so easy, maybe you should write one then, about the things you've had to deal with." She grinned. "*Vegas Vice: The Inside Story.* Has 'blockbuster' written all over it. I could get you some meetings, do a pitch for you. Just imagine it—"

"Okay, okay, point made," he said, chuckling. "So tell me, what made Pearl decide to turn on Dugan? She carried a torch for him even after he married another woman."

"Well, she thought she had his love, and more importantly, his respect." Liza snorted. "Though I'd have had a tough time with that one. But in her mind, she was paying him back for being kind enough to take care of her and love her enough to walk away. She didn't think she was marriage material, anyway."

"And?"

"And then his new wife got a bun in the oven and turned Dugan out of the marriage bed."

Dylan groaned. "Oh no. He didn't."

"Oh yeah, he did. Jerkface," she muttered. "He was fine as long as Elaine was providing for his manly needs. But when that supply was shut off temporarily, he came knocking on Pearl's door again."

"Dumb-ass. Why didn't he just find a call girl or…"

"Or anyone else. I know. I guess he thought she'd welcome him back with open arms. For old time's sake." Liza made a disgusted noise. "What is with men, anyway?"

"Hey," Dylan said. "I take offense at that. Most of us only think with that part of our anatomy—"

Liza folded her arms and gave him a look.

"Most of the time, okay. But not when it's important."

She merely lifted an eyebrow.

Dylan shook his head, laughing as they pulled into the dusty gravel parking lot.

"Where are we?" She looked around. They were at the edge of what looked like a very small, very old town. Only a few buildings lined the main street, and what was there looked mostly deserted.

"Old mining town. Not much left of it these days, but they have the best Mexican food north of the border." He got out and came around to open her door.

"Such a gentlemen," she murmured as he helped her out.

He leaned close. "An excuse to touch you," he said next to her ear. "I want my hands on you, Liza."

There was that pleasurable tingling rush, she thought, then looked up at him and told him exactly what she was thinking. "Then we both want the same thing. Imagine that!"

"I have a really good imagination."

"I imagine you do." She smiled and brushed against him as she moved past him toward the sedan, which had pulled into the lot.

Dylan took her arm and tugged her gently back against him. "In fact, I'm imagining ways to keep you around."

Her heart gave a double thud.

"Well, here's hoping your imagination is as good as you think it is, hotshot," she teased. But as she crossed the lot toward Pearl and Quin, her heart tacked on, *Because maybe if you keep me here long enough, I'll come up with a good reason to stay forever.*

15

"No. Absolutely not." Dylan threw his napkin on the table and pushed his chair back. "I don't have anything set up for that, Quin, and you know it."

The interview was done and Quin had all he needed. In fact, he'd already called in, and a warrant for Dugan's arrest was being processed even as they finished their meal. Dylan supposed he should have seen this little complication coming, but his mind had been too full of getting Liza alone and, frankly, getting some sleep. He'd hoped to combine the two, and forget about Pearl and Quin completely.

Pearl's lip quivered and Liza folded her arms and glared at him. "She can stay with me."

Dylan simply looked at her. "No." He could be stubborn, too.

Liza turned to Quin. "She's a free citizen, right? She can stay wherever, with whomever, she wants, correct?"

"She can, but given the strength of her statement and who she's making it against, it's in her best interest to take the protection we can provide. At least until the trial is over."

"I'm not going back to that town until I have to testify," Pearl stated. "And then I'm heading right back out again. I'm done there." Her eyes started to fill. "It has only bad memories for me. I'm going to relocate.

Somewhere quiet, start over. Florida, maybe. Walk the shore, watch the birds.''

Liza swung her gaze back to Dylan, who was already holding up his hand to stem the tirade that was going to come his way.

''Liza, just because Dugan will get picked up, along with several of his associates, does not mean he can't arrange to send some other little cockroach of his down here.'' He shifted his gaze to Quin. ''I don't want that coming to my town again.'' He reached out for Pearl's hand, and she grudgingly allowed him to take hold of it. He looked only at her. ''This isn't personal. Once the trial's over, you can retire wherever you want. But in the meantime, they have safe places for you there and are much better prepared for this sort of thing than I am.''

Liza snorted.

Dylan glared at her. ''What? What makes you think you can handle something like this?''

''Oh, I don't know. I've managed to keep a seventeen-year-old heartthrob safe from ten thousand—yes, I said thousand—screaming, conniving, desperate, lovesick young girls. And that was in a town that didn't even have a traffic light.''

Dylan didn't blink. ''Yes, but that was for what? A weekend? And those girls weren't killers.''

Liza smiled. ''Oh, you'd be surprised. Some of them were amazingly cold-blooded and calculating. Capable of things that would curl your hair and make you cry for Mama. And it wasn't for a weekend, it was for three months while he was filming a movie.'' She turned to Pearl. ''I'm not the police, and I'm certainly not saying I can do a better job of keeping you safe. But if you really don't want to go back to Vegas until the trial, I'll certainly be glad to do whatever I can to help. Finances aren't a problem for me. We can look into renting a place that's easy to watch, within close distance of the sheriff's department. I've found that sometimes the best place to hide is in plain view. Hard to get you where everyone can always see you.''

Pearl sniffed into a crumpled napkin and nodded. "That's very kind of you."

Dylan swore under his breath. "With Dugan's boat-load of lawyers, we might be talking four months until trial."

Liza sent him a sly smile. "What, Sheriff, you have a problem with me staying in your town for that long?"

"I—no." He was angry; he hated being manipulated. But there was no way he could look at her and honestly tell her he didn't like the idea of having her around. Hell, he'd all but begged her to do just that. He'd just like it better if she wasn't harboring a major mob witness while she did it. "What about the rest of your sabbatical?"

She propped her elbows on the table and rested her chin on her hands. "That's the great thing about sabbaticals. No set itinerary. No one to check with if I want to make a last minute change."

"I didn't think you were planning to be away so long."

"I believe I mentioned earlier that I like to stay until things are finished." She looked at him as if they were the only two people at the table. Hell, in the universe. "I think we both agreed things aren't finished."

Dylan was very aware that they weren't the only two people at the table, and that both Quin and Pearl were watching them with open interest. But four or more months...with Liza right within his reach. Dear Lord, the possibilities were staggering. Of course, the town might never recover. Maybe neither would he. But this wasn't about what he wanted. It had to be about the safety of his people, of Pearl, even Liza herself.

Quin finally piped in before Dylan could say anything more. "Maybe we can work something with the feds. Get her some protection down here. They're going to want in on this now, anyway. Might as well make them earn their way in."

Dylan stared at three hopeful faces and sighed, knowing he was outnumbered. "All right."

Pearl clapped her hands, Quin took out his cell phone and began to make calls...and Liza looked at him and mouthed, "Thank you."

"Just don't make me regret this," he muttered as he stood.

She stood up, too, and leaned over as she pushed her chair in. "I'm hoping neither of us does."

He watched her walk to the bathroom with Pearl, then shook his head. "How in the hell did I let that just happen?"

Quin snorted and shook his head as he tossed some bills on the table. "You've been handled by a pro, pal. Two of them." He nodded at Liza's retreating back. "She's something else, D.J. Where'd you find her, anyway?"

"You wouldn't believe me if I told you. Let's just say she makes a habit of rescuing people."

"Yeah, well, she can rescue me anytime she likes."

Dylan shot him a look. "Find your own woman."

Quin chuckled. "I kind of thought it was like that."

Dylan stared at the closed bathroom door, letting the reality that Liza wasn't going anywhere, at least not for the time being, truly sink in. "Yeah, I think it might be."

"About time, Action Jackson."

Dylan laughed at his old nickname. "Things are different in Canyon Springs. I've toned down my wild ways."

"Maybe. Still, I didn't figure you for the settling down type." He laughed. "Of course, I didn't figure you for the small-town sheriff type, either."

"I don't know about settling down. Nothing's felt settled since she drove into town." Dylan finally smiled. "Harboring Pearl might be tame by comparison."

Quin chuckled and clapped him on the back as they exited the restaurant. "She wants you to keep her here, I say hold on tight. Woman looks at me the way she was looking at you…" He let out a low whistle. "I'd be clinging for dear life. Lucky bastard."

Dylan just shook his head, but that idiotic grin was sneaking to the surface. "You going to stay long enough to help me get them set up?"

"Yeah. I'm waiting on a few responses, but we should be able to get some preliminary things in place by tonight." He raked his fingers through his hair, then stuck out his hand. "Thanks for doing this, man. I know it's not what you wanted, but if these names and dates she gave us play, keeping her from bolting might be the difference between locking up Dugan and half his organization and letting him walk this earth a free man forever."

Dylan gave his hand a shake. "Yeah, I know."

"We owe you one."

He shot him a wry look. "Oh, you owe me so many you can't even keep track of them anymore. I'll let you know when I want to collect."

Quin laughed. "Yeah, next time you need to harbor

some dangerous criminal from Canyon Springs, you let us know."

DYLAN HUNG UP THE PHONE and rubbed his eyes. It had been five hours since they'd dropped off Pearl and Liza—who'd ridden back to town with Quin and Pearl—at her hotel, along with Quin. It was ridiculous how much he'd missed having her next to him on the drive back. Even more ridiculous—what with everything he'd had to do in the past few hours, on as little sleep as he'd had—was just how often his thoughts had been on her. Somehow she'd managed to waltz into town and integrate herself into every corner of his life. He shook his head. She really was something else. And he'd never been so wrapped up in a woman in his life.

Two Federal agents were heading in, and Quin was setting up a virtual command center from a small two-bedroom apartment two blocks the other side of the sheriff's office that Liza had found within fifteen minutes of arriving back in town. Liza had already moved her few belongings there and was busy settling Pearl in with her.

Now that he'd had time to digest the whole deal, Dylan was forced to admit that this was probably the best setup Quin and crew could hope for. Canyon Springs was small enough that, now that they were on alert, it would be difficult for someone new to waltz in and not draw attention. As for the unseen threats, the cops would be watching this time. And with the agents on the job and Pearl's close proximity to the sheriff's office, that shouldn't be too hard, either.

Which left him to worry about Liza. Who was right in the thick of things. Obviously in her element once again. Meaning in control of someone else's life besides her own.

Dylan had this urge to yank her out of there, drag her off to his cave and keep her, handcuffed again if necessary, until she let simply let everything and everyone else go. And why he cared so much whether or not she buried herself behind the needs of someone else, he had no idea. She was obviously good at it, and on some level, he knew it had to be rewarding. But he couldn't shake the feeling that this wasn't what she really needed. Or certainly not all she needed.

He snorted and downed the cold dregs of his umpteenth cup of coffee. Like he had any clue what Liza Sanguinetti really needed out of life. *Besides me in it*, he couldn't help but thinking. Someone to make her take some time for herself, give her what *she* needed. Even if she fought him every step of the way. He grinned despite the fatigue clawing at his every muscle. Right now what Dylan needed was some sleep.

But even as he pulled out of the station and pointed his truck in the direction of home sweet home, he found himself slowing down as he passed by her apartment, fighting the desire to go in and rescue the rescuer. Take her away to a place where she could sit, relax, think deep thoughts, talk, laugh…love. Where there was no one to take care of but herself, nothing to dictate, control or worry about…except herself.

He imagined her on his deck, sipping coffee as the sun rose. In his kitchen…not chained to his kitchen island—although that image was likely to haunt him, pleasurably so, for the remainder of his life—but just puttering about, scrambling an egg, reading the morning paper. He pictured her in his bed. Both with and without the handcuffs.

He grinned and shook his head. He really was tired. But he couldn't help but think his days would never be boring with her in his life, under his roof. Couldn't help but wonder what it would be like to want to get home from work because she'd be waiting for him. Sure, she'd probably drive him and half the town crazy. But maybe he still craved a little crazy in his life.

Sleep, Jackson. To bed. Alone.

So he drove home. And dreamed about giving refuge to a woman who didn't know how to give it to herself. And in doing so, found a way to turn his own refuge into a home.

"WHAT IN THE HELL do you mean, she's gone out?" Dylan pressed his knuckles against his temples and gripped the phone more tightly.

Liza sighed. "Don't worry, Scully and Mulder are with them."

"Scully and who?" He needed aspirin. And more coffee. And then more aspirin. He'd been insane to agree to this arrangement. Three days and he was already losing his mind.

"Yeah, you know, your agent buddies."

"You mean Cassidy and Walker. They're not my buddies," Dylan muttered. "And who exactly is 'them'?"

There was a pause this time and Dylan could feel his neck knot up.

"Well, Avis came by and—"

"No. No, no, no. You are not going to tell me Pearl is off somewhere with my mother."

"Not if you don't badger me into telling you, I won't."

Three days of torture, both in worrying about…well, everything, and in not getting to see Liza, who was too busy bonding with Pearl. And Mulder and Scully. And now, apparently, with his mother. Dylan swore under his breath. "What in God's name is she doing with Avis? I told you I didn't want her getting involved with—"

"Oh, for heaven's sake, Dylan, she's not going to simply stay tucked away here in this apartment for weeks on end. Besides, I explained before and you agreed with me, sometimes the best place to hide is in plain sight."

"Sometimes," he repeated. "Fine. But not with my mother."

"Don't get your handcuffs in a knot. The two of them aren't even in Canyon Springs."

Dylan started to yell, then wisely clamped his jaw tight until he thought he could speak without losing it completely. He'd been doubly insane to think that having Liza in his town was going to be a good thing. He still wanted to get his hands on her, but now he wasn't so sure he didn't simply want them around her lovely neck. "Where...are...they?" he muttered through gritted teeth.

"Heading toward Tucson."

"Out of state?"

"You're yelling."

"I'm not—" He bit off the rest, forced his hands out of his hair before he ripped it out by the roots. "Why?" It was all he could manage.

"They aren't going across state lines, they're merely meeting someone at the border."

"Oh, this eases my mind considerably."

"It's a bird rescue, Dylan. Nothing nefarious."

"How did Pearl end up on one of my mother's rescue missions? Never mind, don't even answer that."

"She was climbing the walls here. And when I talked to Avis earlier, I remembered Pearl talking about retiring to go bird-watching, so I just thought she'd enjoy the company and might get a kick out of seeing her birds. I sort of wanted to see them, too, so—''

"Why were you talking to Avis?''

"Don't sound so suspicious. She wanted to ask me about the festival next weekend. When it got out that I used to handle all sorts of, well, details for people—''

"Famous people.''

"Hey, I didn't tell her that, but she asked me a ton of questions, and what was I supposed to do? Lie?''

"Absolutely.''

"Dylan!''

"Liza,'' he retorted mockingly, though wearily.

"Anyway, I ran into her in town yesterday and we got to talking about this booth she wants to have at the festival. Oh, now don't groan and whine.''

"I'm not whining.'' He couldn't lie about the groan.

"Anyway, she started telling me about these three birds she'd been called on to rescue, and was worried half to death that she couldn't leave, what with all the last-minute festival planning going on. I'd have offered to help with the birds, except I don't know the first thing about handling them. But I do know how to—''

"Oh no.''

There was a pause, then a little sound of indignation. "What?''

"Nothing.''

"Oh no, that was definitely a something. You know Dylan, I thought you wanted me to stay.''

"I did. Do. But—''

"But what? Did you want me to stay hidden away, too? You know, I'm not here simply for your private pleasure.''

"I know that.'' Although his body leaped at the very idea. "It's just that—''

"If I'm going to be here, then I need to be part of the action. I'm no good at sitting still."

"That I understand, but that doesn't mean you have to take charge of the whole town. You've been here less than a week."

She laughed. "What, afraid I'll run for sheriff?"

He laughed hoarsely, then said, "You're not, are you?" He was only half kidding.

"No. I'm not cut out for law enforcement. And I'm not running your town, although I have talked to several members of the city council and you know, you could really stand—"

"Stop. Just stop. What are you doing talking to the city council?"

"Avis was telling me about a slight zoning issue they were having with this one particular idea her ladies auxiliary had come up with for the festival."

"It's next week. Isn't it a little late for—"

Liza just laughed. "Honey, it's never too late."

Dylan let his forehead drop to the stack of folders on his desk. He thought about thumping it against them several times, but figured he was past beating any sense into himself. He blew out a long sigh. "When is Pearl and her posse getting back to town?"

Liza snickered. "Probably not until ten or so tonight, Sheriff. Why?"

"I just figured there had to be a silver lining to this whole situation somewhere. I'm out of here in another hour. Would you like to come up for some dinner?" He thought about offering her the option of going out somewhere, but he wasn't up to sharing her with the town just yet. Not that she hadn't shared plenty of herself with them already, apparently, but he figured they could both use a break from running the town. And he still had this urge to drag her to his cave.

"Dinner sounds nice. As long as you promise to grill only the steaks and not me for getting involved."

"I'll try."

"I'll just distract you if you don't."

Damn if that didn't make him smile. "I'll pick you up in an hour."

"I'll pick *you* up," she said. "Pearl is in the fed-mobile, so I've got my car. I've got to meet—"

"*I'll* pick you up. I have to keep my truck with me. Given our luck, I'll be called out on something or another and I'm not riding to the scene in your little hot rod." Besides which, she was not going to run this evening the way she'd apparently run everything and everyone else today.

"Fine, fine, you can pick me up." There was a pause, then she asked in a sultry little voice, "Will you let me play with your siren on the way home?"

Dylan swallowed, his throat suddenly dry despite the grin threatening. "You're already pushing enough buttons, don't you think?"

Her laugh was deep and throaty. "Oh, I haven't even begun yet. And you're the last one who can talk about being a button pusher."

His lips curved. "I'll be there by six."

"Pick me up at the firehouse. I've got to talk with Tucker about getting approval for—"

"Stop. I don't even want to know. I'll see you there at six, or before, if I can get out of here early."

"Don't forget the handcuffs. It's my turn tonight."

His body went from leaping at suggestive ideas to rock solid arousal, even as the dial tone hummed in his ear. But he was smiling as he clicked the receiver back onto the base and pushed his chair back. "Oh no," he murmured, "you've done quite enough supervising today. Tonight you're mine."

16

LIZA PULLED INTO Dylan's driveway behind him, careful to hide her satisfied smile when he glanced in his rearview mirror. It wouldn't do to be too smug. "Try and control *this* evening, buster," she murmured. Actually, she'd fully intended to ride up the mountain with him as planned, until he'd pulled into the firehouse. She already knew Tucker and Dylan were adversaries, of sorts, but it was almost comical watching Dylan trying not to care that Tucker was all but fawning over her. Liza had already set Tucker straight on her unavailable status earlier, so she'd known even before he sent her a private wink that he was merely giving Dylan a go. Still, it had been fun to watch.

Fun and a little unsettling. Not because it worried her that Dylan was taking their fling too seriously. But because she rather liked the way he snorted and pawed at the ground, defending what he saw as his territory, figuratively speaking. Well, for the most part.

What would it be like to have someone like Dylan trying to run roughshod over her all the time, telling her what was best for her, taming her wilder instincts? Well, not all her wild instincts, she thought with a private smile as she put the emergency brake on and climbed out of the car. She was pretty sure he enjoyed some of her wilder, more basic instincts. Only in private.

She hummed under her breath, thinking it might be

fun to shake up the town sheriff a bit, bring those wild instincts of his out in the open. It should annoy her the way he wanted to tuck her away, make her take some time for herself. As if he knew what was best for her. She could certainly determine when she wanted that time and how to spend it when she did.

Of course, if she'd been all that good at it, she wouldn't have closed up shop and headed into the desert. So maybe he did have a tiny point. And despite his bossy, domineering ways, she had to admit she enjoyed being with him. Even when he was at his most dominating. Sometimes especially when he was dominating, she thought, feeling her skin begin to heat up.

He walked toward her and her gaze shifted to his waistband, where she knew he'd tucked those silver bracelets. She felt a tiny shudder of anticipation run through her at the idea of him taking charge of her the way he had the last time she was up here. But she carefully stoked that anticipation in another direction. Tuck her away he might, but tonight *she* was going to be in charge of whatever private pleasures he had in mind.

Which was why she'd driven up herself. Best he learn right off that she wasn't going to be a pushover where their relationship was concerned.

Relationship. Another little thrill shot down her spine at the idea that she'd committed to spending several months in Canyon Springs. She intended to keep her commitment to Pearl, though she knew Pearl would be fine without her. And to Avis and her ladies club, who'd asked her to help them out with some organizational problems they were having. And then there was the emergency town council meeting tomorrow night that Tucker had told her about, where she should be able to address the auxiliary's concerns, as well as some the

Rotary Club had asked her about after hearing her suggestions to the ladies group.

She hadn't told Dylan about that last part yet. Not that she had to report to him, but since he was going to be at the meeting, she figured it might behoove her to give him a heads-up…that is, if she wanted to keep the opportunity open for some head from him later!

That naughty little thought gave her a naughty little grin, which she kept as she strolled right up to him and slid her arms around his neck. No point in letting him get the upper hand. Or the lower one, she decided, and drew her tongue from the center of his chin up to his bottom lip, which she pulled into her mouth before he could do anything about it. He started to move back, so she inched her fingernails into his hair, raking them lightly over his scalp, and was rewarded with a deep groan. Which she naturally took full advantage of, sliding her tongue in his mouth, teasing his, until he forgot all about controlling anything and let her have her way with him.

When he finally lifted his head, they were both a bit flushed and breathing heavily. "My, my, Sheriff Jackson," she said, striving for casual playfulness, which was a challenge, considering that she wanted to throw him across the hood of her car and straddle him right then and there. "A girl would think you were starving for a bit of attention. You know, you don't have to drag me all the way up here to have your way with me."

In retrospect, she probably shouldn't have provoked him. Only he was so much fun when riled up. Fun, but dangerous when it came to upsetting her plans to dictate the direction this particular interlude would take.

His smile was incredibly sexy. "Oh, but I am starving,'' he all but purred. "Feels like I haven't eaten in days.''

Definitely dangerous.

"And I don't feel like sharing.''

She slid her hands down his chest, preparing to move away and glide up the stairs to the deck in front of him, giving him a nice little view—or should she say, preview—of what she had in store for him. She'd dressed with great care. More for what she'd left off than for what she'd put on. After all, she'd come directly from meetings with both Avis's ladies and Tucker. Liza wondered if Dylan would enjoy knowing that all the while she'd sat there, oh-so-stylishly dressed, beneath it all she was *un*dressed, exclusively for him.

But Dylan locked his hands around her wrists before she could slide around him. He pulled her palms from his chest and pushed them behind her back, which shoved her up tight against him, all her curves and needs tucking tightly against all of his. She tried not to let that little moan of wanton pleasure slip out, but it was damned impossible.

His grin turned downright lethal. "I don't think I can wait another moment to…sate my appetite.''

Any thoughts she had of pushing him away in order to reestablish her control of the evening's activities flew right out the window when he spun her around and pushed her up hard against the side of his truck. Still holding her hands, wedged now between her lower back and the warm metal of the side door, he lazily took a nip of her mouth, then dropped a wet kiss on the curve of her neck. Then, before she could counteract with some kisses of her own, he very slowly—very, very slowly—slid his body down hers until he was crouched in front of her.

He looked up at her, then dropped a carnal kiss right at the juncture of her thighs, her silk skirt the only barrier…and far too much of one, she instantly decided.

"Never tease a starving man," he admonished, then nudged her skirt up with his nose, only to groan in deep appreciation at what he found. "But feel free to invite him in like this anytime you want."

She was saved from having to string even two words together when his oh-so-clever tongue slipped easily behind the tiny triangle of silk masquerading as panties. The delicate threads of elastic holding the ensemble together gave way easily to his teeth, letting the scrap of silk flutter to the ground as he turned his attentions to…sating his hunger.

Liza learned that, out in the open air of the mountains, moans of pleasure echoed almost as loudly as shrieks of ecstasy. He let her hands go, though she didn't move them. In fact, whatever concentration she was capable of was focused exclusively on staying upright under his incredible assault.

He slid his palms beneath her skirt and cupped her buttocks, then slowly nudged her legs farther apart. It was almost as decadent a pose as he'd had her in that night on his kitchen counter, only somehow, despite the fact that she wore more clothing, she felt even more vulnerable. Feeling the night air caress her skin only intensified the slippery coolness of her silk shirt on the rest of her. She wanted to rip it off. No, she wanted him to rip it off, bare all of her to the mountain air…to him.

She had no time to contemplate the wanton way her mind worked when it came to Dylan Jackson. He slid first one finger, then another, inside her, and she climaxed so abruptly it made her gasp in shock.

"Damn," she faintly heard him swear. Then he was

standing, jerking at the snap of his jeans, pulling her thighs up over his hips. "I wasn't going to... Not yet, but—"

"Just do it, for God's sake," she all but growled, never needing anything as much as she needed to feel him fill her up right now. Every nerve ending was still clamoring from her release, and she knew the instant he pushed into her she would very likely—

"Yes! Dear God, yes," she panted as he thrust forward. Stars literally swam as she screamed over the edge again. She crossed her ankles behind his back and held on for dear life as he thrummed inside her, growling in release moments later.

He buried his face in the damp curve of her neck. She tipped her head back and closed her eyes, grinning like an idiot. "I give up," she murmured.

"Give up what?" The words were muffled against her throat.

"Ever trying to be in charge around you."

He lifted his head, chuckling. "Sweetheart, you drove me around like a new car just now."

She laughed. "Well, if that's the case, the ride was a little bumpy, but boy, the jump from zero to sex will take your breath away."

It should have been awkward, pulling up pants and smoothing down skirts, all while standing in his driveway, for Christ sake. But instead it felt...fun. Sexy. Intimate. Maybe having their own private little pleasures wasn't such a bad thing.

"I brought the wine," she said. "But it's still in the car." She shot him a sly grin. "I was so busy plotting your downfall, I forgot it. I guess I should have gotten you drunk first. Maybe I'd have had a shot at the upper hand for a change."

He snagged her arm lightly as she moved past him toward her car, and spun her gently back around and flush up against him. He did that far too smoothly, and she fit him far too well. "Hey."

"Hey, what?" she asked lightly. But her heart had started to pound. A different sort of thunder than it had moments ago in the heat of passion. It was the way he was looking at her now, when passions had been sated. If was far more…intimate than when he'd been deep inside her, driving her over the edge. She worked not to rub at the prickles of awareness that raced along her skin.

"That was… What we just did…" He shook his head, his self-deprecating smile all the sexier for how endearing it was. "I didn't plan that. Attacking you like that. I actually thought we might be civilized about things tonight. Nice dinner, followed by some wine. Then maybe I'd lure you to my bedroom, make slow, passionate love to you." His grin widened. "You know, like real people, instead of the wild animal I seem to be whenever you get within three feet of me."

"Was I complaining?"

"No. And I'm not, either." He laughed. "What guy in his right mind would?" He tugged her closer, tipped her chin up, his smile fading. "I missed you these past couple of days," he said quietly, and quite seriously.

"Yeah?" She traced her fingertips across his cheek. "Me, too. Weird, huh?"

His lips curved just a little. "Not so weird, maybe."

"Then you're not mad? About Pearl staying here with me?"

"Frustrated at times," he said frankly, then dropped a devastatingly gentle kiss on her lips. "But it's worth it knowing that you're still close. That I get to do this."

He kissed her again, nudged her lips apart and sank into her. "This I could get used to," he murmured, finishing with a light kiss to the tip of her nose.

Liza's heart shouldn't have swelled, shouldn't have stuttered, shouldn't have tumbled. But it did. She shoved herself away from that dangerous emotional precipice and did what she always did—let her mouth race ahead of her heart. "Well, you might not be so thrilled when you hear my agenda for the next couple of days."

He winced despite trying to look brave and sincere, and she laughed right in his face. "Don't worry, it's just a town council meeting. How much trouble could I cause you?"

He merely looked at her, then made her laugh again when he said, "I might just have to get a second set of handcuffs. I have a feeling they're going to come in handy while we're together."

Liza's heart stumbled again. *While we're together.* Meaning they wouldn't always be?

What, did you honestly think he was thinking long term? So he wanted to romance you a little instead of rutting like a wildebeest. Did you really think he envisioned wedding bells and diamond rings?

No, she honestly didn't. What terrified her was that, maybe, *she* had been. For a second, anyway. Good thing he'd brought her back to earth before she got too high. The fall hurt a lot less that way.

She laughed, not caring that it sounded brittle even to her own ears, and extricated herself from his embrace. "I promise to behave if you promise to keep me unfettered this evening." She moved past him more assuredly this time and scooped the wine bottle from the passenger seat of the car, carefully walking along the opposite side of his truck to ensure she made it to the deck stairs without being waylaid.

She needed a few moments to regroup, that was all. She was here to have fun. And if she was enjoying the townspeople and getting involved with things besides the sheriff's naked body, then she was damn well going to let herself get involved. Probably she and Dylan would burn out on each other at some point, anyway. If that point coincided with Pearl's leaving to give testimony, then all the better. Liza would depart knowing she was better for having stayed in Canyon Springs.

She felt Dylan climbing the stairs behind her, the heavy tread of his boots making more than the stairs vibrate. Yeah, she'd be better for having known him, for discovering that letting someone else take control every once in a while wasn't the end of the world. In fact, it was kind of...liberating.

"The menu is steak on the grill or pasta in the kitchen," he said, topping the stairs and pausing.

She sat the bottle on the small round table. "Well, I'm not sure I trust myself in your kitchen." Truth was, she wasn't very hungry at the moment. Too many things whirling around in her brain had an unsettling effect.

Rather than head to the door, he crossed the deck toward her. She had a wild thought to run, just race down the stairs, jump in her car and tear down the mountain, keep on driving until she was out of town, out of his life.

Because the way he looked at her made her heart hurt. And she wasn't sure she could manage the pretense of this being another one of her wild flings. It was wild, what happened when they were together, but nothing about Dylan felt remotely flinglike. And when he stopped in front of her, concern in those golden-brown eyes of his, eyes that saw her so clearly it scared her, she doubted four months was long enough to burn him out of her system.

"What's wrong? Did I say something wrong down there? Never mind, I know I did. If it's about the handcuffs, I really didn't mean to insult you about helping in town—"

She laughed and choked on a little sob at the same time. He really was adorable. And wonderful. And sexy as hell. And she wanted him to be all hers. There. She'd said it, even if only to herself. "You didn't insult me. And I'm fine. Just not all that hungry."

He cocked his head and stared at her. "Sure?"

"Yep. Maybe just a glass of wine, out here on the deck?"

He stared at her a moment longer, then said, "Okay." But she suspected he knew she wasn't okay. Not entirely. He went inside for a corkscrew and she turned her gaze to the valley sprawled below.

Okay. She wanted him. Not for a fling, but for the duration, however long that would be. Forever, maybe. If she was lucky. Only for the first time in her life, she wasn't sure how to go about getting what she wanted. Dylan wasn't like anyone else she'd ever met. He wouldn't simply fall at her feet because she willed it to happen. And if she came on too strong, he'd only flip the tables on her. If she tried the timid approach... She stopped right there, since that was simply too laughable to consider. Besides, he'd never buy it, anyway.

Which left...being herself. Whatever the hell that was. But whatever it was, it had gotten her this far.

Damn, but this falling in love stuff was terrifying. She wished she could call Natalie. Nat had been through this...this free-fall-with-no-safety-net feeling. And she'd understand, not question it, as hers had happened just like it was happening for Liza—coming straight at her, speeding into her life like a comet, on a direct collision course with her heart.

It defied every one of Liza's goal-achieving strategies. Instead, it demanded she put it all on the line, throw herself out there and pray like hell that being the vague, undefined entity known as "herself" was enough. Risk the pain of realizing it might not be, not for him. Not that failure itself was all that painful for her. But the broken heart that would come with it would be excruciating.

"Come with me." His deep voice and warm hand in hers pulled her from her thoughts. She turned, expecting to find him holding wineglasses. But he was empty-handed, except for her. He turned, pulling her along behind him. She went silently, curious about what he had up his sleeve this time.

It struck her, as they wound their way into his living room, how comfortable she was, how much trust she'd built up in him. Here she was, halfway through his house, and not once had it occurred to her to try and wangle the scenario to her advantage. Or, more to the point, to her control.

Maybe, she considered, her heart had already figured out what her head had taken a bit longer to realize. That whatever he did with her, for her, to her, was to her advantage. That he was a man who had, if she thought about it, always put her needs first. Sometimes knowing what those needs were before she did.

So when he led her up the curving wrought-iron staircase to the loft above, she went along willingly. Anticipating whatever he had planned…without a thought toward trying to take over. Because she finally understood what he'd been trying to tell her all along. That this wasn't about who was on top. This was about giving in, not only to him, but to herself. It was about trust, and knowing it was as important for him to give as it was for her to learn to take.

My God, she thought with a happy little grin. *I think I finally grew up.*

17

DYLAN STARED AT THE SCENE he'd set, smiled ruefully, suddenly feeling stupid, then stepped aside so Liza could see. Her gasp of surprised pleasure made taking the risk worthwhile.

"I know they're not all that pretty. Mostly I keep them for when the power goes out."

She turned away from the lit candles that dotted the nightstands, dresser and windowsills. "They're beautiful." She moved into his arms. "And so are you."

He smiled. "Yeah, I'm a regular Don Juan." Then his smile faded and he pulled her more tightly against him. "I know it sounds foolish, and you've probably been wined and dined by men better at it than me, but—"

She pressed her fingers to his lips. "Maybe so. But there's calculated seduction, and then there's…well, you."

Dylan laughed. "Gee, thanks."

"No, that's not how I meant it." She tried to wriggle free, only he didn't let her.

He wanted her right where he could touch her, hold her, smell her, taste her when he felt like it. It should alarm him that he'd become so obsessed so quickly, but he didn't care.

"I just meant, well, you've already had me, and given

what just happened in your own driveway, it's a safe bet you could have me again." Her dry smile faded. "So there was no need for all this, and yet you did it anyway. That's what I meant. It's more romantic than any polished and perfected little scene, because you wanted to do it for me, just because."

Dylan grinned. "Well, there might have been a little calculation involved."

She cocked her head. "Oh?"

He shuffled her backward, until the mattress bumped the backs of her legs. "I thought that maybe with all this flickering candlelight, I could distract you long enough so you'd let me do this." He pushed her back and fell with her onto the bed, careful to lever himself so he didn't crush her.

"This?" she said, a bit breathlessly.

He leaned in, trapping her hands beside her head. "Yeah," he said quietly. "No cuffs, no games, no power struggles, just…this." He lowered his head and took her mouth, gently this time, exploring what was there instead of simply invading it.

When he shifted his attentions to the fine line of her jaw, then her neck and that delectable little curve of her shoulder, she sighed. "I'm liking this."

"Good," he murmured, "because I have a lot more of it in mind."

This time they undressed each other. Slowly. Lazily exploring every nuance, every dip and sinew. By the time Dylan pulled her beneath him, he didn't think he'd ever felt so deeply connected to anyone. And when he slid inside her and she wrapped herself tight around him, he couldn't ignore the sensation that he'd come home.

"Liza," he whispered, as he thrust slowly, distinctly, inside of her.

Her eyes fluttered open and he thought he might drown in what he saw there. "Mmm," was all she managed in answer.

You're mine, he thought, and for a split second he thought he'd said the words out loud. Maybe he should. He felt like shouting them. And he knew it wasn't just the way she contracted around him, holding him inside her like they were built to fit as exactly as they did. Because he felt just like this sitting at his desk, thinking about her.

He was in love with her. It was crazy. And it didn't matter. His head knew. And now his heart did, too.

"Hold on to me," he told her. And she did. He moved deeper, never once wavering from her steady gaze. Then he rolled to his back, pulling her on top of him. Her eyes widened in surprise, then they both groaned as she settled her weight on him, and he sank even more deeply into her.

"And just when I was getting used to being on the bottom," she quipped, then gasped as he lifted his hips.

"I like keeping you off balance," he said, his own lips spreading in a wide grin.

She clamped her knees to his sides and rode him steadily, making him gasp and buck instinctively. "Better watch out, I'm a fast learner."

He rolled her to her back, causing her to shriek with a little laugh, her head almost off the bed. "So we'll teach each other," he said, then paused in midthrust, surprised at the fleeting expression that had crossed her face. "What?"

"Don't stop, I'm fine."

He trapped her face in his hands. "No, you avoided the question earlier. Now tell me. Am I moving too fast?"

That got a dry laugh out of her. "I don't think either of us can claim any kind of patience."

"Then maybe it's that I'm presuming too much." He thought she hadn't understood the depth of what he was feeling, that he'd masked it well behind the need of his body for hers. But he already knew nothing got past her. He shouldn't have been surprised that this hadn't, either. "I know it seems too soon," he said, "but it's just the way it is. I'm not making any demands. But I won't lie and tell you I'm not already planning to find a way to keep you here long enough so that when the time comes and Pearl's done her thing, you won't even think about leaving."

She said nothing, simply stared at him, her expression for once unreadable. His heart was pounding, and not just because she felt so damn good and he'd been so damn close to climaxing before he stupidly decided to have this little talk. "You know, I've faced down whacked-out perps waving loaded guns, and never felt quite this nervous. Tell me what you're thinking."

It was another moment before she spoke. "I'm thinking you should finish what you started, then we'll talk."

His body urged him vehemently to take her suggestion and run wild with it. But something told him if he let them drift back to the physical now, an important, maybe life-altering moment would be forever lost. He might get her like this again, but she'd be prepared next time. And the time after that. "That's exactly what I'm asking you," he said. "To stick around long enough for us to finish what we've started here."

"You're really not talking about sex, are you." She hadn't made it a question.

He shook his head. "I'm talking about this." He bent down and kissed her, gently, reverently, then lifted his head just enough to look into her eyes. "I'm falling in love with you, Liza. I think maybe I was the moment you got out of that death trap you call a car. And it's not about this." He moved inside her, making her gasp. "Although it's certainly a side benefit."

She arched one brow and wrapped her legs more tightly around his waist, lifting her hips, coaxing him deeper, so his body would simply take over, bypass all the cerebral stuff. And she almost succeeded. Almost.

His jaw was strained with the tension of not giving in to what he so badly wanted…and what they both would so thoroughly enjoy. "You want to run every last committee in town, that's fine," he growled. "You're not happy unless you're running something." He grunted a little when she simply squeezed her inner muscles, tightening her grip on him by way of agreeing with him. "Very funny."

She managed to smile up at him, but she was trembling, too.

"But you can't always be in charge. You need to learn how to take. And I want to be the one who brings you to that place. Where you can let it all go. Trust that I'll handle it. Handle you. Just let go." He kissed her again, more urgently this time, and he began to move as well. "Just let it go." He looked down at her, thrust again, and again. "Come home to me. Let me be that for you."

She thrashed her head from side to side as he continued to drive her, with his body, with his words, until she screamed, "Yes! Okay, dammit?" She was gasping; his hips were pistoning. "Yes, *yes!*"

He took her over the edge, not surprised that she took him with her. He collapsed next to her, pulled her against him and tried to remember how to breathe.

Eventually his heart slowed and he felt her own breathing even out. He stroked her hair and wondered if he hadn't just ruined what might have been a wonderful couple of months by pushing her too hard, too fast.

"Did you really mean it?" she asked softly.

He thought she was dozing, so her quiet question startled him. He continued to fiddle with her hair, concentrating on the drowsy weight of her limbs draped across his, and how right this whole thing felt. "I meant everything I said. Which part are you asking about?"

He started to shift so she could lift her head, but she pressed her cheek firmly to his chest, keeping her gaze averted.

"I'm...my family doesn't exactly have a good track record when it comes to long-term commitment. In that respect, I don't fall far from the tree."

His heart skipped a beat. He willed it to smooth out. "You strike me as a risk taker."

"In some things."

"But not with this sort of thing? Then how do you know you won't be good at it?"

"I've...I have no strategy for this. No method of success to copy, no pattern to follow." She finally lifted her head and looked at him. "What if I can't figure out how to make it work?"

He smoothed her rumpled curls. "I'm new at this, too. We'll figure it out together."

"I'm not an easy person to deal with."

His grin came naturally. "I think it's one of the things I enjoy most."

She snorted. "That's the recent double orgasm talking."

"Could be."

She swatted him on the chest.

He trapped her close with one strong arm. "I can't claim to have a mind totally unfogged by recent activities, but I do know that I've been with women who were simple, easy to get along with, go-with-the-flow types."

"And?"

"And it was…boring. Or at the very least, not stimulating."

"And I am?"

"Oh, definitely. And no, I'm not talking about sex this time, either."

She settled on his chest, propping her chin on her hands. "Well, that will get old, let me tell you."

He took her face in his hands. "Well, why don't we just find out for ourselves, okay?"

She frowned. "You're really serious, aren't you?"

"Is it so unbelievable that I could fall in love with you? Do you see yourself as unlovable?"

"Yes. I mean, no. I mean…" She sighed. "I don't know what I mean. I never really looked at it that way. But then, I never thought about permanent, personal type relationships." She grimaced. "That was half my problem—I never thought about anything personal. I was all-business, all the time."

"So this wasn't part of the sabbatical plan, I take it? You want to move on then, see if anything else strikes your fancy? Fills your soul better?"

"It would be smarter to figure out what I wanted before I got to the *who* I wanted part."

"Sometimes we don't get to be in control of that, either."

She rolled her eyes, then rested her cheek on his chest, looking away once again.

The silence stretched out and he appeased his growing anxiety by toying with her curls, playing with one dark coil, then another. "If you want to go," he said at length, "then I won't stop you." He wove his fingers deeper, urged her to shift and look at him. Only when she had did he add, "But I can't promise I won't come after you."

Her gorgeous eyes widened. "You wouldn't. You have work here, a life here."

"I do. But I also know a once in a lifetime deal when I see it. A job is just a job. And Canyon Springs isn't going anywhere. But you…" He brushed a fingertip down the length of her nose, let it pause on her lower lip, then caressed her chin. "You could be everything."

"You don't mean that."

He grinned. "Try me."

Liza did sit up then, despite the strong band of muscles binding her to his side. She swung her legs over the edge of the bed and tried like hell to get her mind to stop jumping and focus. Dear Lord, had he really just told her she was the one for him?

It was like a dream come true. Her heart was pounding, urging her to do the happy dance. But how did she make herself believe in it? Sure, she knew he meant what he was saying. But he was in lust, puppy love, early hormonal crush, when everything was sexy and nothing imaginable could go wrong.

He said he'd follow her. And she'd be lying if she said she wasn't a bit seduced by the thrill of a man wanting her badly enough to fight for her. To pursue her, dog her heels and wear her down until she confessed that, yes, dammit, he was everything she wanted.

Did it really have to be hard? And what exactly did she want him to do to prove this wouldn't all turn out badly? Sign an agreement?

But this wasn't a business proposition. It was a heart reaching out. Taking the risk. He couldn't be that confident. This had to be hard for him, too, right?

"Aren't you scared?" she blurted out.

"Terrified," he confirmed solemnly.

She looked over her shoulder. Damn but he looked good, all sprawled and naked in those sheets. *This could be yours, every morning and every night.* It was like being told you might hold the winning lottery ticket.

But then again, you might be one number off. And lose everything. Because that's what this was. Winner take all, loser go home with nothing but a broken heart.

"I hate to lose," she muttered.

"So do I."

She slid off the bed, but he snagged her wrist, made her turn around. "I don't expect a life commitment right this very second, you know. In fact, I hadn't planned on telling you anything about the way I felt." He smiled that disarming, cocky-but-self-deprecating smile of his. "I was going to wear you down with great sex until you were hooked on it, and pray like hell you'd end up sticking around for more."

"Setting yourself up as an orgasm pusher with me as your junkie. Well, that's a first."

"Would it have worked?"

She laughed despite herself. "Might have."

He pulled her back on the bed. "Then forget everything else I said and let's go back to plan A."

He tickled her, dragging her on top of him, making her giggle—giggle, for God's sake!—and also giving her the perfect out to a situation that had started as sexual and somehow turned serious. As serious as it gets.

But he'd risked a lot by being honest. It was only fair that she do the same. So she snagged his teasing hands and waited until he was looking directly at her. "Okay. You got yourself a deal."

"Orgasm pusher?"

She shook her head. "Relationship instigator."

He stilled, then his face split wide in a grin like she'd never seen. But hoped to see again. He rolled her to her back. "I promise I'll go more slowly from now on."

"And ruin everything?" she joked, only her throat had somehow gone tight. His eyes were all dark and serious, and he looked like a man who was about to—

"Okay, then I love you. There. How's that for fast?"

She couldn't breathe. "A minute ago you were falling in love with me."

"I landed."

She swallowed. Hard. "Oh."

"Yeah, I know. Scary doesn't even come close to describing it. But what's a guy to do?" His smile faded and he pushed the tangle of curls from her face. "It's just how I feel. You take your own time, do this your own way." Then he grinned and this time it was purely sexual. "But be warned, I don't play fair."

"Why Sheriff, whatever would the citizens of your fair land think?"

"That I do whatever I have to to get the job done."

"So now I'm a job?"

He laughed. "Oh no, you're pure adventure." And then he was kissing her, teasing her, proving to her exactly how he intended to wage his campaign of winning her heart.

What he didn't know—and she didn't intend to tell him, not just yet, anyway—was that he was closer to succeeding than he knew.

But she could save that little announcement for later. He slid down her body, kissing her navel on the way. Much, much later.

18

"No. ABSOLUTELY NOT." Dylan felt like a broken record. "Because I said so." He sighed and held the phone away from his ear for a moment. "I know she went with you to get the rescue birds, and it went fine. And I know she's become fond of them and I'm glad she's helping you out, even though I'm not fond of her putting you in jeopardy." He clenched his jaw as his mother continued fighting her case. "I don't care if the agents are there, it's not the same as keeping her safe, and you safe by default. Just because the—" He widened his eyes and looked at the phone.

"Hang up on you again, did she?" Liza asked.

He just glared at her and replaced the receiver with a sharp click. "None of you seem to grasp the importance of keeping Pearl close at hand where we can best control her surroundings. Maybe we should all drive by what's left of Mims Motel on a daily basis as a reminder."

Liza stood and walked around his desk to knead Dylan's shoulders. He tried to remain stiff and unyielding, but, damn, she knew just where to—

He stood up, making her hop backward. "Oh no, you're not going to get around me so easily this time."

She smiled sweetly. "Why? It's worked so well all the other times."

Dylan didn't even bother to argue. Mainly because she

was right. "When did I lose control of this relationship, anyway?"

Liza laughed in shock. "Exactly who carried me upstairs last night and deposited me in a tubful of warm water and made me sit and sip a glass of wine—slowly—before forcing me to submit to being tortuously washed with an incredibly soft washcloth?"

Dylan tried not to smile, really he did. "I'm such a cad, I know. You had a screaming headache after that town council meeting, which, by the way, I tried to tell you would be a nightmare. But would you listen to me?"

"No," she agreed readily, "I didn't listen. But I got my way in the end, didn't I? Avis and her friends will be able to have that salsa-eating contest and the board of health is okay with the booth setup. Everyone happy. So what if I had to endure four hours of mind-numbing debate over the color of the table swathing and who will give the first speech of the day? It was worth it."

"Because you got your way in the end."

Liza smiled. "You know me so well."

It had been only a week since the first time he'd carried her to his bedroom…and she'd never exactly left. With the agents in place, Pearl hadn't seemed to mind, and Liza still spent a good deal of time with her every day. God knows Dylan wasn't complaining. At least not when Liza and he were both home. Away from home? Well… "That's what scares me," he grumbled. Because the more he knew her, the more he couldn't stand to be away from her.

She wove her arms around him from behind and toyed with his badge. "You didn't seem too scared when you pulled me out of that tub and took me up against the wall of your bathroom." Her hands drifted downward.

"And I surely enjoyed the way you sipped your wine off of me."

Jesus. His entire body stiffened, some parts more painfully than others. He carefully removed her clever little hands and stepped away. Before he ended up risking his badge and taking her right on his desk. "Don't you have some part of this town you haven't run roughshod over?"

She gave him a wide-eyed, innocent look, then laughed and reached up on her impossibly high heels and kissed him on the cheek. "I only stopped by to say hi on the way to getting my nails done."

"Didn't you just have them done last week?"

"And your point is?"

He shook his head. "None, apparently. Except to be thankful I was born a man."

She stepped closer. "I'm thankful, too."

He laughed, but held her away. "You can show me your appreciation—with those shiny red nails, if you want—but later. I know you're already running half the town, but I have to keep the rest of it safe."

"And don't think we don't appreciate that. In fact, I plan to show you just how appreciative I can be. But only after I get these cuticles attended to. You know, Minnie is a dream find for a manicurist. She does makeup, too. She could be raking in a fortune in Hollywood. I even offered to help her out."

"No kidding."

Liza just looked at him. "But she's happy here. Go figure."

Dylan knew she was tweaking, but it wasn't the first time he'd wondered if someone like Liza, who was used to moving in distinctly faster circles, could ever truly be happy in Canyon Springs.

"Anyway, Minnie was saying last week that she'd really like to expand to the space next door, but the guy who owns the place, Dick Harbert, was giving her a hard time about paying for the repairs herself. I spoke to Tom Connelly about it and he's going to meet me at Minnie's later to see if he can help her out."

"Tom is an estate attorney. How is he going to help...?" Dylan held up his hand. "Never mind. I don't want to know. Can't you even get your nails done without taking over something?"

Liza stepped closer, straightened his badge, gave him that look that made his already hardened body jerk a little harder. "I like helping people. Can I help it if I'm good at it?"

He couldn't deny she was right. It was almost terrifying how embedded in town matters she'd become.

"Not bad for a former showgirl from Vegas, huh?"

Dylan did smile then. Ever since Avis had let it slip that Liza used to work with Very Famous People, she'd been the buzz of the community. It had only made it easier for her to insinuate herself into just about anything she wanted to insinuate herself into. Which seemed to be every damn thing.

And yet the energy she'd created, just by, well, being herself, was undeniably affecting everyone in a favorable way. Himself included, no matter how much he grouched. He did that mostly for effect, anyway. Someone had to keep her balanced. "By the time Pearl gives her testimony, they'll be erecting a statue in the town square in your honor."

She laughed. "Don't be silly." She ran her hands down over his belt buckle and stroked him swiftly with those perfectly fine looking nails of hers. "Your town square's not nearly big enough."

She left him as she usually did—speechless and hard as a rock. "I'm sure you'll find a way to rectify that little injustice before dinner," he muttered, then found himself smiling as he sat down behind his desk. She really was something else. And she was his. At least for now. Just thinking about what came after dinner, when it was his turn to make *her* crazy...well, suddenly he didn't mind so much how she filled her days.

He snatched up the phone and punched in a number. But that didn't mean he was going to roll over and play dead regarding all of her little schemes. "Patterson? Sheriff Jackson here. Any chance we can move Ms. Halliday and your two agents closer to your home base in Tucson? We're slated for a number of festivities here shortly and I'd appreciate it if— What? Oh. Yeah, I see. No, no, I understand. I'll find the additional security necessary." Dylan swore under his breath as he hung up, then lifted the receiver again. He wasn't the only one with troubleshooting capabilities.

"Quin? Hey, it's D.J. Any word yet on trial date? I've got my manpower stretched to the limits here and—"

"Actually, I'm glad you called," his former colleague answered. "Things are going crazy up here. I should have something for you shortly."

"Crazy how?"

"Good crazy, man. Listen, I don't have time to explain everything at the moment. We've still got eyes on Dugan's usual suspects, and there doesn't look to be anything headed your way from our end." He laughed. "Right now, he's got a number of other problems to attend to."

"Such as?"

"Well, we had hoped some of Pearl's dates and names

would give us a bit of ammo, but it's been the start of an avalanche. We turned Morty.''

"No shit.'' Mortimer was Dugan's right- and left-hand man. "How in the hell—''

"Later, I really have to roll. But the rats are jumping ship in droves now. The way things are going, there might not even be a trial. If we're lucky, he'll be begging us to deal by the end of the week.''

"That's the best news I've had in what feels like a decade.''

Quin laughed. "Liza making things interesting for you down there?''

Dylan started to make some smart-ass remark, but what came out was, "Yeah. In fact, she is. But I'll be a lot happier if this thing gets tied up.''

"Well, keep Pearl close and tight for at least a few more days. Right now, I'm betting we bring her up here early and her part will be over with. I'll call as soon as I hear.''

Dylan hung up, feeling as if he'd just lost a two-ton weight off his shoulders. The festival was set to launch Friday, and Avis wanted Pearl to stay at her house and bird-sit for her so she could be more involved in the various booths and activities she'd set up with her ladies group. Dylan just wanted to take Liza out, eat some good food. Mingle with the townsfolk while he kept an eye out for his deputies, who were in charge of the event. Maybe do a bit of dancing, then drag her home when things began to slow down.

He did not want to worry about Pearl and his mother.

But that wasn't what was really bugging him. The reality was things were coming to an end where Pearl was concerned, and far more swiftly than he'd expected. Every day that passed with Liza only left him wanting more, craziness and all. He'd already figured that at the right moment, he was going to ask her to stay. Permanently. He'd just thought he'd have a whole lot more time to pick that moment from. In fact, he had sort of hoped that if he waited long enough, Liza would come to that conclusion on her own.

Whether or not she realized it, Liza was definitely finding her place in Canyon Springs. Headaches and all, he was all for her involvement in the community. She'd also definitely made a place in his heart. He was all for that, too. The burning question was, had he made a place in hers?

LIZA TWIRLED and looked at the way the flared skirt skimmed the backs of her thighs. "It is kind of cute." She smiled at Kendra, the shop owner and designer of a number of the fashions displayed therein. "You really have a good eye. Ever thought about heading to New York?"

Kendra blushed, but laughed. "I thought about going to school there, many moons ago, but decided I'd rather run my own modestly successful place and be my own boss."

Liza nodded. "Smart girl." She stepped back into the dressing room and slipped the soft red fabric over her head. "I'll take this and the other two outfits hanging on the door. You going to the festival opening tomorrow night?"

Kendra took the dress as she handed it over the curtain. "As soon as I close up. I'm supposed to help the fire marshal with their safety booth. I'm handing out those stickers you put in bedroom windows so they know where people are sleeping in case of a fire."

Liza smiled to herself. Kendra sounded awfully

dreamy about handing out stickers. "Have you known Tucker long?" She slipped out of the dressing room in time to watch Kendra's face register surprise.

"I guess *you* would know him, since you're living with Sheriff Jackson."

Liza didn't bother to blush. She was technically still living in the apartment with Pearl, Mulder and Scully, but she had been spending her nights up in that A-frame. It didn't surprise her that word had gotten around. "You know, I used to think there were no secrets in Hollywood, but they could learn a thing or two observing how small towns operate."

Kendra laughed. "I don't know anything about Hollywood, but I'm guessing it's probably like a small town of its own, in a way." She bagged Liza's purchases. "And no, to answer your question, I don't know Tucker Greywolf personally." She fluttered her lashes. "I've lusted from afar, however." She shrugged and blushed a little. "Then I decided it was silly to sit and watch him flirt with all the other women in town and not do something about going after getting his attention focused where I want it. Which is on me."

"Smart and talented. I'm liking you better all the time," Liza said.

"Yeah, well, I'm not sure if I can parlay handing out stickers into a date." She grinned and winked. "But I'm sure going to give it my best shot."

Liza handed her a credit card. "My money's on you."

Kendra finalized the sale, then handed her the garment bag, a considering look in her own pretty brown eyes. "I'm thinking the same about you. You know, the whole town is wondering about you and the sheriff. You've really stirred things up around here."

Liza smiled, unoffended by the frank comment. "I

guess I haven't exactly been hiding my light under a basket, huh?''

"Hardly," Kendra said wryly, then they both laughed. "Not that anyone's complaining. We're enjoying watching Sheriff Jackson go down for the count. I was beginning to think the man was a monk."

It was all Liza could do to keep a straight face. *Boy, does he have all of you fooled,* she thought. But wisely said nothing, happy enough to be the one who'd "defrocked" him.

"So," Kendra added, more boldly now, "are you going to stay? Give our hunk of a sheriff a run for his money?"

Despite her growing daily schedule, Liza had been thinking about little else lately. She slid the strap of her purse over her shoulder. "It's beginning to look that way, isn't it?"

Kendra beamed a smile and shot a thumbs-up as Liza let herself out of the shop. She paused outside the door. *What have you just gone and done?*

But she knew exactly what she'd done. And she was pretty sure Kendra was already on the phone telling someone about it, who'd tell someone else. By the time she and Dylan showed up at the festival together tomorrow, the town would have a pool going on the names of their first children.

She laughed and swung the bag over her shoulder as she strolled down the street toward her car. Funny, but she didn't feel the least bit concerned about that.

Not that she was planning on having kids anytime soon. She was still coming to terms with the idea of having a man in her life on a permanent basis. But no amount of rational analysis about what she should do, or should feel, based on the short time she'd been here, refuted the basic fact. And that was that Dylan Jackson was perfect for her.

He didn't let her push him around…or he did, but in the right ways. And he pushed back…in the right ways. She smiled and squirmed a little in the leather seat of her car, just thinking about how right his ways were.

But even more than that, she'd found herself here in this little town. It amazed her on an hourly basis, but she was thriving here, in ways she hadn't expected to. She'd meant what she'd said earlier. She was good at helping people, but here it felt more…specific. Worthwhile. She supposed because she was around to see the direct benefit of her assistance, and to enjoy the real friendships that were already developing because of them. What she did mattered here, because she mattered here. Or she was starting to.

She looked around as she pulled out and headed toward the apartment. "Liza Sanguinetti from Canyon Springs, New Mexico," she murmured, testing it out. Yeah, it even sounded like home.

19

DYLAN CHECKED IN with his deputies one last time, then went off to find Liza. His visions of spending a lovely evening enjoying the festivities hadn't exactly panned out as he'd hoped. He hadn't even seen her, though he had spoken to her via Tucker's radio at one point, hours earlier. At the time she was manning a booth for Tucker on the festival grounds so he could go dancing with someone named Kendra. Whatever. Liza was in her element, and Dylan was glad she was having a good time.

But he also hadn't minded when she stipulated that she would be making up later for their lack of alone time. In fact, he was looking forward to it.

He was exhausted. It had been a long, fourteen hour shift. After putting in a day behind his desk, he'd been off and running in ten different directions once the festival had begun. He'd been on and off the radio all evening with one minor thing after another, culminating in a call from Quin thirty minutes ago, which had dragged him back to the station. But that particular distraction had been well worth it.

It was all over. Dugan's organization was in shambles and he was begging to take a deal. No trial. Pearl was free to go.

As was Liza.

"Heard you were looking for me."

He turned to find Liza leaning against one of the trees

lining Main Street. In fact, it was the very tree he'd been stuck in the day he'd first met her.

She caught him looking up, and her lips curved. "Seems like a long time ago, doesn't it?"

He nodded. She did that fairly often—read his mind. It had stopped surprising him. In fact, he found he rather liked it. "In some ways, it does." He stepped closer to her. "In other ways, I still feel like I've barely gotten to know you." He pulled her into his arms.

"What other ways?" she asked, sliding her arms around his waist.

He felt that jolt of pleasure he always felt when her body molded to his. He didn't bother to hide it. "Like that. Every single time, it does that to me. That still feels new."

She looked up at him, a considering look on her face. "Maybe it will always be that way." She pressed her face to his chest. "I feel it, too."

Her voice had grown uncharacteristically soft. His heart skipped several beats. He'd wanted this moment, but he wasn't prepared, hadn't thought of what he'd say. But it was likely to be his best chance, so he took it. "Maybe we should find out."

She looked up at him, but before she could say anything, he had to tell her. "I heard from Quin tonight. Dugan won't be going to trial. They had him cold, so he took a deal. It's all over."

Her eyes lit up and she pulled out of his arms to clap her hands. "Pearl is a free woman?"

"She's always been a free woman."

"You know what I mean. Oh, I can't wait to tell her."

"She knows. I called at the house." Where she was watching his mother's birds. Another battle he'd lost. Right at the moment, looking into Liza's shining eyes, he didn't mind so much. Although it should horrify him to think he was actually getting used to being ganged up on by the women in his life.

"Is she staying?" Liza asked. "Do you know? I have to talk to her."

Dylan grabbed her waving hands and pulled her close, tucking them beneath his arms. "She'll still be here tomorrow. You can talk to her then. Right now I want you to talk to me."

She smiled up at him, then must have seen something in his eyes, because her smile faded. "What's wrong?"

"That's just it. Nothing. Except you leaving. That would be wrong." She started to talk, but he shook his head. "Let me get this out."

She merely looked at him, but nodded.

"You told me you were looking for something to fulfill yourself. Well, I don't know if you've felt it, or noticed it, but this town sure has. You've made a place for yourself here, Liza. Just ask anyone. In fact, I've never seen someone who could waltz into a place and claim it as thoroughly as you have Canyon Springs."

"Thank you," she said, but he couldn't read anything else into her tone. "What about you?"

"What about me?"

"I agree with you, about the town. I like it here. I like the people here. When I help them, it feels…I don't know, more personal. Meaningful. I'd like to find a way to do that in a more official capacity." When his eyebrows lifted, she smiled and said, "I'm still working out the details."

His heart, which had stopped momentarily, started again, in double time. She was staying. Had he heard her right? He couldn't be sure, for his pulse was thundering in his ears.

"But, more importantly," she continued, "I'm starting to build friendships here. The real life kind I've only felt with Natalie. I like it." Liza's smile turned wistful. "Remember when I told you I was envious of your extended family, of having so many people connected to you that you could turn to? Well, that's sort of what I feel I can have here. Not merely business contacts, but people I actually care about, who might actually care about me."

"Then you're staying." He wanted to hear her say the words, so he could start believing his best wish had come true.

"That depends. You never answered me."

"On what?" He tried not to sound panicked. He sounded panicked. "What didn't I make clear?"

She laid her hands on his shoulders, then lifted the tips of her fingers to brush at the sides of his face. "You said I claimed the town as mine. Although I think they've claimed me just as thoroughly. Was that your only concern—about me abandoning the people I've started to help here?"

"No. They could live without you, if they had to." He pulled her hands together and clasped them in his, then kissed her fingertips. "But I can't. You claimed me just as thoroughly, perhaps more so. I know you're going through big life changes, Liza. But I want to be one of them. In fact, I want to be the main one. I'm finding I'm selfish like that where you're concerned. Normally I'm a patient man, but with you, I don't want to be. I love you. I want all of you, all the time. And I don't want to wait."

"Well, that dovetails nicely with my plans then," she said, her smile bright, but her voice a bit wobbly.

"It does, does it?" he asked, his heart as wobbly as

her smile. But every other part of him was racing ahead. "And here I thought I was doing the planning, the asking."

"Are you? Are you asking me? I could have sworn you were telling me."

"I've learned with you that telling is sometimes more effective than asking."

Her brows arched and she tried to pull her hands away.

He held on tight. "You know I'm right."

She pulled again.

"Don't make me use the cuffs," he warned, knowing she could see the teasing glint in his eyes. Just as he knew she'd give it right back to him. He wasn't disappointed.

She pushed up against him and moved her hips just right. "Maybe I'd enjoy that, Officer." She wiggled a little and enjoyed the hell out of the tight groan she got from him. "I did the last time, remember?"

He could barely string words together. She did that to him, too. God bless her. "Yeah." It was all he could manage. How did she make her hips do that, anyway?

"So, why don't you take me home and tell me what else we're going to be doing for, oh, the next forty or fifty years?"

"I seem to recall you telling me once that I didn't need to drag you all the way up the mountain to have fun with you. That our pleasure taking didn't have to be so private." He spun her around and pulled her up tight against him, then pressed his lips just below her ear. "And now we'll have plenty of time to play at home. Years."

"Oh?" Her breathing was just a little shallow, a little quick.

Keeping her off guard was a real challenge. One he hoped he was up to for, oh, the next forty or fifty years. Someone had to be. "Did I mention how desperately in love with you I am?"

"I think maybe you mentioned something about that." She tried to wiggle those hips against him again. "Desperate though, huh?" She made a little purring sound and shifted closer.

He managed to shift away just in time. "Oh no, you don't. Not this time." He slipped back until the shadows beneath the tree swallowed them up. Holding her hands in one of his, he used the other to slip his tie off.

"What are you doing?"

He looped the tie around her wrists, then pulled them over her head and looped the other end over a low branch.

She tensed, but didn't pull away. "You wouldn't."

He wondered if she could see his grin in the dark. "I would have asked you up in the tree, but as I recall, you're not a climber."

"Dylan," she yelped as he began unbuttoning the top of her dress. She was squirming, but not trying to get away from his reach. "Anyone could walk by." The excitement was clear in her voice.

"Then I guess you're just going to have to be really quiet."

Whatever she might have said died on a low hiss as he pulled one puckered nipple into his mouth.

"Dear God, you always taste so damn good."

"I'd taste even better at home in your house."

"Our house." He closed his fingertips around her other nipple and continued to taste the first one. "And you taste just fine no matter where we are."

"Dylan, please—"

"Thank you, I think I will." He slid his hands beneath her dress and drew his palms along her thighs. "What surprises do you have for me tonig— Dear God."

She chuckled then, but he didn't mind the little self-satisfied noise. He was too intent on crouching down and taking advantage of the nothing she wore beneath her dress.

"I thought you might like…" The rest came out in a long, low moan. "Have I mentioned how much I love you?"

He stood up and quickly unlooped her from the branch. "In fact, I think you neglected to ever let that slip." He tried to sound nonchalant, teasing. But the fact of the matter was, they were words he'd been dying to hear. And they'd sounded way better than even in his best fantasy. And he'd had…oh, one or ten.

She smiled up at him. "I hope you know how amazing this feels for me."

"I think I have a clue."

"Maybe we were meant for this—two people who make a habit of rescuing others, rescuing each other. That's how I feel, Dylan. Like I've been rescued, and at the same time, found the place I was always meant to be in."

"As long as it's right here—" he pulled her mouth to his and kissed her hard and fast "—then I agree one hundred percent." He kissed her again. "Tell me again."

"I love you, Dylan Benjamin Jackson."

"Damn, but that's good. I'm warning you right now I'm going to need that fix often."

"So now I'm your pusher and you're the junkie."

Dylan grinned. "A love junkie, that's me. Lock me up."

She arched her brows. "Speaking of which...when *does* it get to be my turn? You keep promising, but then we keep ending up in some derivation of this." She wriggled her still-bound hands.

"My intentions are always good," he said, taking hold of his knotted tie. "And you don't seem to complain."

"Well, no, but—"

He cut her off with a hard kiss. It was all sinking in now, that she was his and was going to stay his, for as long as he loved her, which would be forever. Filled with the heady rush of it all, and maybe a little drunk on the power of it, too, he made the instant decision that they should begin their life together the way he meant to continue it. Her taking control of every other thing...and him finding a way to get her to take whatever he damn well wanted to give to her, when he wanted to give it.

He turned and pulled her after him.

"Where are we going now?"

He'd have smiled if he hadn't been in almost physical pain from how badly he needed to be buried inside her right at that very moment. "Town bad boy I might have been, but no way am I roughing up that sweet skin of yours against that tree." He tugged her toward the curb, where his truck was parked.

"Yeah, Mr. Bad Boy," she teased. "You talk big about taking risks, but we both know you'd rather keep your pleasures—and those smiley-face briefs—private."

He opened the back door, gripped her hips and put her up on the back seat. Grinning, he dipped in for a kiss and didn't come up again until she slumped weakly against him. "That, too," he responded with a grin. "When it comes to you, I'm not going to be big on sharing. When you're not running the town and I have my time with you, I'm going to have you, and have you often. All to myself.'' He traced a finger up the inside of her legs, then shifted them into the truck before he lost what little control he had. ''I'm greedy that way.''

He was buckling her in when she said, ''Um, Dylan, my wrists are still—''

''I know.'' He closed the door and hopped in the front seat and gunned the engine. ''Lean back and relax.'' He glanced in the rearview mirror. ''You're not leaning.''

''Is this a proposal or a proposition? Because, I can tell you—''

''No, that's just it. You're going to let *me* tell *you*. Now lean back.'' He looked in the mirror until she did. ''Now—'' he pulled out and slowly drove out of town, the opposite direction from his house ''—while we drive, I'm going to tell you exactly what I'm going to do to you. How I'm going to do it. How I'm going to enjoy doing it. For how long I'll do it…and—''

She was already sighing and relaxing back in her seat. ''I do love a man who knows how to push me around.''

''As long as it's this man you're loving.''

''You're the only one I ever have.''

He slowed the truck a little and looked back at her. ''I know exactly how you feel,'' he told her.

She smiled, then stretched and let her legs slide open just a bit. He bit down on the inside of his cheek and forced his attention back to the road. He had a feeling their lives were always going to be a battle for control.

He could hardly wait.

''So, tell me, are we always going to do wild and crazy stuff like this, too?''

''I've discovered I like taking you off guard.''

''Honey, I like you taking me just about any way you want.''

He grinned. "I've discovered that, too. Which is what makes you—and doing this—so irresistible. Now, have I mentioned just how I'm going to peel that dress off of you later?"

"No. No, I don't believe you have."

"With my teeth."

He heard the satisfied little gasp and smiled at the dark road ahead.

"I want you to imagine how that soft dress will feel, being slowly pulled across those perfectly beautiful nipples of yours. I might even drag it down, slide it slowly between your legs."

She whimpered. "Just make sure you don't take too long telling me," she warned, her voice all soft and needy. "You did leave my hands bound in front, you know."

He chuckled. "You take charge of this and you'll end up having only yourself to blame when you're done before I get started."

She thumped the back of his seat with her foot, but smiled at him. "You derive way too much pleasure from bossing me around, you know."

"Hey, the way I look at it, you get to boss everyone else around all day. Someone has to be the boss of you and let you off the hook some of the time."

"And you'd be the guy for the job?"

He just glanced over his shoulder and smiled at her, then turned his attention back to the road. He had no idea where they were headed. But then, that was why he'd fallen in love with her in the first place.

"Then I'm going to get a bottle of honey," he continued. "And heat it up...."

"Definitely the guy for the job," she murmured happily, managing to unbuckle the seat belt so she could stretch out until she was lying along the seat, bound wrists over her head. "Tell me more."

Dylan was pulling over and climbing in the back not ten miles later.

"What about the honey?" she murmured as he climbed on top of her.

"Who said I'm done yet?" he said as he slid into her.

"Not me," she groaned. "But then, you're in charge."

"Yeah. And don't you forget it," he said, pushing deeper as they both laughed. "And don't let me forget it either."

"That'll be my pleasure."

"No," he managed to say as she tightened around him, "that'll be ours."

The Trueblood, Texas
tradition continues in...

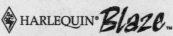

TRULY, MADLY, DEEPLY
by Vicki Lewis Thompson
August 2002

Ten years ago, Dustin Ramsey and Erica Mann shared their first sexual experience. It was a disaster. Now Dustin's determined to find—and seduce—Erica again, to prove to her, and himself, that he can do better. Much, *much* better. Only, little does he guess that Erica's got the same agenda....

Don't miss Blaze's next two sizzling Trueblood tales:

EVERY MOVE YOU MAKE by Tori Carrington
September 2002
&
LOVE ON THE ROCKS by Debbi Rawlins
October 2002

Available wherever Harlequin books are sold.

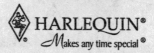

HARLEQUIN®
Makes any time special ®

Attracted to strong, silent cowboys?

Then get ready to meet three of the most irresistibly
sexy heroes you've ever met in

THE SILENT

Type

From bestselling Harlequin Temptation® author

VICKI
LEWIS
THOMPSON

These three lonesome cowboys are about to find some
very interesting company!

Coming to a store near you in August 2002.

Who was she really?

Where Memories Lie

GAYLE
WILSON

AMANDA
STEVENS

Two full-length novels of enticing, romantic suspense—by
two favorite authors.

They don't remember their names or lives, but the two
heroines in these two fascinating novels do know one thing:
they are women of passion. Can love help bring back the
memories they've lost?

Look for WHERE MEMORIES LIE in July 2002—
wherever books are sold.

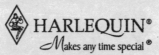

HARLEQUIN®
Makes any time special ®

Visit us at www.eHarlequin.com

BR2WML

Princes...Princesses...
London Castles...New York Mansions...
To live the life of a royal!

**In 2002, Harlequin Books lets you escape to a
world of royalty with these royally themed titles:**

Temptation:
January 2002—*A Prince of a Guy* (#861)
February 2002—*A Noble Pursuit* (#865)

American Romance:
The Carradignes: American Royalty (Editorially linked series)
March 2002—*The Improperly Pregnant Princess* (#913)
April 2002—*The Unlawfully Wedded Princess* (#917)
May 2002—*The Simply Scandalous Princess* (#921)
November 2002—*The Inconveniently Engaged Prince* (#945)

Intrigue:
The Carradignes: A Royal Mystery (Editorially linked series)
June 2002—*The Duke's Covert Mission* (#666)

Chicago Confidential
September 2002—*Prince Under Cover* (#678)

The Crown Affair
October 2002—*Royal Target* (#682)
November 2002—*Royal Ransom* (#686)
December 2002—*Royal Pursuit* (#690)

Harlequin Romance:
June 2002—*His Majesty's Marriage* (#3703)
July 2002—*The Prince's Proposal* (#3709)

Harlequin Presents:
August 2002—*Society Weddings* (#2268)
September 2002—*The Prince's Pleasure* (#2274)

Duets:
September 2002—*Once Upon a Tiara/Henry Ever After* (#83)
October 2002—*Natalia's Story/Andrea's Story* (#85)

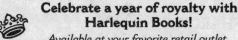

**Celebrate a year of royalty with
Harlequin Books!**

Available at your favorite retail outlet.

HARLEQUIN®
Makes any time special ®

Visit us at www.eHarlequin.com

HSROY02

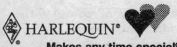